CRAGBRIDGE HALL

THE INVENTOR'S
SECRET

CRAGBRIDGE HALL

THE INVENTOR'S SECRET

CHAD MORRIS

ILLUSTRATED BY
BRANDON DORMAN

SHADOW
MOUNTAIN

Text © 2013 Chad Morris
Illustrations © 2013 Brandon Dorman

Visit us at ShadowMountain.com

This is a work of fiction. Characters and events in this book are products of the author's imagination or are represented fictitiously.

First printing in hardbound 2013.
First printing in paperbound 2014.

Library of Congress Cataloging-in-Publication Data
Morris, Chad, author.
   The inventor's secret / Chad Morris.
      pages cm — (Cragbridge Hall ; bk. 1)
   Summary: When twins Abby and Derick start junior high at the prestigious academy their grandfather founded, Cragbridge Hall, they discover firsthand the dangers of time travel and must find a way to save their parents, who have been sent to the Titanic the night it sank.
   ISBN 978-1-60907-326-8 (hardbound)
   ISBN 978-1-60907-875-1 (paperbound)
   [1. Space and time—Fiction. 2. Boarding schools—Fiction. 3. Schools—Fiction. 4. Twins—Fiction. 5. Brothers and sisters—Fiction. 6. Grandfathers—Fiction. 7. Inventors and inventions—Fiction. 8. Titanic (Steamship)—Fiction.] I. Title.
   PZ7.M827248Inv 2013
   [Fic]—dc23   2012041691

Printed in the United States of America
R. R. Donnelley, Crawfordsville, IN

10   9   8   7   6   5   4   3

To Shelly, Kirtlan, Maddie,
Kimball, Cannon, and Christian.

Thanks for believing.

CONTENTS

Contents

1

GRANDPA

Abby waved at various security cameras on the front porch. She knew they were just machines, but she waved just the same. They wouldn't notice her sandy blonde hair, her light runner's build, or her brown eyes. They simply scanned her, matching her fingerprints and facial features to those authorized to enter. Abby heard the locking mechanism slide open, and a thin light above the door handle turned green. She opened the door and stepped in, her twin brother, Derick, and her parents only a step behind her.

"Hello, Grandpa," Abby called out.

She loved the smell of Grandpa's place—a mixture of hot cocoa and ready-made dinners. There was also a hint of old smell—like the carpet and furniture hadn't been replaced for decades—but she chose to ignore it.

The floorboards creaked as the family passed the living

room and walked down the hall toward the den. Abby couldn't remember for sure, but she thought the house was built way back before the turn of the century—like 1997 or something. Funny that the man famous for making the greatest leaps in modern technology lived in such an old, dusty place.

As they neared the den, Abby saw her grandfather sitting in his favorite chair in a room lined with bookshelves. A couple of slightly newer couches and a pair of tall lamps were the only other pieces of furniture in the room. Cracks lined the neglected brown leather chair like the wrinkles that covered Grandpa Cragbridge. Wrinkles had been cured back in 2047, but Grandpa wanted to age naturally.

He looked up from the journal he was scribbling in and raised both of his boney hands. "Two of the most promising students in the world! Good to see you." Grandpa set down his journal, picked up his cane, and hoisted himself up. As usual, he wore a simple collared shirt and the blazer he'd received when Cragbridge Hall had opened years ago. The school crest featuring a watchman's tower was embroidered next to the lapel. His bald head reflected some of the light, and a white beard covered his face, except for his chin. Abby always thought he looked a little like an old explorer. "You didn't wear your jackets?"

Abby and Derick had both received similar blazers when they had been admitted to the school. "We're only required to wear them on special occasions," Abby said. "Not orientation."

Grandpa looked down. "Well, I guess much of my life

must be a special occasion, then." His bushy white mustache couldn't hide his smile. "Are you ready for this?"

"I hope so," Derick said, standing a little taller than Abby. "I've never been excited about school before. I always liked it, but this is a whole new level."

Grandpa grinned and then turned to Abby for her answer.

"I . . ." Abby grabbed her sandy blonde hair and nervously twisted it into a temporary ponytail. "I'm . . . hoping for the best." Not only was she going to attend a new school, but it was the premiere junior high in the world. Yeah—in the entire world. She had the reputation of her genius grandfather to live up to, and she would be living away from home. And of course, there was the fact that she didn't even deserve to . . . She didn't want to think about it.

Grandpa lowered himself back into his chair and rubbed his bald head with one hand. "I've arranged it with security so that you can visit me whenever you want. You have permission to leave the grounds as long as you're back before dark."

"Really?" Abby said, feeling like a weight had been lifted from her shoulders. "Thanks, Grandpa. I . . . might need it."

"Of course. I think the academy owes me," he said, and winked. Grandpa's inventions had not only made the school possible, but they'd given it notoriety and acclaim. There was a reason it was called Cragbridge Hall.

"I'm sure your inventions are seriously amazing," Derick said.

"Yeah, I can't wait to see them in person," Abby added. When she was younger, she used to imagine contraptions with screens and gears and lasers. Of course, as she grew older, she began researching them. She'd seen photos online, but that was nothing like experiencing them for herself.

"I'm sorry I couldn't show them to you before. One day you'll know why." Grandpa looked up at Derick and Abby's parents. "Can you believe it?"

Dad laughed. "I wish the academy had been open when I was a kid."

Mom smiled and wiped a tear from her cheek. Maybe it was as difficult for her to send her kids to live away from home as it was for Abby to go.

"We are proud of you both," Dad said. He gave Abby a quick peck on the forehead, then grabbed Derick by the shirt, pulled him in, and kissed the top of his head. Derick let out a cry as shrill as if his hand had been dipped in a bucket of maggots.

The twins' father bolted down the old hall with Derick chasing close behind. Abby knew how this would go. They would chase each other around, one would try to get the other in a wrestling hold, and then Dad would probably cheat by tickling, which, of course, would provoke Derick even more. The whole thing would end with violent laughter.

"I'd better referee," Mom said, and walked down the hall.

"Boys." Abby shook her head.

4

Grandpa laughed, wheezing between chuckles.

There was a moment of silence, and then a playful scream from Abby's father echoed down the hallway. He and Derick were running into the basement.

Abby took a step closer to her grandpa. "Thanks for getting me into the school."

Grandpa looked sternly back at her, "I didn't 'get you in.' The admissions review did. Just because you're my granddaughter doesn't mean you get special treatment."

Abby smiled. "Grandpa, you're a genius, but you're a terrible liar. I got a rejection letter. Then a week later, I got my acceptance. I don't think schools like Cragbridge Hall change their minds like that unless someone is pretty persuasive."

Grandpa paled for a moment but then waved off his granddaughter's accusation. "It doesn't matter how you got in." He stood and slowly made his way to one of a series of old pine bookshelves. Books were packed tightly along most of them, with an occasional knickknack wedged between volumes. He probably had more real books than most libraries. "Come here. I want to show you something." Grandpa pointed to a small frame between *To Kill a Mockingbird* and *The Three Musketeers*. It could easily fit in the palm of his hand. Inside the frame were dark splotches interconnected on a lighter background, looking kind of like a maze. "That," Grandpa said, pointing at the strange mass with his boney finger, "is a slice of Albert Einstein's brain."

Abby stared back incredulously. "You're kidding me, right?"

"Haven't I ever told you that story?" Grandpa asked. He shuffled back to his old chair and began, not waiting for a response. "In a small town classroom, a teacher asked what the students knew had happened recently in current events. One child mentioned that Albert Einstein had died. Another raised his hand and said, 'My father has his brain.'"

"What?" Abby said in disbelief.

"The boy wasn't lying. His father was Thomas Harvey at Princeton Hospital. He performed the autopsy on Einstein, and he took the liberty of keeping the famous scientist's brain."

Abby raised her eyebrow. "Are you just trying to distract me? I know you got me into school."

"Excuse me," Grandpa said. "I was telling you about one of the great relics of the world."

Abby sighed. "Alright, Grandpa, let's talk about the brain. How did you get it?"

"Good question," Grandpa said, apparently satisfied. "Once, Einstein and I had a . . . disagreement. It was about relativity. Anyway, he got upset with me and said he wanted to give me a piece of his mind." He paused. Abby sighed—she should have seen it coming. He began to laugh, his giggles coming out as more of a light wheeze. "A piece of his mind," he repeated between chuckles.

"C'mon, Grandpa."

He was a genius in many areas, but comedy was not one of them.

"Alright. Alright." He waved his arm, but still snickered for nearly another minute before continuing. "I have a few friends in the scientific world, and someone thought I deserved to have it." Grandpa got up and walked a few steps toward the shelf, his cane knocking against the wood floor before each step. "Pieces of it ended up all over the place, given as gifts to other scientists." He picked up what looked like an old photograph from another shelf. "This is a picture of about one fifth of his brain. But look here. *This* is what I wanted to show you. Do you see that groove?" Grandfather pointed to a certain part of the brain. "That is the inferior parietal lobe—the part of the brain most used in mathematics and spatial thinking. Einstein's is shorter than most people's but fifteen percent wider."

"Is that why he was a genius?" Abby asked.

"Maybe, or perhaps his brain became stronger because he worked so hard and learned so much, and because he practiced thinking so well."

"This is great," Abby said. "But I'm no Einstein. I couldn't even get in without—"

Grandpa slammed the bottom of his cane onto the floor. "Abigail Cragbridge, you are just as good as, if not better than, every other student in that academy. When they said 'no,' I had to prevent them from making a terrible mistake. You'll be one of the best things that ever happened to that place."

"You don't have to—"

"I'm completely serious," Grandpa interrupted. He grabbed Abby's face by the chin. "You have heart, Abby. The kind of heart some teachers and academics can only dream about. And I'm not saying that because you're my granddaughter. You meet your challenges head on. I remember when you struggled with algebra. You spent hours every night studying and doing homework. The time you wanted to take guitar lessons, you saved up for months to pay for them. And when that Greenwich girl spread that dastardly gossip, you stuck it out with dignity. Eventually, you two even got along."

"Yeah, things ended up okay—"

"*You have heart.*" Grandpa's eyes didn't flinch. "I know it better than anything I've discovered, better than anything they've ever called genius. I'd stake all my reputation on your success."

Abby swallowed hard and blinked several times to keep tears from forming. She turned back to the jar.

"Einstein said that he had no special talent," Grandpa continued, "but that he was passionately curious. Very few people are born extraordinary. You have to earn it. And you, Abby, have the heart to earn it."

Dad and Mom walked in, with Derick a few steps behind. They were all breathing deeply—the aftereffects of a good laugh.

Abby quickly wiped her eyes.

"Give Grandpa another good hug, and let's get out of here," Dad said. "You don't want to be late for orientation."

"Wait just a minute," Grandpa said, his brow wrinkled. "Derick, come over here by Abby. I have something for the two of you."

Derick obediently stood beside his sister as Grandpa moved over to the fireplace. He picked up a brass-handled shovel and a poker from a matching set. He shoveled away the pile of ashes to one side of the fireplace, then pushed the tip of the poker into the corner of one brick. With a whir and a click, the brick rose out of the floor, and a small metal box appeared beneath it. Grandpa stooped and picked it up.

What kind of a gift did Grandpa keep buried underneath a brick in his fireplace?

"Are you sure?" Dad asked Grandpa, looking at the box.

"Yes, I am," Grandpa said confidently. "Now, could you grab me a towel?" Dad jogged into the other room.

Grandpa turned to the twins. "I'm very proud of both of you. I've decided that you're mature enough for a few very special gifts." He wiped the beginnings of sweat from his brow with the back of his hand.

Dad returned with a towel, and Grandpa used it to clean any last traces of ash and soot from the box and from his hands. He set the towel aside, then opened a flap, revealing a lock screen. After a couple of keystrokes, the entire casing unlocked. The box was made of thick metal, and Abby couldn't see inside it.

Grandpa reached in and pulled out two thin metal bands. "These are history attachments for your rings. Just slide them inside your existing rings." He handed them to the twins. "They allow you to tap into my database, which means that you have access to some history not yet charted and open to the public. You'll learn more about what that means after school starts. The attachments will allow you to access my personal files and memories through your rings. I have not kept an adequate journal, but in some ways, this is much better."

He returned to the box and removed two metal lockets, both attached to thin chains. "And I want to give you these." He handed one to Abby and the other to Derick. Abby's locket was heavier than she expected it to be. It had ornate designs around the front, but the locket itself was a simple flat circle.

"I want you to put those somewhere very, very safe—preferably, you'll wear them. And you'll need to check them every day."

"What do you mean?" Derick asked.

"Look at your locket every day," Grandpa said. "If nothing has changed, then continue with your studies as before. But if something does change, you may be desperately needed. The locket will tell you what to do." He wrung his hands. "I get especially nervous at the beginning of every school year. It would probably be the best time to . . ." He let his sentence trail off as he became lost in thought.

"To what?" Abby asked.

"Please keep your lockets a secret—I cannot stress that enough. No one should know about them, especially not the teachers," Grandpa said. "Do you have your book collections with you?"

"Yes," Abby said. "You insisted."

"Even though no one else in the world uses actual books anymore," Derick added.

"They should," Grandpa said. "Nothing beats paper."

"Time to go," Dad interrupted.

"Wait," Derick said. "What's inside the lockets?"

Grandpa gazed into Derick's eyes, then into Abby's. She wasn't sure what she saw in his eyes—concern? Love? Fear? Grandpa let out a sigh. "I hope you never have to find out."

ORIENTATION

The history classroom looked normal—except for the full-sized pirate ship emerging from the front wall. The new seventh graders of Cragbridge Hall gasped in unison, their eyes wide and mouths open. Abby sat awestruck as the old wood soon surrounded her and the other rows of students, like a ghost ship. She had heard tale after tale about the amazing learning devices at the premiere school, but this was her first experience with living history.

Abby could hardly stay in her seat. She was finally seeing one of her grandfather's inventions in action. Abby pushed a strand of hair away from her eyes and tucked it behind one ear. She didn't want any distractions. She looked over at Derick. He no longer spoke with the boys sitting next to him. His blue eyes stared ahead, mesmerized.

The teacher, Mr. Hendricks, paced in his button-down

shirt, slacks, and shiny loafers. "Welcome to orientation. Because history is your first-period class, I have the pleasure of helping to prepare you for the school year that begins tomorrow. But first, a little history." He narrated as they watched. "You are about to see one of the most infamous villains from the past few centuries. His name was Edward Teach, a pirate in the early 1700s. The episode you are about to watch happened off the coast of North Carolina in late November, 1718. Teach caused great damage by ransacking ships, setting them on fire, and sinking them. He threatened many people's lives, but he never killed his captives. He famously sailed a ship called the *Queen Anne's Revenge*, but today you'll see him in a smaller vessel—the *Adventure*."

Abby instinctively rubbed the ring on her index finger, which turned on all the rings she wore on her fingers and thumbs. The virtual screen in her contact lenses flicked on. With a swipe of her finger, she set the screen to appear only in the upper left-hand corner of her vision. Each ring had a sensor that traced that finger's movement. She could easily type, select, and change programs with them.

Abby virtually typed a few notes: *Edward Teach, 1718, off the coast of North Carolina, The* Adventure.

How many of the students were actually listening to the teacher's words? Part of her didn't want to; it was hard to listen to a lecture with a pirate ship in the room. The other part of her knew she had to focus, had to learn.

More of the ship glided into view. It moaned and creaked under its own weight, swaying from side to side with the waves. The deck wasn't crowded with pirates like Abby would have imagined. She estimated there were fewer than twenty. As she watched the straggly characters, one man caught her attention—he demanded it. A tall, broad-shouldered man with long, dark hair and a matching beard gazed intently in front of him. His beard was braided into two long strands that moved stiffly as his head swiveled to bark orders. He wore black boots that came up to his knees, and a long dark coat.

Draped across his wide chest was a leather sling holding two pistols in holsters. A third holster hung empty, the pistol in one of the pirate's hands. His long cutlass was in his other. Jutting out from under his hat and along the bottom of his beard was a series of lit fuses. It was a fire hazard if Abby had ever seen one, but clearly the pirate wasn't afraid of danger. Smoke curled up from the fuses, surrounding the man's head in a dark cloud and making him look like some sort of demon. He was the most intimidating person she had ever seen.

Abby looked again at Derick. This time he whispered something to the dark-haired boy sitting next to him, then quickly looked back at the menacing pirate.

Derick and Abby had been at Cragbridge Hall for under an hour. From the time their parents had dropped them off at the great gates until now, they'd only had time to leave their suitcases with a supervisor at their dorms before coming to orientation. Yet Derick had already managed to make some friends. Abby had barely even said hello to anyone.

Mr. Hendricks continued. "Very few people know him

by the name Edward Teach. You may recognize his pirate name: Blackbeard."

A murmur of recognition spread through the class.

Before today, Abby hadn't realized that Blackbeard was a real person. For all she knew, he was just a character from old novels and movies.

"*Now!*" Blackbeard yelled, and his crew lit fuses in bottles filled with powder. The fuses sparked and sizzled as they flew over the students' heads, presumably to attack someone behind them. Explosions boomed, and then dust and smoke fogged over the classroom. Students shifted in their seats to look at the back of the room.

Blackbeard squinted, trying to make out details of something in front of him. A partial smile turned only one end of his mouth. "Ready the hooks!" he shouted. Several men grabbed long ropes with eight-inch iron hooks on the ends.

Another ship floated into view. It came from behind the class, drifting closer to Blackbeard and his crew. The hooks flew over the students' heads, ropes trailing behind, and grabbed at the rails of the other ship, clawing into the wood. Soon the two ships met, filling the classroom. The ropes held them close together.

Blackbeard screamed and lunged over the side of his ship and onto the deck of the other vessel. He fired his pistol at the first movement visible through the haze. Ten men followed him, each shooting on the attack. But as the smoke cleared, only Blackbeard's pirates were on the bow of the other ship. His head twisted in every direction, searching for his enemy.

Across the deck, the door to the hold flung open. Shots blared, and yells rang out throughout the history room. The marauding pirates had walked right into an ambush.

With swords raised and guns firing, the action paused. A ball hung suspended in the air about a foot from a gun's barrel. Mr. Hendricks walked into the middle of the image. The pirates, the ships, the water were all frozen.

"The ship that Blackbeard is attacking, *The Pearl*, is captained by Lieutenant Robert Maynard. He's the one in the uniform at the head of the men who burst out from behind that door." Mr. Hendricks pointed him out. "Maynard hid more men there than Blackbeard had expected. This is the day that will put Robert Maynard into the history books."

Abby had never heard of him.

Mr. Hendricks sent the scene rolling again with a flick of his finger. His rings controlled the images like a remote control.

Blackbeard pointed one of his pistols at Maynard and fired. The lieutenant fired back. Blackbeard's shot buried itself into the banister behind Maynard at the same time as the pirate himself stumbled. Blackbeard had been hit at point-blank range.

He only staggered for a moment. Blackbeard's lip curled, and he charged Maynard, his cutlass slashing in front of him. The steel of swords collided, anger and adrenaline fueling the fight. The two men attacked and defended in a deadly dance across the blood-stained deck. The other soldiers and pirates fought fiercely around them. Abby scarcely knew where to look, so she tried to look everywhere at once. Her head swiveled from one battle to another, but her attention always returned to Blackbeard.

His long arms wielded his weapon well. He was strong despite his wound. With a furious grunt, the pirate's sword clashed against Maynard's, breaking it in two. Several students gasped, and one girl even screamed. Maynard backed up quickly, desperately. He had no chance without his sword. Blackbeard lunged. Someone else's blade slashed from the side—and the entire scene quickly faded away.

The class groaned in disappointment. Students' questions filled the room. "What happened?" "Did he die?" "Who won?"

Mr. Hendricks shushed the class. "You know very well that Cragbridge Hall does not show gratuitous violence. This is as far into the battle as you can watch." Their teacher stood tall and handsome, with short, dark hair tipped with gray. "The sword you saw save Maynard belonged to one of his men. Several others from his ranks also attacked Blackbeard. We don't know which blow was fatal, but by the end of the day, the pirate had five gunshot wounds, and several deep gashes. This was the last day of the infamous Blackbeard the pirate."

"You mean, he died?" a boy in the back row blurted out.

"I thought I heard something," Mr. Hendricks said, motioning that the young man needed to raise his hand. "Though we are an institution with amazing and exciting learning devices, we must still keep order."

The same boy lifted his arm in the air. "So Blackbeard died?" he repeated sheepishly.

THE INVENTOR'S SECRET

"Yes." Mr. Hendricks paced to one side of the room. "That is part of why I'm showing this episode for orientation. Blackbeard was a villain. He broke the rules. He stole and plundered what he had not earned and did not deserve. A person cannot live that way and get away with it forever."

"But . . ." another boy started, then caught himself and raised his hand.

Mr. Hendricks called on him.

"But he was so awesome," the boy defended.

"He may have been 'awesome,' but he was also a villain. He should have been caught sooner." Mr. Hendricks paused. "Much, much sooner. But at the end of the day, he *was* caught. Maynard threw Blackbeard's body into the sea and hung his head from the bowsprit of his ship."

Several girls winced. "Disgusting," a blonde a few rows to Abby's left whispered. Abby thought Blackbeard probably deserved what he got, but she was glad she hadn't seen it.

"His head was later placed on a stake near the Hampton River to warn all pirates," Mr. Hendricks continued, pacing up the row. "The message was that the pirates had to change, or they could expect the same fate. Which brings me to one point of our orientation." Mr. Hendricks pointed to a digital poster on the wall with a three-dimensional image of Blackbeard. A few of the fuses under his hat still burned. His cutlass was raised in front of him, his strong arm holding it forward. But he was also weak, injured. Beneath his determination, Abby could see surprise, and maybe even fear.

"I keep this picture on the wall to warn you. You do not

want to be like Blackbeard. Sometimes bright young people believe they are above the rules. They think they can take advantage of the system. At times, they even delude themselves into thinking they should. Believe me, you are not above the system. If you break the rules of this academy or the rules of this class . . ." Mr. Hendricks didn't finish his sentence. Instead, he ran his finger across his throat.

Abby froze in shocked silence. No one in the class made a sound.

After several moments of tension, Mr. Hendricks laughed. "That's sign language for suspension or dismissal," he teased. "Did you think I meant something else?"

Abby exhaled, and several other students did the same.

Mr. Hendricks gestured for the class to stay quiet. "But I'm not joking about suspension or dismissal. You must keep the rules. And for you to keep the rules, I'd better make sure you understand them."

As Mr. Hendricks went through the rules, Abby took copious notes. She knew most of them from the virtual orientation tour, but rewrote them to make sure they were seared into her memory. Breakfast was at 7 A.M. sharp. Each of their seven classes began on the hour, starting at eight, with a one-hour lunch at eleven. Those in the higher grades ate at noon. If tardy or truant, students received two warnings before detention. After three detentions, they would be suspended. If the problem continued, they may be expelled. The highest penalties would be enforced against cheating.

The library, the commons, and even the gym and the fields were all open areas after school if not occupied by a team. Students had to pass through several levels of security as they entered, both to keep the students safe and because of the great inventions at Cragbridge Hall. This meant that students could leave the school grounds only with permission and on special occasions. Dinner was at 6:00, curfew at 9:00. All students had to be in their rooms by curfew. Lights would be turned off and doors locked at 10:00.

Abby looked over at Derick, who hadn't even turned on his rings. She hated his excellent memory. He didn't take many notes about anything. She had to read, study, and pound information into her brain, while her twin brother often glanced over the textbook the night before and still got the class high on a test. She never scored higher than he did.

"Any questions?" After Mr. Hendricks waited an uncomfortably long time, he continued. "That is it for orientation. You'll return here for first period tomorrow morning, and I'll go over another set of rules."

Abby thought she could feel the class weighed down by the drudgery of the regulations.

"You will need to follow those rules meticulously when it is your turn to use . . . the Bridge." The general feeling quickly changed as excited noises spread through the room like wildfire. They were going to get a chance to control the world-famous device that had just allowed them to see a pirate battle.

JACQUELINE

S o," Abby said, seeing that Derick had finished his conversation with a few other boys. "What do you think?"
She felt grateful to know one person in the room. At least
she had someone to wait for.

"Incredible," Derick answered. He waved good-bye to
his new friends, and the twins walked out of the history
room, into a great hallway. The ceilings were several stories
high, and a long sunroof let in the twilight.

"Yeah," Abby agreed. "I don't think this place could be
any more amazing."

"Sure it could," Derick said, one eyebrow cocked between his dark hair and blue eyes. Abby knew a joke was
coming. "They could let us paint murals on the walls and
give us all amusement parks, and x-ray vision . . . Oh! And
pet dragons."

Abby hit Derick—not a full-blown punch, but not just a playful kidding around hit, either. It was a hit only a sister could give and not be considered abusive. "You're so weird," she said.

They passed a series of digital images posted on the wall like paintings. Abby guessed they all portrayed Shakespearean plays—*Romeo and Juliet, Julius Caesar*. The last one showed a man in a large storm. Abby didn't recognize it.

"But I'm right," Derick responded. "I'd love a fire breather or a dragon that could become invisible and turn people to stone with its tail. You'd probably have a little pink dragon with rainbow scales that spit flowers and cried candy hearts."

Abby hit Derick again. How could he come up with funny things to say so quickly?

"Always resorting to violence," Derick said. "You're lucky I don't have my dragon yet." There it was again. Did he even have to try to be funny? Abby could sometimes come up with something witty, but by that point she'd missed the chance to say it.

Derick pushed open the large doors, and they left the Hall—the building that housed the history classes, the commons, and the cafeteria. It's official name was Cragbridge Hall and was the original building of the entire school. As the school grew, other buildings were added, but the entire academy kept the name. They walked down the steps and onto a path surrounded by grass fields and shrubs carved into a variety of shapes. One shrub looked like a bear on its hind legs, and another was trimmed to look like Abraham Lincoln.

"Well," Derick finally said, pointing down the path to the left, "I guess I should head to the boys' dorm—unpack and stuff." He waved good-bye. "Try not to do anything too stupid. I'm your twin, so people assume things."

There was something in his smile, or maybe in his eyes, that made Abby think he wasn't completely joking. "Thanks," Abby said. "Your confidence is inspiring."

"I lift people," Derick said sarcastically. "It's what I do." He headed down the other sidewalk.

Abby slowed her pace as she watched him go. She didn't know how Derick could seem so casual about living away from home for the first time. They were at the premiere secondary school of the world—the pressure was on. He should be nervous. Then again, Derick succeeded at everything.

It wouldn't have been so completely annoying if he wasn't her twin. He hadn't lived longer. He hadn't attended a different school. She had no excuses. The truth of the matter was, they both had the same experiences in life— same family, same school, even the same vacations—yet he outdid her at everything.

Abby made her way to the younger girls' dorm on the other side of the playing field and raised her hand at the scanner as she approached. She couldn't feel it, but she knew it was doing its work. She didn't even have to slow down before the doors opened.

Ninth graders were busily talking in the halls on the first floor. There were hugs and squeals as girls reunited after the summer break. They didn't have to attend the orientation, so some were just arriving, suitcases dragged behind them. Abby looked at the smiles, braids, pressed skirts, beads, sandals, and boots. She suddenly became self-conscious about her jeans and fitted T-shirt. Abby saw every shade of skin, and guessed the girls came from all over the globe. They all looked so mature and ready for the world.

It took Abby a moment to reorient herself. She had only been in the building once before to drop off her luggage. She opted to take the stairs instead of the elevator chute. Sure, the chute would bring her to both her floor and then across to her room, but she wanted to stretch her legs and look around. She peeked out of the stairwell to look at the second floor—more of the same crowded hallways.

Abby continued up to the third floor, her new home. She tried not to think about the house she grew up in, which was less than a half-hour drive away, and Grandpa's house, less than a mile away. She didn't want to feel the pangs of homesickness, not on the first day.

She pushed the door open and stepped onto the third floor. It was different from the lower two stories. There were a few loud conversations, but the seventh graders were definitely quieter than the eighth and ninth graders. Abby imagined most of the girls would be like her, not knowing anyone else.

Abby had to turn on her rings to check her room number: 326. As she walked down the hall, she heard a girl speaking to her mother. Abby thought about using her rings to sync up to her mother's rings to talk to her, but decided against it. She had only been gone for a few hours. Syncing up now would look wimpy. Out of another room came some sort of syncopated music. Whatever it was, the lyrics were not in English. Eventually she approached her room. The door was partially open. She figured her new roommate was inside. Abby paused and took a deep breath. She twisted her hair into a ponytail, then tapped her knuckles on the door as she entered.

A girl with long, black hair that fell flat and shiny down to her shoulders turned around. She was unloading one of five suitcases opened on the floor and bed. That was three more than Abby had.

The girl held a skirt and a hanger. "Hello?"

"Hi! I'm Abby. I guess we're roommates."

"Oh." Her smile revealed perfect teeth several shades whiter than was naturally possible. "I'm Jacqueline." Her voice was filled with energy. She surveyed Abby from bangs to sandals, a head-to-toe evaluation. "Nice to meet you." She offered a hug. Abby accepted, though it felt incredibly awkward. "So, tell me about yourself," Jacqueline said.

"What do you want to know?" Abby had no idea where to start.

"Where are you from?" Jacqueline asked.

The girls exchanged answers. Jacqueline was from New Hampshire. "So what did you do to get into Cragbridge?" Jacqueline asked.

"What do you mean?"

"You know," Jacqueline answered. "Aside from grades

and citizenship, they look for the whole 'ambitious youth,' thing—'trying to excel and to contribute to the world.'"

"Um," Abby hesitated. What could she say?

"Okay, I'll go first," Jacqueline said. "I was a student body officer, and I played cello in the New Hampshire Youth Orchestra." She spoke and moved with a poise and grace that surprised Abby. "But my real claim to fame is that I have my own fashion line—Jaq-L. Have you heard of it?"

"Of course I have," Abby blurted out. She had seen it on several teen-based sites. She'd heard it was designed by a girl her age, but she never imagined she would be roommates with her. "I think one of my tops is a Jaq-L."

"That's fantastic!" Jacqueline sifted through her suitcase and picked out a red shirt, which had layers around the neck that draped down in different levels. "Here, have this one. It should be about your size."

"Thank you!" Abby said, thrilled. "It's beautiful." She thought about asking Jacqueline to sign her new shirt, but wasn't sure if it would just wash out. She could picture telling her friends back home about her roommate. They would be so jealous. Abby hung her new shirt on a hanger in the closet and turned to her packed suitcases.

"I'm glad you like it," Jacqueline said. "So what about you? How are you 'excelling and contributing to the world'?"

Abby pulled her Cragbridge blazer from her case. "What? Oh. I do okay in school. I'm decent at track. And I was part of a service club." It all sounded so ordinary coming out of her mouth.

"You're just being modest. 'Okay' and 'decent' don't get anyone into Cragbridge."

Abby looked at her jacket, slowly threading the hanger into its sleeves. "Hopefully I'm a bit better than okay." She placed the jacket on the rack, wondering if she deserved to have it. "My twin brother is here, though," Abby tried to change the subject, "and he is a genius. Perfect grades. Aces every test. He designed a virtual program that supposedly could train him to be a samurai. He wants to market it to the video game crowd. He's done it all."

"He sounds great. I'd love to meet him."

Hoping to keep the conversation away from her, Abby asked if Jacqueline had brothers. Then she asked about the rest of Jacqueline's family, her business, and her future. She even asked if Jacqueline had left a special boy back in her hometown.

"You still haven't answered *my* question," Jacqueline said. "What makes you special? We're roommates. We're destined to be best friends and know everything about each other. You might as well just come out with it." She sat on her bed, gazing at Abby, ready to listen.

She had a point. She would find out sooner or later.

Abby clenched her teeth for a moment. "I'm not like my brother. I don't have a list of accomplishments." She exhaled slowly. "I'm just average."

"Whatever." Jacqueline stood and hung up another skirt. "So do I have to guess?" When Abby didn't respond, Jacqueline kept on going, "You probably like invented some new math formula and run a four-minute mile."

"No," Abby said quietly. "I didn't even get straight As. And I couldn't break any team records. Well, I got close to one, but that's it."

"You're just holding back."

"Part of me wishes I was . . . or were, or however you say that," Abby said. "But I'm here, and I'm hoping to keep up."

Jacqueline looked at her for a moment, gave a half-smile and turned back to her clothes. As she put the second shoulder of a blouse on a hanger, her hand slipped, and the shirt fell. It landed on top of Abby's suitcase. "Sorry about that," Jacqueline said.

"Don't worry about it," Abby said.

When Jacqueline picked up the shirt, she noticed Abby's name on the suitcase tag. "Your last name is Cragbridge?" She pointed at the tag.

"Yeah," Abby said.

"Are you related to *the* Oscar Cragbridge?"

Part of Abby did *not* want to answer. She loved her grandfather dearly, but she didn't want to be known as just the inventor's granddaughter. She wanted to stand on her own. Abby wanted to change the topic, but could see no way around it. Jacqueline would find out sooner or later. "Yes, I am."

Jacqueline stopped putting her things away. "He founded this school," she said slowly. Abby could almost see Jacqueline's mind working. "Wait a second." Jacqueline's eyes narrowed. "You had average grades, but you're the granddaughter of the man who founded this school." She began to speak louder. "Gee, how did you get in?"

Abby twisted her hair into a ponytail. "Um . . ."

"That isn't fair," Jacqueline said. She began unpacking quicker. Her trained hands pulled clothes from her case and hung them in the closet with surprising speed. Her brow furrowed more and more as she worked.

"I'm sorry," Abby said. "I can't say that I'm a complete fan of the situation either. I'm kind of nervous that—"

"Just let me think for a second," Jacqueline said, cutting her off.

Abby sat on the edge of her bed, quietly hoping for the tension to fade.

After several minutes, Jacqueline broke the silence. "Do you know how many of my friends applied to Cragbridge?" Abby didn't answer; she could guess it was a lot. "Tammy got perfect grades her entire life, and she was declined. Amiya was the junior racquetball champion of the United States and a mathlete. Jared was published in the fifth grade."

"I'm sorry," Abby said. "I don't know how the admissions board works, and I'm sorry your friends—"

"No. Don't even say it." Jacqueline was nearly shouting. She reached into the closet, found the shirt she gave Abby, and ripped it off the hanger. "I'm taking this back."

Abby couldn't believe it. Minutes ago it seemed like the two of them were going to be fast friends. Now, it was shaping up more like archenemies.

"In fact," Jacqueline said, "this isn't going to work." She pinched a series of Abby's clothes between her two arms, and lifted them from the bar in the closet. She walked outside of their dorm room and dropped them on the floor. "There is no way I can room with you."

Abby stood there in shock. Was this really happening? "What do you mean?" she asked. "Let's talk about this for a—"

"No. No talking," Jacqueline interrupted. "This . . . is . . . over!" She grabbed the rest of Abby's clothes and threw them in the hall. Abby walked to the hall and started to pick them up. Several girls peered out of their doors, watching the commotion. When Jacqueline came back out, pushing both of Abby's suitcases out of the room, she noticed the gathering crowd.

"This girl," she said, pointing at Abby, "got into this school because she's the granddaughter of Oscar Cragbridge. She didn't work for it. She didn't earn it." Jacqueline looked into the eyes of the other girls. "She's taking the spot of someone else who got denied—maybe one of your friends— because she got a free pass." Jacqueline shook her head, then disappeared back into the room.

Abby looked into the eyes of the girls in their doorways. Some looked on curiously; some scowled.

"I really have worked hard," Abby said in her defense. "It's just that . . ."

Jacqueline returned, holding one final suitcase.

"Let me take that," Abby started, trying to grab her suitcase. "Some of my things are very special to—"

"I don't care," Jacqueline said. "My friends are special to me, and thanks to you, they aren't here."

"Where am I going to go?" Abby asked.

"Don't care," Jacqueline said. "Maybe you should try a normal school, with people who do normal things. You might fit in there." Jacqueline slammed the door. The lock clicked behind her.

Abby met the gaze of several girls staring at her from the hallway. No one asked if she needed help. Instead, most of them glared at her. They probably had friends who had been rejected too. One by one, they all went back into their rooms, some of them following Jacqueline's lead by slamming their doors.

Lights flashed in the hallway. Ten seconds later, the door to leave the floor automatically locked: 10:00 curfew.

Abby could feel tears building up, threatening to stream down her face, but she closed her eyes and refused them. Then she wiped them away. She was not going to break down just because one drama queen overreacted. Then again, that drama queen had just kicked her out of her own dorm room. Now where was she going to sleep? What should she do with her things?

Abby remembered the Cragbridge student-body helpline. She blinked and sniffled as she turned on her rings. She searched her history until she found the sync code. Within a moment, she was looking at a tired, middle-aged woman.

"Cragbridge Hall. How can I help you?" the woman said. The words rattled out of her mouth without feeling. A small earpiece that accompanied the rings allowed Abby to hear what the woman said.

31

"I . . . I've been locked out of my room," Abby said, careful to maintain her composure.

"It's past curfew dear, and Cragbridge has strict rules. You'll just have to sleep in the hall tonight. That will help you learn to be in your room tomorrow."

"But my roommate—" Abby started.

"No excuses," the woman said, looking stern. "You have to take responsibility for your own actions. Now try to get some sleep."

"But—"

"Is this an emergency?" the woman asked. "Is there a fire? A flood?"

"No."

"Then night-night. I'm not going to send the teacher in charge of your floor over just because you were irresponsible." The woman closed the sync.

Abby exhaled, trying to keep the tears from returning. Deep breaths. Wipe eyelids. She tried not to think of home. She tried not to think about what it would be like when everyone else woke up and found her and all her stuff in the hall.

Abby nestled against her things and hoped tomorrow would be better.

THREE DAYS UNTIL
THEY ARE DEAD

Oscar Cragbridge woke up suddenly from pain running up his spine. His lower back was stealing his sleep again. In some ways, he could thank his herniated disk. It had kept him up many nights that had then led to great discoveries.

As he propped himself up on his bed, he was careful not to twist his back. With a wince, he stood. A tingling sensation went down one leg. The disk had pinched a nerve.

He thought back over the previous day, and a smile crept over his face. He was so proud of his two grandchildren. Now that he looked back on it, he thought they were more of a marvel than anything he had ever invented.

He heard a faint click. Oscar's eyes grew wide. They were here.

What could he do? He couldn't write a message to

those he trusted to come to his aid; those who were after him would simply find and destroy it. He couldn't sync, or they would check his history and hunt down whoever he'd talked to. Maybe he could leave a clue. He grabbed his electronic reader from the nightstand. He only used it when he couldn't sleep and didn't want to make his way to his bookshelves.

He opened the cover and scanned the book titles. He selected one, and then unselected it. He set the reader in the middle of his bed, and then made the bed over the top. It was a sloppy job, but he didn't have time for anything else.

Oscar walked out of his room and into the hall. He heard a swoosh like a rustling curtain. Something pricked his neck. A second later, he fell unconscious on the hallway floor.

• • •

Oscar woke up with a pressing headache. It felt like his skull had his eyes between vises.

"I must apologize for such a rude awakening," a thin voice said.

Oscar's eyes could not seem to focus, but he made out a slight man in front of him. He had slicked-back gray hair, and he wore a classic business suit. He sat in Oscar's old chair with two figures flanking him. Both were dressed completely in black, with neither of their faces exposed. Oscar guessed that one of them had shot the dart into him.

Oscar thought of all the security measures to his house. "How did you get in here?"

"There are ways to get in anywhere," the man said. "There are ways to do anything."

Oscar blinked several more times. The tranquilizer was wearing off. He might know . . . yes, he was sure of it. His whole body tensed as he recognized the man. "Hello, Charles." He clenched his eyes closed for a moment, trying to get rid of the haze from being unconscious. "Did you decide to spend your fortune breaking into old men's houses? I know you want to revolutionize the world, but I thought you'd have something a little nobler in mind."

Charles Muns smiled. "We're getting to that," he said. "I have made a discovery—quite a discovery."

"You mean the scientists you pay made a discovery," Oscar corrected. He tried to keep his body from tensing. He knew where this was going, but refused to show any sign of it.

"That is very fitting, giving credit where it is due," Charles admitted. "They have discovered why no one but you has been able to make a Bridge."

Oscar glared at Charles. His heartbeat quickened.

"It turns out that you have discovered more than you have let on," Charles said. He began walking down the hall. "Please follow me." The two men in black stood behind him. Oscar didn't move.

"They are more than willing to *help* you," Charles said.

Oscar Cragbridge found his cane and, holding the

35

familiar carved handle, gingerly got to his feet. He walked slowly, fighting the dizziness. Eventually he walked down the stairs.

The heavy metal lab door stood wide open. Oscar tightened his jaw.

The small group entered the room, passing a series of complex devices attached to several points on both the door and door frame.

"You have a rather thorough security program. It took me longer than I expected to get past it."

The large room was filled with screens, gadgets, tools, metal scraps, and gears. Plans and blueprint sketches lined the walls and were scattered across a round table in the center of the room. Several heavy doors stood along one wall, but the largest along another.

"Sadly, tonight we only have time for what looked like the most important door." Muns led them to the largest door. Thick locking metal bars and fixed gears showed its strength on its face, yet it stood slightly ajar.

Oscar gasped.

"Yes," Muns said. "Quite an accomplishment to open this one. I was pleased to confirm my suspicions that you have a copy of the Bridge in your basement. It really makes things much more convenient."

"Changing the world, one trespass at a time, are we?"

Charles didn't respond, but led the group inside. He walked over to the controller and punched in specific dates.

Within moments, the ghost of a large ship protruded from the front of the room. It was at least four stories tall and close to three football fields long. What looked like four stout towers blew dark steam as the vessel drove forward.

"I believe you recognize the infamous ship," Charles said, gesturing toward the vessel.

Cragbridge nodded.

"And the day you are seeing right now is April 12, which is, of course, quite close to its infamy."

"Did you really break into my home to give me a history lesson?" Oscar asked.

Charles didn't answer the question. "I noticed you didn't sign the official reports about what the Bridge does. Your honesty would not let you."

Cragbridge sat coolly, careful not to change his expression.

"That's a decent poker face, Oscar, but it will soon go away. Though my scientists cannot duplicate your Bridge, they've managed to create a concentrated enough energy burst that . . . well . . . I think you'll want to see for yourself." Charles pointed to a part of the huge ship.

Cragbridge watched very closely. He saw upper-class Americans in suits and dresses. Couples strolled the deck together. Others lined up to enter the dining hall. He knew that millionaires, Broadway producers, authors, a United States presidential aide, the Countess of Rothes, and even a silent film actress were all on board, but he recognized no one.

"Watch," Charles said, moving the perspective of the Bridge like a camera angle down through the stories of the ship. He pointed at a couple in the boiler room. The woman sat still with her head in her hands. The man paced back and forth.

Oscar Cragbridge looked for a moment. His mouth dropped, a hollow groan seeping out. He pointed a quivering hand at Charles and yelled, *"What have you done?"* He raised his old body to his feet. He took a step toward Muns, ready to get in one good hit with his cane.

The two men in black quickly seized Cragbridge by the arms.

"Calm down, Oscar," Charles said, and slowly walked beside the image he'd pointed out.

"W—w—why?" Oscar whispered, his body trembling.

"Why?" Charles repeated. "I think you know why."

Oscar spoke through clenched teeth. "You can't do this. It will change everything."

"That's the idea," Charles retorted. "I am not afraid of change. Which brings me to my point—I need you to tell me how the Bridge works. And looking at the ship, this means you have an ultimatum. Remember, it is April 12."

"Three days," Oscar whispered.

"And then they're dead," Charles finished. "Think about it."

GHOST OF THE PAST

Calm down, calm down," Mr. Hendricks said, motioning with his palms. "I told you I'd teach you how to use the Bridge today, and I will, but you'll have to listen first." He paced the front of the classroom.

Abby had never been so excited in her life. She sat up straight, and her heart raced, which is why her yawn felt so out of place. She hadn't slept well in the hall, although that had more to do with Jacqueline's words than it did the hard floor. She'd woken up early and put all of her stuff in a linen closet. Then she'd left a message with the help desk for the dorm supervisor, and was told that they would take care of it tonight—they would straighten out the whole situation.

"It is a privilege to use the Bridge," Mr. Hendricks continued. "And if ever you break the rules, that privilege can and will be revoked. It is to be used for study, not for entertainment, practical jokes, or to try to impress someone you think is cute." There was probably a story or two behind each of the examples.

"You may use the Bridge labs across the hall as long as one is open. They are available for an hour before school, during lunch, and after school until an hour before curfew. You'll also notice that we have a station for each of you in this room." Mr. Hendricks pointed to twenty booths lining the classroom. They were large enough to fit four or five people. "These can be used during the same hours. We have several hundred booths total, and they are all connected to one great Bridge—the actual Bridge."

A boy with dark black hair raised his hand. "Where is the actual Bridge?"

"Good question," Mr. Hendricks said. "I don't know. As you can imagine, an invention like the Bridge is priceless, so it is kept somewhere secret to ensure its protection and working order. It works best when undisturbed. The more people who fiddle with it, the higher the chance that it won't work. I believe only Oscar Cragbridge and possibly a few others know exactly where it is."

It all sounded so mysterious—and Abby's grandfather knew the secret. She wondered whether her parents did.

"Anyway, the location of the Bridge is of no concern to you," Mr. Hendricks said. "But what should matter to you is that though you may have to wait your turn, usually most people can be accommodated at a Bridge lab. There are also Bridge labs in your dormitories. They can be used for homework during after-school hours, but keep in mind that they get crowded near midterms and final exams."

Viewing living history for homework—it sounded better than any assignment Abby had done before. Memories of last night and the things Jacqueline had said returned. Maybe she shouldn't be allowed to do homework on the Bridge. Maybe she shouldn't be here at all. Maybe it would be better if someone else—someone more qualified—took her place.

"In a minute," Mr. Hendricks said, walking to the back of the room, "I'll invite you to take your place in front of one of the Bridges, but first let me explain them to you."

It all felt surreal. Abby had heard her father, her mother, and her grandfather talk about Cragbridge Hall, but she was actually here. She had seen a pirate ship sail through her classroom, and she was about to be briefed on how to use the Bridge for herself.

"The Bridge is just a nickname, of course, called after its inventor—Oscar Cragbridge." Abby felt a sense of pride rise inside her. Derick sat up a little straighter in his seat. "It just so happens that we have his grandson and granddaughter in our class. Abby," Mr. Hendricks pointed at her. She shyly smiled and looked around the room. She noticed a few girls scowling back. "And Derick." Everyone seemed to beam at him.

Mr. Hendricks approached one of the terminals. "Its real name is the Historiographic Visualizer. I personally feel that *the Bridge* is much catchier."

A girl two seats in front of Abby raised her hand. "How does it work?"

"I can't go too deeply into the science," Mr. Hendricks replied. "I am only a historian after all, but I can conceptually explain it." He drew a line across the white screen at the front of room by selecting a color and skimming his finger across it. "This line represents us in time. We are here one moment." He made a mark toward the beginning of the line. "Then a few minutes later we are here." He drew another mark farther down the line. "Every day we move farther on in time. We grow older, and, in my case, better-looking, with every day." He smiled at his own joke.

"Now this next part may be confusing, but I'll try to make it understandable." He pressed another mark on the far end of the line. "We are here, and . . ." Hendricks changed a setting on the screen, then moved his finger again across the length of line that came before his last mark. The line faded; Abby could barely see it. "We cannot retrieve one year, one day, one moment that has passed." He pointed to the faint hint of where the line had been. "But we can remember it." He paused for effect. "It's like time itself has a memory. The Bridge can read it and display it for us. You'll notice that it is just a ghost of what once was. We cannot prove how reliable the memory is, but so far, it has never been definitively contradicted."

Abby wasn't sure that she understood any of the explanation at all.

Another hand went up. "I read that Oscar Cragbridge compared the Bridge to how a botanist reads the rings of a tree. Each ring tells a story, and a botanist can go to each ring, though some grew years ago, and tell facts about it."

"Yes," Mr. Hendricks agreed. "I've heard him use that metaphor several times. The bottom line is that there is nothing like the Bridge in the world, and because of your place in this academy, you have the opportunity to use it. Very few people outside this institution ever do." The words hit Abby hard. She closed her eyes, and wished back the guilt.

Mr. Hendricks walked to the nearest booth. "You'll step inside." He opened a steel door and stepped in. After a muffled whirring sound, Mr. Hendricks appeared in front of the class. "I know this will be a little strange at first, but I can use the projector to show you how to work the Bridge from inside it. First, if you'd like to, sync your rings to the Bridge. It is very similar to syncing to your music files, or movies, or books, but syncing to the Bridge is only available inside the Bridge lab. If you don't want to sync, you can use the screen built into the Bridge."

Mr. Hendricks pointed at a screen. "Perhaps at one time, someone used the keyholes you'll see on the console, but we do not anymore. I prefer the sync, but for ease here, I'll show you on the screen." The screen flicked on in front of him. His name registered, and he entered in a password. "You'll have your own ID. Of course, we can track what you watch and can revoke your Bridge privileges at any time. As long as you're using it to learn, you should be fine."

Mr. Hendricks moved his fingers, and another image appeared on the screen. "Here are the Bridge controls. You scroll through the display like this . . ." He moved his finger down the screen, and the log entry changed. "The first column selects the event or log entry you want to see. The second shows you the date, and the third shows the specific hour, minute, and second. The majority of the time, you can simply select the log entry, and the other two will automatically fall into place. Of course, many events can happen over a long period, so sometimes it's helpful to fast-forward or rewind the entries to watch the most significant parts. Some entries are even put together as a series of the most important events to save you time. Oh, and as I'm sure you've heard, you cannot see every event in history. It must be a logged event."

Several students raised their hands.

"I cannot see if any of you have questions, because I'm too lazy to turn on my monitor in here, but every year at this point, someone asks why it must be a logged event. Though I do not have a complete answer, I do know that there are limitations both to the ability of the Bridge, as well as what we allow at the academy. First, the Bridge cannot go more than roughly three and a half thousand years ago, and it cannot show anything that happened in the last fifty years. Second, there are privacy and appropriateness issues. We cannot allow you to roam wherever you want, or—perhaps it would be more accurate to say *whenever* you want—throughout history to look at anything. Some of history is violent, indecent, and grotesque. Some of it just simply should not be seen again, but rather studied in books. Years of work by Oscar Cragbridge, and Abby and Derick's parents, have logged these entries, and I believe you'll find that the vast majority of historically significant events have been logged. If we have missed one, simply put in a request, and often within a month or two, your request will be made available—sometimes sooner."

Abby had heard that her parents logged events in history for Grandpa's invention, but now that she had seen them, she had a new appreciation for their work. It all seemed more real sitting in a classroom surrounded by access to the Bridge.

"When you have chosen the event you want to see, simply select this button." Mr. Hendricks pointed to several buttons at the bottom of the screen. "For example . . ." Mr. Hendricks pushed one.

In an instant, the room changed. The ceilings looked taller, and there were two curved rows of tables with wooden chairs behind them. A dozen men gathered at a higher table at the front of the room. More men were scattered throughout, speaking with one another, seated and resting. Most of them wore long wigs, buttoned jackets, tall socks, and buckled shoes.

"This is Independence Hall in Pennsylvania," Mr. Hendricks said. "You may recognize a few of these men signing the Declaration of Independence."

A feeling of awe grew inside Abby. She felt a chill witnessing such a monumental event. History had bored her in class before, but watching it was different. She saw men willing to risk their lives to start their nation—her nation. If the British could seize them, they'd be hanged for signing

the Declaration. The first man Abby recognized was a bald one with spectacles—Benjamin Franklin. She looked for George Washington, but then vaguely remembered that he wasn't at the signing; he was already fighting for their independence. She wondered which man might be Thomas Jefferson.

The image faded, and a new one appeared. Lines of Roman buildings, with white pillars and terra-cotta roofs came into view. A deafening boom thundered throughout the room, and Abby covered her ears. In the background, a looming volcano spewed flame, rock, and smoke miles high. Intermingled with the flames was a cloud of stones and ash. Even though Abby knew it was just a shadow of history, the scene terrified her.

"This is the famous eruption of Mt. Vesuvius in A.D. 79," Mr. Hendricks explained. "The volcano is spewing out molten rock at a rate of over a million tons per second. The cloud is more than twenty miles high. Pompeii, the Roman city you see in the foreground, was completely destroyed— buried in over four meters of rock and ash."

"And for another example," Mr. Hendricks flicked his fingers again, and the room was suddenly part of a crowd in a large, circular theater.

An actor onstage cried out, "It is certain I am loved of all ladies, only you excepted: and would I could find in my heart that I had not a hard heart; for, truly, I love none."

A woman responded, "A dear happiness to women. I had rather hear my dog bark at a crow than a man swear he loves me."

The crowd in the theater surrounding them erupted in laughter.

Abby couldn't understand all of what the actors meant, but she knew they were making fun of each other. Only after the woman had finished her lines did Abby realize that the actor was really a young *man* dressed up as a lady—gross. She had heard they used to do that in Shakespearean plays, but she wasn't very excited to see it.

The scene continued, but now without sound, as Mr. Hendricks explained, "This is the Globe Theater just outside of London. It had to be outside the city limits, because acting was quite controversial in those days. This theater later burned down. It is where many of William Shakespeare's plays were performed during his lifetime."

The Globe Theater disappeared, and the real Mr. Hendricks emerged from out of a Bridge booth. "Now," he said, clapping his hands. "It's your turn."

ORDINARY

Buffalo Bill shouted, his bushy mustache moving with his words. "And now, the extraordinary sharpshooter Annie Oakley." The crowd erupted into applause.

In the last few minutes, Abby had learned about Buffalo Bill's Wild West Show. The group had toured much of America and Europe, and an important part of the show was the young woman named Annie Oakley.

"You'll soon see why Sitting Bull calls her 'Little Sure Shot,'" Buffalo Bill announced.

Abby watched as Annie Oakley, dressed in a cowboy hat, a long-sleeved dress, and boots, stood in the middle of the stage. She had to be in her late teens or early twenties. The crowd roared as Annie raised her rifle and tossed her long, dark hair.

A man on one side of the stage held a series of glass

balls. Annie cocked and readied her rifle against her shoulder. After she nodded, the man threw the balls, one after the other, into the air. Annie shot each before they could hit the ground. They shattered into hundreds of little pieces. It was quite a show, and Abby couldn't help but think, *Quite a mess to pick up later*.

After several seconds of applause, Buffalo Bill raised his hands and waited for the crowd to calm. "Annie will now shoot a dime from ninety feet away!"

A dime? Really? It would be difficult to even *see* a dime from that distance.

The same man as before held up a dime between his finger and thumb. He threw it into the air. There was only a moment as the target flipped end over end, before Abby heard a bang almost immediately followed by a ping. Impressive.

After the applause and another announcement, the man threw a face card into the air. Annie shot it five or six times before it could hit the floor. But Abby was most impressed when Annie shot the ashes off a cigarette that the man placed in his mouth. Annie Oakley was definitely talented, and the man who trusted her had to be extremely brave . . . or extremely stupid.

"Wow," Abby said, walking down the hall minutes later. "She could hit anything. Apparently she started shooting when she was six, after her father died and she needed to help her family eat and pay the mortgage."

"That's pretty cool," Derick said, walking with a small backpack over his shoulder. Some kids still used them.

Derick carried his art gear and a little extra food in it—he couldn't make it all the way to lunch without getting hungry. "I watched Neil Armstrong walk on the moon. It was epic. If I could jump as far as they could in low gravity, I could practically dunk a ball from the three-point line. But then again, I might be easy to guard moving as slowly as they did up there."

"I wonder if I'll ever get used to this kind of stuff at school," Abby said.

"Sure you will," Derick said. "It'll just take a little time." He paused for a moment. "So is your roommate pretty?"

Abby didn't feel like talking anymore. "Why do you care?"

"I'm your brother, so I should get to know her. You know, to make sure she's good enough for you."

Her brother was at least partially joking around, but Abby didn't feel like discussing her roommate.

Later Abby would decide that she should have said that Jacqueline was bald with a couple of splotches of hair, had a hunchback and a goiter the size of a second head, but she didn't think of it in the moment. She didn't say anything.

Derick looked back at Abby. He must have noticed her reddening eyes. "You okay?"

"Yeah," Abby lied. She inhaled long and hard, and then told her brother about the night before.

"Really?" he asked.

Abby nodded.

"Wow. She didn't even give you a chance."

"Maybe she's right," Abby said. "Maybe I don't . . ." She didn't finish.

"Oh, c'mon," Derick said. "Of course you got in because you deserved it." There was something about the way Derick spoke—his voice was flatter than normal—that made Abby wonder if he really meant what he said. "Should we go down to the office and complain or something? Or we could call Grandpa. Maybe he could punish her by forcing her to watch the history of crochet . . . or . . . fishing."

"No," Abby said, smiling slightly at her brother's joke. She took another deep breath. "I'll be fine."

They walked for another ten yards in an uncomfortable silence before Derick broke it. "So what class is next for you?"

"English. How about you?"

"Music and then zoology," Derick said, his face brightening. "I can't wait for zoology."

"Do you think the rumors are true?" Abby asked, thinking about what she had heard about the inventions they used to learn about animals. Grandpa was partly responsible for them as well as for so many other things.

"Everything else has been better than I expected," he said. "I don't see why zoology would let me down." He gazed at a device in his hand. It flashed and vibrated, showing that it was time for him to turn right. It was the new way of guiding seventh graders around campus. Abby heard that originally the orientation committee had requested personal holograms of Lewis and Clark to guide new students, but the administration thought the idea belittled history.

"Looks like this is where we split up," Derick said. "Have a good time. You'll show them."

"I'll try," Abby said, and turned left.

She checked her orientation device. Her unopened mail messages showed in the corner. A new one appeared from Jacqueline. The subject line read, "Sorry." Abby let out a huge breath. What a relief. Jacqueline had been under a lot of stress. It was probably her first time living away from home as well. Abby could give her the benefit of the doubt.

She clicked the message open. The file had the face of a dark-skinned girl with large pretty eyes. Her name, the file labeled, was Kyra. The message held some sort of information sheet. The girl spoke three languages and had become a successful computer programmer. During sixth grade, she did freelance CGI work for a major firm.

The next sheet showed a boy who had already sung in the Metropolitan Opera House seven times before he turned twelve.

Next was a girl who won the national debate tournament.

Abby flipped through several more sheets. She read about kids who made inventions, played stringed instruments, and crossbred birds into a new subspecies. After the last of twelve information sheets, she read a single line.

I'm sorry. I'm sorry you're here instead of these people who were turned down. Go home, Miss Ordinary.

MS. ENTRESE

Oscar Cragbridge winced and opened his eyes. He coughed as he breathed in dusty air. Wherever he was, it smelled of drywall mud. He looked around the best he could with a stiff neck. He was lying in a simple twin-size bed, but it was somewhere much larger than a bedroom. Off to the side, he saw a wooden chair, painted black. He looked up to see a series of mounted lights. They were rather like simple stage lights. Where was he? The last thing he could remember . . .

It all came flooding back. They had come for him.

Oscar heard footsteps.

"Good morning, sir," a voice said. "You've slept in, which is quite understandable, under the circumstances."

Oscar rubbed his eyes and slowly sat up. He looked at a man with thick eyebrows and a flat nose. He wore a black suit. "I'm sorry. You're probably very uncomfortable," the man said. "But we had to travel during the night, and we couldn't have you making noise and drawing attention to us, so we tranquilized you again. You probably don't recall that I explained this all to you hours ago."

The man did look familiar. Not like Oscar had seen him often. They were definitely not friends.

"Feel free to walk around. My team and I will keep you safe. This is going to be your quarters until you tell us what we want to know. Of course, you may remember that you have fewer than three days to do so."

"Where am I?" Oscar asked.

The man smiled. "I think once you let yourself fully wake up, you'll recognize the place, despite the remodeling. I was told that it would be a fitting location for you, should you decide not to tell us anything."

Oscar looked around and suddenly remembered.

• • •

Abby walked down the hall, trying not to think about Jacqueline—trying not to think about others who were more qualified than she was to be at Cragbridge Hall.

After several classrooms, the corridor opened into a large common area. Tables filled one end of the large room, and the other had large steps with a statue in the middle. A replica of Grandpa Cragbridge, chiseled out of stone, looked over her. He wore stone glasses and a suit—complete with his Cragbridge Hall blazer. He somehow managed to look both dignified and casual at the same time. Seeing his face calmed her nerves.

Abby remembered her grandpa's words. He believed she could succeed. She took a deep breath and moved on down the hall, glancing at her guidance system. She turned left and then right, and walked into her next classroom. As with most classes, desks stood in rows. The floor gradually sloped downward, so that those in the back could see the front easily. Several digital posters lined the walls. Abby recognized a few pictures of great works of literature—a woman with a scarlet letter on her dress and a sweeping view of a massive whale coming out of the ocean.

Abby found an empty seat and sat down.

Immediately after the tardy tone hummed, the teacher stood from behind her desk and began speaking. "Hello. I'm Ms. Entrese," she said. She wore a black dress with a blacker belt, black nylons, and black shoes. "I am here to be your guide through the great world of irony, symbolism, types, foreshadowing, metaphors, conflict, mystery, and resolution." She annunciated every word carefully, and her voice fluctuated dramatically as she spoke. Ms. Entrese probably had some experience onstage.

Abby glanced around the room. Jacqueline sat on the other side, four rows to her left. Abby's stomach rolled as Jacqueline glared back. Abby quickly looked away, back to the teacher.

"Today, I would like to introduce you to one of the great inventions we have here at Cragbridge." She pointed to one of the boys in the front row. He seemed startled. "Your brain," Ms. Entrese said. She pointed to several other students' heads. "I say 'introduce you' to this invention, because in this class, you will be asked to use your brains in a manner different than you ever have before."

Ms. Entrese pointed to a simple chair with a tall back. It was made of cedar wood and lined in places with a dark metal. "This chair," she said, "is another of Oscar Cragbridge's inventions. The Chair will unlock what really goes on inside your mind." She pointed to a blonde girl. "For example, Carol, please step forward."

Carol responded quickly. "Um . . . how did you know my name? Not that a teacher shouldn't know my name, but I was just a little surprised. It is our first class with you." She spoke rapidly, without stopping to breathe between sentences.

"I simply studied your picture in the registry," Ms. Entrese said. "I've studied all of your pictures and all of your names." She rattled off several names of students in class. "I used my mind." Ms. Entrese patted the Chair. "Now, have a seat."

Carol walked to the front of the class. "What do I do? Is the Chair going to tell me my future or electrocute me or something? I guess it wouldn't kill me, because then you'd be in *huge* trouble, because—"

"Just sit," Ms. Entrese interrupted. "And think."

"About what?" Carol asked. "Because if I'm thinking about *trying* to think, I don't think it will work very well. Wow, I said the word *think* a lot there. Sorry for the repetition." Carol's hands moved in quick gestures as she spoke.

She sat down before continuing. "Or should I think about something completely random, like a buffalo in a tutu?" Suddenly on the screen behind Carol, an image appeared of a buffalo curtseying in a pink tutu. The class gasped and clamored with excitement.

Carol whirled around to see her imagination in action. "What? You can see my thoughts? That's awesome!" She paused for a moment, and the buffalo grew a clown nose and huge shoes. Then it sprouted a purple afro and began an amazingly agile disco dance. The class laughed and cheered.

"That's enough, that's enough," Ms. Entrese said, blowing a stray hair out of her eyes.

Carol began prattling on again. "So if I think about the trip I took with my parents to Cancun, or the time when Ben Tristen kissed me in the third grade, which, I might add, wasn't as bad as I anticipated—I thought it would be all slobbery and stuff . . ." The corresponding images appeared on the screen. "Or my first night here." Carol appeared, unpacking her things. Then another image of her talking with a roommate. Abby just hoped Carol hadn't been one of the girls who witnessed Jacqueline kicking her out of her room last night. She didn't want that on the screen for the whole class to see.

"Yes," Ms. Entrese said. "Exactly. The Chair could be used for many purposes—"

"You could interview criminals with this thing," Carol interrupted. A new image appeared: a man with a blond beard and scraggly hair seated in front of a police officer. "Or even better, you could interview cute boys." Now the screen showed several boys, including one who sat in the back corner of the room. The class erupted.

"Calm down, calm down," Ms. Entrese said. "The situations you described may or may not be useful. The person in the Chair still controls their mind, and if they are bright enough, there would be no way of knowing whether they are showing the truth or something imagined." She sighed for a moment, looking tired of explaining. "The Chair is useful here at the academy to show literature." She handed Carol a book. "Read the marked passages."

Carol looked down, cleared her throat, and began to read:

"'Second to the right, and straight on till morning.'"

Abby recognized the words almost instantly, and apparently, so did Carol. A boy, wearing a mix of animal skins and leaves, with curly auburn hair, stood on the screen. Abby smiled as she realized that the boy had the same face as the boy in the back of corner of the room that Carol thought was cute.

"Wait for a moment," Ms. Entrese said. "Notice how this image isn't nearly as clear as those we saw when Carol pictured a memory. See how part of it is completely out of focus? As Carol practices more, she will learn to fill in the image with more detail." She nodded at Carol to continue reading.

In the next passages Peter, Michael, John, and Wendy whooshed across Carol's version of London. They flew between chimneys and circled church spires. They were all dressed in their night robes. Abby was surprised when, at a certain point, John shifted his momentum, and his long nightshirt blew up and exposed his underwear. She hadn't considered how hard it might be to fly in a nightshirt.

Carol read how the group of children in their pajamas continued to fly and fly. It took days to get to Neverland. They had to snatch food from birds, and they tried not to fall asleep—sleeping could kill them. As soon as they were unconscious, they dropped like stones. Abby had no idea it had been so dangerous to go to Neverland. She had seen a few movies, but they always left that part out. Perhaps she needed to read the book.

"Not bad, Carol," Ms. Entrese said. "The book was obviously *Peter Pan*. Who wrote it?"

Several in the class answered, "James Barrie."

"Yes," Ms. Entrese said. "I gave you a rather easy one to start. James Barrie, a Scottish novelist and playwright, wrote *Peter Pan*. Actually, it originally was a play that was adapted into a novel in 1911. It was first titled *Peter and Wendy*."

Ms. Entrese stood behind a podium near her desk. "The power of literature is its ability to create pictures with words, but those pictures only form in the mind of the reader. The Chair helps us practice our ability to understand literature and grasp the author's meaning, or at least to solidify our own interpretations."

"Abby, your turn," Ms. Entrese said, pointing to the Chair.

Why her? Somehow, Abby had known it was coming. She slowly got up and walked to the front of the room. Her heart pounded, and her nerves tingled all over. Was she going to be able to do this? She didn't have the same type of genius mind as the others. Ms. Entrese handed Abby a book, opened to a page with marked quotations.

Ms. Entrese spoke to the class. "Robert Louis Stevenson wrote the rough draft for *The Strange Case of Dr. Jekyll and Mr. Hyde* while sick in bed; he finished it in fewer than three days. He revised the manuscript for several weeks, and it was published in the late 1800s."

"Now before you begin to read this one, Abby, I should prepare you. It's a little more complex than a few kids flying through the sky. We will launch right into the text, so you'll need a few points of reference. The character we'll read about is a good and respectable scientist. You may want to begin by imagining someone you think is good and respectable, someone you admire and look up to."

Almost instantly, Grandpa Cragbridge appeared on the screen behind Abby.

"Oh," Ms. Entrese said. Abby saw her teacher's face flash with surprise and then . . . was it contempt? "He is definitely a scientist, just like our good doctor in the story. There are some who would disagree about his ethics and reputation, but this classroom would hardly be the place for that."

Abby didn't know what to think. Everyone she had ever met loved her grandfather and had nothing but compliments and praise for him. Ms. Entrese didn't seem to be in that camp.

"Now," the teacher continued, "you will not want to

make him look like Oscar Cragbridge, so maybe change your doctor's appearance."

As Ms. Entrese spoke, Abby reformed her image. A younger doctor began to take shape. He looked taller and stronger than Grandpa.

"Very good," Ms. Entrese said. "Now you may begin."

As Abby read aloud, her doctor mixed a vial of liquid. It boiled and smoked for a moment before he grabbed it and swished it around. He waited until the smoke dissipated, exhaled, then downed the liquid in one long gulp. As she read on, the scientist hunched over, a grimace on his face. He clenched his teeth and tried not to scream.

"Very good," Ms. Entrese said. "Now you'll be reading about how the formula changed the doctor's looks. So class, be patient with her."

Abby read how the doctor felt evil, ten times more than before. She discovered as she read that he had actually *become* evil—that was what the experiment did. A good, respectable man transformed into the evil that had been hidden somewhere inside him. As he changed, he shrank and became demented. He also looked younger, his evil side being much less developed than his good. Abby imagined the man hunched over, his teeth yellow, and his hair long and wiry. Dirty stubble sprouted from his chin. Abby didn't enjoy imagining the evil side of someone.

The class watched as Abby continued to read, imagining the hideous, evil form lurching over to a cabinet, drinking one more vial, and buckling to the floor. His legs flailed in every direction, his arms gripping his stomach. At last, his jerky movements slowed, and once more, he was the doctor she had pictured at the beginning—though much paler, and sweat streamed down his brow.

"Decent," Ms. Entrese said. "This book is an allegory for the evil that lurks in even the very best of us. We all must fight to keep it contained. If we let our guard down . . ." Ms. Entrese spoke slower. "If we ever let our guard down, it may catch us unawares." She began looking above her students, avoiding their eyes. "And as you will see later in the book, it becomes harder and harder to leave that darker side alone. The evil will grow stronger." As she finished her statement, her eyes glossed over for a moment. She blinked several times, then simply said, "It is a fine book."

She turned to Abby. "As you continue reading, though, there is more to Mr. Hyde—that's the name given to his evil side. He is a secret. The doctor wants to hide him, to control him. You may want to think of something in your life you would like to keep secret."

Almost instantly a picture of a letter appeared. Abby panicked. Before anyone could read that it was a rejection letter from Cragbridge, she tried to think of something else—anything else. The locket her Grandpa had given her flashed on the screen. Not that. She shouldn't show that, either. Abby cleared her mind, but out of the corner of her eye saw Ms. Entrese watching the screen intently.

"Sorry, Abby," the teacher said. "I didn't mean for you to picture them. That is a small hazard of the Chair. If it helps, I don't think anyone in the room could tell what those things were. Use whatever it was you thought about to help you as you conjure up Mr. Hyde again."

Abby returned to the book, but she couldn't help but think of Ms. Entrese watching the screen and noticing the locket. It appeared on the screen.

"Are you distracted?" Ms. Entrese said. "I told you, none of us could recognize what you thought of."

Abby tried to clear her mind, but she was afraid something had gone wrong. She remembered Grandpa telling her not to show the locket to any of the *teach* . . .

Abby stood up to cut off the Chair.

SQUIRREL
MONKEYS

Derick walked down the hall in the science building, his backpack over one shoulder. Brick walls gave way to large windowpanes, showing a room the size of a basketball court. As Derick looked through the glass, he saw something that could have been out of an African safari. The ground was sand and dirt. Several trees stood tall, with leaves that formed a tremendous umbrella for shade. A glass roof allowed the sunlight to shine on the entire room. His heart beat faster as he searched the room for movement.

There it was! A rhino shook its head to shoo a fly away. It lay like a large boulder near the pond. Another rhino rested against the trunk of a tree. Another one lazily moved toward an alcove in the corner of their large living space. A zoo inside of the school! And if the zoo was real, then . . .

Derick quickened his pace down the hall. The next

room looked like a jungle. Tree after tree filled the area, and trails and brush covered the ground. At least eight gorillas moved around the room, resting along the floor or climbing the trees. One sat with his large black back against the glass. They looked powerful, yet agile. Derick thought they would have to be some of the most intimidating creatures in existence. He rapped his knuckles against the glass. The creatures completely ignored him.

The next room held lions sleeping next to a pond. A giraffe habitat was in the following room, where they ate leaves from tall trees. Finally, Derick found a room with a series of three trees swarming with small monkeys. Their bellies were gray, but a bright, tannish yellow color covered their backs, arms, and legs. They scurried quickly from place to place and swung with agility from branch to branch. The tops of their heads and their snouts were a darker brown, but pink lined their eyes and ears. It was almost as if they were wearing light, furry goggles. Derick paused to look at a monkey eating some sort of small green fruit.

The moment Derick saw the next room, he stopped, his mouth gaping. The room looked like a large warehouse, with rows and rows of storage space, but instead of boxes, there were animals. Each lay lifeless in their sections, like merchandise ready to be sold. Rows of monkeys identical to those in the trees here stood on shelves. Lions stood motionless on all fours. They looked like stuffed beasts in a museum. Giraffes lined one column, and several massive rhinos stood along the back wall. Varying types of birds, squirrels, and other animals lined the next rows. Even a variety of fish lay on shelves.

"Avatars," he whispered, and quickened his pace.

Derick walked between two large open doors, noticing what looked like a complicated locking mechanism on both of the doors. They were open now, but he could imagine they stayed locked up tight after hours. The avatar lab must have cost billions of dollars; of course the school took all possible precautions to keep it safe.

As Derick filed into a line, he could tell he had to enter through another set of doors. Each person in line had to answer several questions before continuing on into the lab. Derick had to wait. When no one entered the line behind him, he figured he'd probably spent a little too much time entranced by the animals and avatars.

"Hand up," a boy said with a slight accent that Derick couldn't place. The boy had olive skin and long, dark hair pulled into a ponytail. He was probably a few years older than Derick and was wearing a name badge that read "T.A.—Rafael."

Derick raised his hand, and a beam scanned it.

"Looks like you're clear," the boy said. "Do you promise to follow all the lab rules?"

Derick hadn't expected such a greeting, but responded with, "Sure."

"If you break a rule, do you understand that you could be dismissed from this academy, and, depending on the nature of your behavior, even prosecuted by the law?"

"Really?" Derick asked.

"Yes," the boy replied, not a hint of a smile or joke on his face. "Avatars can be weapons if used inappropriately. We have taken every precaution to keep them safe here. The glass you saw on your way in is several times stronger than brick, and it's laced with alarms. You can only be allowed in if the professor or I let you in from the inside. Only those who are completely trusted have access."

"You have that kind of clearance?" Derick asked. "Aren't you just a student?"

"Yes and no," the boy said. "I'm a ninth grader and the teacher's assistant."

"Give me a year or two, and maybe I can be an assistant too."

The boy's lips curled into a half-smile. "*Vamos ver.*"

Derick couldn't understand the words, but there was something about the boy's expression that gave Derick the impression that he had no chance of being a teacher's assistant. "Can I go in now?" Derick asked.

"If you understand the seriousness of the responsibility," the boy said, "you may enter. If you prefer not to, we can have a counselor transfer you to another class, like pottery or modern dance." Derick thought the boy was just provoking him now.

"No, thank you," Derick said. "I'm in all the way."

The boy tilted his head to the side and let out a small huff. He flicked his finger across a screen, which made several clicks. The next set of doors opened, and Derick entered into a large classroom.

"Take your seats. Take your seats," a man in slacks and

a blue button-up shirt said. Derick couldn't tell if the man's short hair was blond or white—likely a decent mixture of both. "Pick any seat. You won't be in it long." He waited for all the students to sit. Derick picked the closest one he could find, which was at the edge of a middle row. "I'm Dr. Mackleprank, your zoology teacher." He spoke casually and sat on top of a desk at the front of the room. "And you've all met my assistant Rafael, or Rafa, for short."

He pointed to the boy who questioned Derick on the way in. *He's Brazilian*, Derick thought. *That would explain why the initial "R" is pronounced like an "H." I wonder what part of Brazil he's from?* Derick had learned that pronunciation rule after watching Brazil play in the World Cup last year.

"Rafa took roll and made you agree to follow the rules before you could even come this far. Thank you, Rafa." The boy nodded back at the professor.

"You'll find that Rafa is somewhat of a prodigy in the subjects we'll study in here. He can be of great use to you. I suggest you follow him very closely." The teacher surveyed the room for a moment. "In this class, we will strive to make the world of animals come alive for you. To pass, you'll need to know anatomies, behavior, habitat, and more for several species. You know, of course, that technology has given you a great advantage. You will have the chance to earn an opportunity to use the avatars and to interact with real animals. It is a scientist's dream and your privilege here."

Dr. Mackleprank swung his feet off the desk and moved toward the center of the room. "If the concept of an avatar is unclear to some of you, I will explain. An avatar is almost like another body for you, another form, which you control. In this case, we have made intricate robots to perfectly replicate animals. They move like animals. They imitate breathing and eating like animals. They can even make the same animal sounds. You control them from a lab, but when you are hooked up to our system, you see what they see, feel what they feel. Yes, the program is that accurate—for all intents and purposes, you become the animal."

Derick had hoped the avatar rumors were true, but he felt shocked by the magnificence of it. He would even be able to feel what the robots felt—incredible.

Dr. Mackleprank continued. "You must pass thorough exams before ever being allowed into the animal habitats. Not only will you need intellectual knowledge, but you will also have to prove competency with your particular avatar. Real monkeys can pick out a clumsy fake any day, and they will treat you as an outcast." Dr. Mackleprank paused. "I've decided that to help you begin, and to motivate you with your studies, we will start with an avatar experience today."

This was going to be the best zoology class ever.

"You have probably seen the variety of avatars we offer here," Dr. Mackleprank said. "But don't get overly excited. They are very difficult to control, so you must start off with the easiest to move. For example, it would be nearly impossible for one of you to learn to fly an eagle as a seventh grader. Which do you think would be the easiest to learn how to use?"

Derick raised his hand, but Dr. Mackleprank called on a girl a few seats away. "The gorillas," she guessed.

"Yes," Dr. Mackleprank said. "As primates, humans and gorillas have similar movements. Gorillas will be much easier to learn to control than lions or giraffes. However, because you could do serious damage with a gorilla before learning good body control, you will begin with squirrel monkeys."

A boy with red hair raised his hand. Dr. Mackleprank nodded, and the boy asked how fast they would likely be able to progress to using other animals.

"Good question, and a good one to get out of the way. As seventh graders, you will probably only gain experience with the squirrel monkey. It takes time to get used to controlling an avatar, and once you've mastered one, learning others becomes easier. After the monkey, gorillas are the next step. Then the four-legged animals, then those that swim, and finally, if you are especially proficient, years from now, you may begin flight."

Derick imagined how amazing it would be to fly, even if it was through a robotic avatar. He didn't care if it was with an eagle or a sparrow; he just wanted to fly. He vowed that he'd get there.

"The majority of students who begin flying do so only by entering the accelerated high-school program here at Cragbridge."

Dr. Mackleprank clapped his hands. "Now before we get ready for your first experience in the lab, I must once again stress the importance of the rules. The mere invention of avatars is potentially dangerous. If the wrong forces could imitate our technology, they could work horror by stealth and disguise. A dog could be a spy, a bird an assassin. The main inventor of our avatar, the woman who worked with Oscar Cragbridge, is currently in a highly protected area because of her work. And Cragbridge Hall is well-secured for that reason. You all know of the heavy guard detail at every entrance and exit. The air space over the school is monitored and guarded. The government monitors our use of the avatars, which may be utilized only for educational purposes. For all of these reasons, you must obey completely. Understood?" Dr. Mackleprank waited for the students to nod. "Good. Now follow me."

He guided the students into the adjoining room. Hooks lined the wall, holding what looked like masks and dangling black strands of thick fabric. "These are your avatar guidance systems," he said, gesturing to the items hanging from clasps on the wall. Not every clasp held gear. Perhaps they didn't have enough, or perhaps some were being repaired. "I will show you how to put them on. Then we'll issue one to each of you."

Dr. Mackleprank pressed his finger against a sensor, and the clasps opened, allowing him to pull the gear free. He stepped into a series of straps like he would into a pair of pants.

Two slipper-like ends went on his feet. Several thin black strands wrapped around his legs. Thicker straps crossed his ankles, knees and waist. Dr. Mackleprank threaded his arms through another series of straps with gloves at the ends. He had straps over his wrists, above his elbows, and on his shoulders. He attached a series of thicker straps across his chest. Finally, he put on a mesh mask with a reflective visor.

"Now it's your turn," Dr. Mackleprank said. "Please, wait patiently until you receive yours." Both Rafa and Dr. Mackleprank quickly went to work assigning each of the students their equipment and helping them put it on. Once he was outfitted, Derick felt like he was wearing some sort of Halloween costume.

"I know they feel uncomfortable at first," Dr. Mackleprank said, "but eventually you get used to the suits. There have been attempts to use visual sensors without a suit and have the avatar mirror your movements, much like the video game units that came out in the early 2000s, but they simply aren't sensitive enough." He surveyed the room. "Are we ready?"

"Yes," Derick said, several others echoing his enthusiasm.

"Not likely, *rapaz*," Rafa said quietly, standing close to Derick.

Dr. Mackleprank led them into a long hall, segmented into small booths. It reminded Derick a bit of the Bridge.

"Everyone line up so that you can see this one booth," Dr. Mackleprank said. "Rafael, would you mind demonstrating in a moment?"

"Not at all," Rafa said. "*Meu prazer*."

"Let me explain how you control an avatar. First, we suspend you in the air." He pulled a cord from the ceiling and hooked it to the back of Rafa's harness. "The harness makes you lighter on your feet. In this case, we'll rig it to tip

73

you forward slightly to compensate for the squirrel monkey's tail. You need to be free to move your appendages in every direction, but it is the fact that you can feel what the avatar feels that makes this successful. As you walk, it walks, but you will feel your feet hit the ground. Without that feeling, all of you would fall. If you reach up and grab a tree branch, the avatar will as well, and you will feel the branch in your hand. If this sensation did not happen, it would be nearly impossible to accurately control an avatar.

"Once you're ready, you initiate the system by pressing the button behind your neck. You will only have access to squirrel monkey avatars for now, so you don't have to worry about choosing an animal. The avatar will be placed by our program into your private practice room, and then you can begin."

"But there are no windows. How do we see the avatar?" a girl, with what Derick thought was an Asian accent, asked. Derick had also noticed that the booths were solid walls.

"You don't have to see the avatar from the outside," Dr. Mackleprank said. "You will be seeing the world through its eyes. Oh, and to end a session, simply press on the same button on the back of your neck."

After a few minutes, Derick was hooked up. He pressed the button at the back of his neck to log on. A quick pain behind his eyes forced them closed. His head ached. Derick recoiled for a moment, then slowly opened his eyes.

It was like nothing he had ever experienced before.

The most massive tree Derick had ever seen stood in

the middle of a space the size of a soccer field. It must have been ten stories tall. Derick turned his head, which made him lose his balance and nearly fall over. Pesky tail. Plus, his head felt off balance. Maybe it was larger in proportion to his body than he was used to. He looked down at his hands—furry. He rubbed them against his chest—furry. He rubbed them on the top of his head—furry. He felt like a walking rug. His nose, however, was cold and clammy. Derick was a squirrel monkey.

"Students," he heard Dr. Mackleprank's voice saying, "I'm speaking through a sound system that your ears pick up in your booths, not the monkeys'. That will be important for when you want to join the real monkeys. We can't have them hearing our instructions and being wary of new visitors.

"You'll notice that many things look very large to you. Squirrel monkeys are only twenty-five to thirty-five centimeters tall, so, as you can imagine, you're looking at the world from a whole new perspective. Everything will seem much larger."

Derick began to take a few steps. It felt good—completely strange, awkward, and imbalanced, but also agile and light. He nearly fell to the left, but after spreading his arms as a counterbalance, he managed to stay upright. He was learning to walk all over again.

Derick heard Mackleprank again. "Off to one side of the room are a series of bars you can use to practice climbing and swinging from branches. Squirrel monkeys live in the canopy of tropical forests in Central and South America. So obviously, much of their lives is among trees.

Derick turned toward the bars and toppled onto his side. Getting up was a bit of a chore.

"I'm sure you've now felt the imbalance a tail causes. I've seen several of you already fall over. Don't worry; the tail takes getting used to. Squirrel monkeys don't use their tail for climbing, so you won't have to worry about learning to control an entirely new appendage that way. Just use it for balance. Once you are in a tree, you'll find it to be quite an asset. Balance is everything in a tree. When you become more advanced in your skills, you may learn to use the tail as a sort of tool, but that won't come for a while."

Derick walked forward again. After a few moments, he began to increase his speed, leaning forward a little farther than he was used to. He turned to the left and had to compensate for the tail, but continued his jog.

"Practice, practice, practice. We isolate you for now, but you'll need to be good enough that you can move fast. Squirrel monkeys are prey for falcons, snakes, and felids. They also live in large groups of up to five hundred, which means you must be able to keep control of the avatar despite the chaos of the other monkeys.

Derick reached the bars. He jumped and sailed higher than he expected. He wasn't sure if a squirrel monkey's muscles were stronger, or if his body was lighter, or a combination of both, but soaring through the air was a pleasant surprise. Until he caught the bar in the belly, which nearly knocked the wind out of him. He managed to hold himself there while he regained his breath, and then pulled himself up and jumped to the next bar.

"Start with major movements now, and we'll gradually work our way to fine motor skills, which squirrel monkeys use to eat fruits, insects, seeds, leaves, and nuts, among other things."

Derick leapt for the bar above him, and then the next. He felt limber, quick. Being a little monkey was addictive. He could feel the air through his fur, which he thought might make him feel like he was going faster than he really was. He jumped higher and higher. Then, one bar from the top, he lost his grip. He flailed his limbs in a panic as his avatar fell toward the ground.

GYM

Abby's father walked down a hall of the ship with doors on both sides, his wife a few steps behind. He tried every door handle. He needed just one to be unlocked. He had found one earlier, but discovered someone else inside.

"Sorry," he'd apologized. "Wrong cabin." He hoped they didn't realize he didn't belong there at all.

Wrong cabin. Wrong floor. Wrong ship. Wrong everything.

It had taken the two of them a few hours to realize how bad it truly was—to figure out where they were. And when they did . . . he could still feel the paralyzing fear. He couldn't think about it. He had to do what he could.

Now in a different hall, he twisted another knob. It didn't give, but when he pushed, the door swung open. Whoever's cabin this was, they'd locked the door, but they hadn't pulled it completely closed. He quickly stepped in and looked around. No one. He motioned for his wife, Hailey, to follow him in.

"I don't want to be a criminal," she said.

"Me, neither," Jefferson Cragbridge responded. "But we can't walk on the decks dressed like this. People will ask questions we can't answer."

They still wore their pajamas from last night, when a group of men somehow got through all the security in their house and took them hostage. Jefferson had fought with everything he had, and so had his wife. A few of the men would have a couple of dark bruises and deep scratches for the next couple of weeks.

But in the end, both of Abby's parents were tranquilized. They woke up on this ship—one of the very worst places to be.

"Even speaking with someone could have terrible repercussions," Jefferson said. "We have to blend in." He opened a suitcase and carefully rifled through the clothes.

"Are you sure it wouldn't be better just to hide in the boiler room?" Hailey asked. "We only have to avoid a few maintenance men there."

"We've stewed over this enough," he answered, pulling out a shirt and then a pair of khaki pants. "I don't know how they trapped us here, but I know this is dangerous—not just for us, but for everyone, everywhere. Our only hope is that those with the lockets will discover us, and for that to happen, we have to get up on the deck where they are most likely to search for us." He changed into the shirt from the suitcase.

"Do you think our kidnappers found *our* lockets?" she asked, a quiver in her voice.

"No," Jefferson responded. "We were smart to hide them where we did."

"But even for the others that have them, the lockets probably haven't even—"

"They will soon," he interrupted.

Hailey finally surrendered and looked in the woman's suitcase on the other side of the room. After pulling out a simple dress, she asked, "What about your dad? Do you think he's okay?"

"He's safe, if that's what you mean," he answered, now buttoning a pair of pants. "But I'm sure they're holding us here as collateral. If he wants to save us, he'll have to tell them his secret."

"There's no chance he'd do that."

"No," he said, folding his old clothes. He paused for a moment, "Not even to save us. Though it will rip at his heart, there is too much on the line."

Hailey, now wearing the dress and holding her night-gown, looked back at him. He could tell she was thinking. "Jeff?"

"Just a moment," he said. "Let's get out of this room first." They put the suitcases back exactly how they found them and left the cabin, locking the door behind them. With a little luck, the owners wouldn't even realize their clothes were missing, or they'd think they had just forgotten to pack that dress or that shirt. Then again, unless the owners were going to wear the clothes very soon, it didn't really matter.

As they climbed the stairs, Hailey began again, "But there are others with lockets. They could follow the clues to save us."

"Yes. And that's what we have to hope for. But they'd have to work fast and—against all odds—find out where we are. It's our only chance, and it's a long shot."

"The twins have lockets."

Abby's father didn't speak until after they emerged onto one of the decks of the ship. He leaned on the railing and spoke softly. "For them to figure everything out and face all the challenges needed to reach us would take everything they have," he admitted. "And there are obviously those who would try to stop them. Whoever these guys are, they won't give in easily. I'm not sure Derick and Abby stand much of a chance. They probably have no idea how much is at stake or how much their lives are about to change." He dropped his pajamas over the edge of the ship.

His wife looked down at the ship's sleek floorboards. "How much time do we have?"

"Two and a half days, and then . . ." He didn't finish the thought; he didn't have to. They both knew that they, along with over a thousand others, would be dead. He grabbed his wife's nightgown from her hand, threw it over the railing, and watched it fall into the ocean.

• • •

After Abby received her school-issued gold-colored T-shirt and blue shorts with gold trim, she found a locker. She changed and stepped into the largest room she had ever seen. It was like several gymnasiums combined. Most of the room looked like a regular gym. The south wall, however, did not. It was a mountain. Trees sprouted out sporadically along the rocky terrain, and stone steps carved a trail up the face.

As Abby gazed in awe at the gymnasium, she heard a voice. "Hey there."

Abby turned to see a smiling blonde girl—Carol from English who had imagined a buffalo with an afro in a tutu. She used the vast majority of her arm to give an enthusiastic wave to Abby.

"Hey," Abby answered simply.

"Sorry about Ms. Entrese. It was mean of her to suggest that you think about secrets. I couldn't tell what they were, but I could tell it bothered you. I would have stood up from the Chair too. I mean, I probably would have thought of the time when I secretly borrowed my sister's training bra and wore it to school when I was nine. Or maybe when I hacked into my school's computer system and changed my file so my birthday was listed every other month. I know I probably shouldn't have done that, but they gave out those king-sized candy bars, and I'm a sucker for chocolate. Or maybe when I purposely messed up this scene in acting class about six times. Brian Colfer had to hold me for the whole scene, and I didn't mind the practice." Carol spoke even faster now that she wasn't in front of the class.

Abby smiled. "I guess they aren't secrets anymore."

"Oh, I don't really care if they're secrets. It's just what I thought of," Carol said. Anyone who spoke as much as Carol probably couldn't keep many secrets. "So are you excited for gym? I can't wait. It's good to get up and move around, you know. Plus, all the guys are wearing these cute gym shorts. Can't complain about that. I mean, I guess you could, if you were blind or something."

"You sound really excited about this place," Abby said.

"Might as well be," she responded. "Beats complaining or moping. That's what I think, anyway. Someone else may disagree, but they're probably the moping type—know what I mean?"

"I guess you're right."

"My name is Carol Reese. It's nice to meet you." She offered her hand with the same enthusiasm she'd shown waving earlier.

"Abby." She shook Carol's hand.

"Abby what?" Carol asked.

"Um . . . " Abby hesitated. "Do you promise not to make a big deal out of it?"

"What? Your last name? Is it like McSweaty, or Butts, or Booger or something? I really did meet a boy with the last name Booger. He was nice, but I wasn't going to marry him. He's off my list. I can't have the last name Booger. *Mrs. Booger*," she said as if considering it. "No way."

"No. It's just—"

"I promise," Carol interrupted, and crossed her heart. "Poke a thousand needles in my eye. That's if a thousand could fit, which I don't think they could, but it does sound very painful, which is the point, right?"

Abby surrendered. "My last name is Cragbridge."

Carol's eyes widened, and she started hopping up and down. She looked like she was going to scream, but she bit her bottom lip, which only allowed a happy hum to escape. "You mean you're related to Oscar Cragbridge?"

"He's my grandpa," Abby said.

"Wow." Carol shook her hand again. "Oh, that's why you pictured him when you were in the Chair! I can't believe it."

"I can't believe you have this much energy," Abby said, watching Carol jump.

"Hey, it's better than being boring," Carol said.

"True," Abby agreed.

Carol calmed for a second. "Oh! I heard a rumor that a girl in our year got into school because she was related to Oscar Cragbridge. She didn't have good grades, or high accomplishments, or anything. And she is like pure evil. I think my roommate added that last part though. That rumor doesn't have anything to do with you, or some evil cousin or something, does it?"

Not again. And just when she seemed to be about to make a friend. "I . . . I think so. I mean . . . yes. But I'm not evil, and my grandpa seems to think I deserve to be here even though I'm just kind of average."

Carol paused for a moment, then shrugged. "I guess that's cool. I mean your grandpa's a genius. So I'll trust his judgment. Plus, in a way it makes you stand out. In a sea of people who are geniuses and standouts, you're ordinary. That almost makes you extraordinary."

Abby knew Carol was trying to help her feel better, and it worked, at least a little. There was no harsh judgment in her voice. No threats. In fact, for the first time, Abby felt close to accepted.

Two coaches approached the class. Most of the clumps of students stopped chattering and looked up. "Welcome to physical education," a large voice boomed. It came from an equally large man. He wore black exercise pants that swished as he walked, and an extra-large blue T-shirt that tightly lined his mounds of muscle underneath. The T-shirt had the words "Cragbridge Hall" printed in bright white letters. He was twice as wide, and a head taller, than most men Abby had seen. She guessed he was in his late forties, maybe early fifties, but still in great shape. "Gather round." He motioned with his hands, and the students quickly obeyed.

A trim woman stood next to the man in a matching uniform. "I'm Coach Adonovich," she said, putting her hand on her chest. She spoke confidently with a thick Russian accent. "And this is Coach Horne. Your parents would quickly recognize him as the United States gold medal weight lifting champion in three Olympics, but that was probably a little before your time."

Coach Horne broke in. "And Coach Adonovich has been a top world gymnast for the last decade. She's only recently retired from her professional career to teach here."

Coach Adonovich smiled briefly, then continued to address the class. "We have many advantages here at

Cragbridge Hall," she said. "One of them is you. You have been admitted to this fantastic school because of your overall education. It is not just your academic grades. You have all met a minimum standard in physical education. That is extremely important. Your brain works better if your body is in good condition."

Coach Horne took over. "Every day when you come to P.E., we'll have a challenge for you—one that will not only maintain your good form, but also teach you. Before we get to our first activity, you'll need to stretch. Let's start with the calves." He put one leg in front of the other, stretching out the back one.

Abby, Carol, and the rest of the students followed his lead.

"So where are you from?" Carol whispered, switching to stretch her other leg. She was going twice as fast as the coach, which wasn't surprising.

"I grew up about forty miles from here. You?"

"Antioch, California," she said simply. "It's in the Bay area. I love it—especially going down to San Francisco, but it's really hilly. I mean, you're going up and down *all* the time."

"So what did you do to get into Cragbridge?" Abby asked. It felt good to be on the other side of the question.

"Oh, I've done some acting—a few low-budget web series. Nothing on the prime sites, but I don't think it counts."

"Wow. That's incredible."

Carol smiled. "Thanks, but statistically speaking, that doesn't make me more likely to succeed. In fact, it just makes me more likely to eventually have a large lawsuit against my parents, get a criminal record, abuse prescription drugs, and get divorced more than three times in my adult life."

Abby laughed, now stretching both her arms high above her head like the coach demonstrated.

"Alright. Now for today's challenge," Coach Horne called out. He moved his fingers, which were obviously synced to a school network. Images of Chinese boys surrounded the group. Coach Horne was using the Bridge.

The boys all wore loose yellow outfits with what looked like white socks tied with black straps. Were the straps to keep their socks on? Abby had no idea. At a word from their instructor, they broke into a series of kicks, punches and jumping twirls. The oldest of the group looked about fifteen, and the youngest could not have been older than four. They all moved with amazing agility and grace.

"These boys study at the temple at Shaolin," Ms. Adonovich called out. "One day they hope to become monks there."

Several of the virtual boys came forward. One by one, they did a series of flips, kicks, and handstands that caused the students in the gym to cry out with applause. Two Shaolin boys climbed a sixteen-foot wall along one side with only their feet, then turned to sit on the top of the wall. What looked like the oldest of the boys seemed to be lost in meditation. Several others approached with spears held up. The oldest boy then lay on multiple spear points while the others carried him that way for half a minute.

When they set him down, he didn't have a scratch on him. Again the class clapped.

"It sounds like you're impressed," Coach Adonovich called over the gathered students. "There is a way these young men become so physically fit and mentally strong. They wake up every morning at 4 A.M. and run up a larger version of this hill." The coach pointed to the mountain behind her. She nodded to Coach Horne, who moved his fingers again. The virtual boys began running up the pale carved stairs. "This is the easy part," Coach Adonovich continued. "It gets tougher when they come down."

"Follow the boys up the mountain," Coach Horne said, then blew his whistle.

The mass of students moved toward the stairway. Several boys tried to prove their prowess by sprinting up the stairs. Abby and Carol jogged from the middle of the mass of students. Abby felt good to be doing something she knew how to do; she'd run every day for several years now. She loved it. Running helped her get out her discouragement, and it focused her mind.

Carol looked over at her. "I still can't believe that you're related to—"

"You promised not to make a big deal out of it," Abby interrupted.

"I guess I did. But I don't think I am making a big deal out of it. I'm ecstatic. I mean, he's the most influential scientist in history. He's not like my granddad at all. My granddad is likely to sit around and play his old video games—the ancient kind where they used little controllers."

Abby laughed. That didn't sound like her grandfather at all. The two girls passed several other students, and then a girl burst by them.

Long dark hair swooshed past them—the same hair Abby had seen as she was locked out of her own dorm room.

"I thought you said you ran track," Jacqueline said over her shoulder.

More emotions surged through Abby than she knew she could feel. All the stress and difficulty of the last twenty-four hours seemed to rush over her. She hadn't realized Jacqueline was in the class. For a moment, Abby wanted to slow down and nurse the growing pit in her stomach, but then she realized she was supposed to be getting out her energy, relieving her stress. And Jacqueline just gave her a very good reason to run harder. Abby looked at Carol.

"You know, I'd love to chat with you, but right now . . ."

"You really want to beat Miss Prissy up to the top?" Carol asked. "She doesn't seem nice. I mean what's the deal with, 'I thought you said you ran track'?" Carol moved her head in exaggerated sweeps to flip her hair.

"She's kind of ruined my last day and a half. I could use this."

"I'll try to keep up," Carol said.

Both girls nearly doubled their speed, pressing up the stairs. They passed student after student. Abby looked at Jacqueline's back; the sight fueled her legs. She pressed harder, but made sure to pace herself. She didn't want to run out of steam before the top.

"I don't buy . . . that stuff about you just being . . .

ordinary," Carol said, starting to get winded. "You're not even . . . breaking a sweat."

"Then what is this watery stuff . . . coming out of my pores?" Abby asked.

"You know . . . what I mean," Carol said. "It's just an expression. Like . . . like . . . I can't really think right now . . . We're running too fast . . . It's shutting off my . . . brain."

The two girls had been running long and hard enough now that they could no longer talk. They increased their speed to yet another level. They would have to in order to catch Jacqueline. Abby pushed herself harder. She thought of Ms. Entrese. She thought of giving away the secret of the locket, and she ran even harder. She thought of how intimidated and scared she was to be at Cragbridge Hall and pushed harder again. She thought of sleeping in the hall. Her legs pushed more.

They passed runner after runner as they approached the top. Jacqueline was now in the lead, with a couple of boys a few steps behind. Abby thought her lungs would burst. She passed one boy, then another.

Jacqueline looked over her shoulder, saw Abby, and moved faster. Abby was at her heels. Carol gave out a slight grunt and tried to keep up. Abby bit her bottom lip, only half a step behind. The three pushed on in a dead sprint, the top of the synthetic mountain quickly approaching. Soon there was only a matter of inches between them.

Abby could almost taste victory. She wanted it. She had pushed herself this far, and she wasn't about to let her goal slip out of her reach. She tried to dig deeper, to find a place in her muscles she had not yet reached—to simply will them to go faster and push more.

Jacqueline turned her face sideways. "Never," she said, and her lips curled up into a half smile. "You're not in my league." She increased her speed, not thirty steps from the top.

Something in Abby popped. Something that had been holding back her last bit of strength burst open, and desire surged through her body. She could not stand to lose—not today. This girl had just unleashed everything Abby had. Her legs pushed, her heart pumped stronger and faster.

There were ten steps left. Eight. Five. Three. Abby leveled with Jacqueline, and pushed into a slight lead. She was going to win.

Jacqueline flung her arm to the side, hitting Abby in the stomach. Her breath escaped, and she faltered for a split second.

Jacqueline sprinted past, winning the race.

Abby slowed after reaching the top, glaring at Jacqueline. Soon Carol joined her. All three walked around, waiting for their hearts to slow down.

Jacqueline beamed at Abby. "Good try," she said. "But maybe you don't belong on the top."

"I'm in the best shape of my life, and I couldn't keep up," Carol said. "I'm impressed with both of you. Except . . . for your cheating thing." She pointed at Jacqueline. "That was . . . really low. I mean . . . are you like a second-grade boy . . . who just can't stand to lose? No offense, but it was really immature." Though Carol was winded, she still managed to speak fast.

"Are you with her?" Jacqueline asked. "I wouldn't hang out with her . . . You'll get dumber by osmosis."

Abby glared at Jacqueline. "Have you always cheated to get to the top?"

Jacqueline huffed. "It's not cheating if you win." The way she said it, Abby was sure she believed it.

Just then, someone Jacqueline knew finished the run, and her face went from anger to delight. "Good job, Kevin," she congratulated. There was no sign that she had just been spitting darts at Abby and Carol.

One after another, all of the students made it to the top. Both of the coaches had also made the run, trailing in the rear to make sure all the students made it.

"Very impressive, ladies," Coach Horne said, looking at Jacqueline, Abby, and Carol. "Now that we're all up here, watch as the virtual monks show you how to go down." Coach Horne flicked a finger, and the monks began to crawl down the stairs on their hands and feet. They looked like skinny human spiders.

"You're kidding," Abby said.

"I hope so," Carol offered.

"Nope, that's the way," Coach Adonavich answered. "Works your feet and heart on the way up, your arms and thighs on the way down."

Abby wouldn't be challenging Jacqueline on the way down.

THE LOCKET

"I'm glad they don't try to teach us about famous chefs while they give us food," Derick said, emerging from the cafeteria line with a plate of fajitas and a cup of horchata on a tray. "It might just overload my brain."

"I don't know," Abby said. "It might be kind of nice. I like anything about food." She opted for the mandarin chicken salad and apple juice. They found an empty table in the commons and sat on opposite sides.

"So how is your first day going?" Abby asked, still a little flushed from gym class.

"We got to watch a little Mozart and some B.B. King in music," Derick said. "I liked them both, but there's just something about a big black man with a guitar." He panto-mimed the famous Blues guitarist swaying with his guitar. "And zoology was *amazing*! Dr. Mackleprank says I'm a fast learner too. Maybe a natural." He raved about his time with the squirrel monkey avatar for the next several minutes.

He didn't tell Abby that he'd made the avatar fall from the top of the climbing gym, and Dr. Mackleprank warned him that if he broke it, he would spend the rest of the semester reading zoology textbooks.

Carol bounced down the space between benches, holding a tray of her own. "Hey, Abby," she said. "I don't mean to interrupt, especially if you and your friend here are talking about something private. Especially if he is your boyfriend. And if he is, all I can say is 'wow.' You've been here for a day, and you've already hooked up with a good-looking kid like that. I'd applaud, but I don't want to drop my fajitas."

It was almost like Carol didn't realize that Derick could hear everything she said. "He's my twin brother," Abby explained.

"Whew!" Carol looked from Abby to Derick several times. "I mean, now that I look at you, I can tell that you're family, but I couldn't at first." She raised an eyebrow. "And that means you're not her boyfriend."

Abby let her brother sit in the awkward moment for a few seconds before saying, "This is Carol." She turned to Carol. "Have a seat." Abby moved over, but Carol sat down next to Derick.

"Nice . . . to meet you," Derick said. It came out as more of a question than a statement.

"Pleasure's mine." Carol set her tray, heaping with food, on the table. "I just couldn't choose, so I talked the lady into giving me both kinds of fajita and a full salad. Which is fantastic, because I'm soooo hungry. I think I'd be really dangerous right now at an all-you-can-eat place." She spoke as fast as ever.

"So you didn't tell me you had such a good-looking brother," Carol said, picking the onions out of her fajitas. "I mean he's no supermodel, but close enough, you know? Plus, he's here, so he probably has brains, which is always a bonus." Abby couldn't stop herself from cringing a little. Carol turned to Derick. "Unless, of course, you're like a super genius and want to spend all day talking about physics equations and math theorems, and then we might as well call it off right now—*boring*! I mean, snorefest 2074. You know?"

"You speak faster than most people can think," Derick said.

Carol blushed slightly. "Thanks."

She launched into another flood of thoughts, but Abby didn't pay attention. She felt something. It took her several moments to pinpoint what it was. She put her hand to her chest. Something moved underneath her hand, like an insect had crawled under her shirt. She almost screamed.

But it was no insect. The locket her grandfather had given to her was . . . moving. She almost pulled it out from under her shirt but remembered that Carol was at the table.

"What's wrong?" Carol asked. "Oh, does it have to do with the locket you want to keep secret? I mean, I don't mean to be nosey, but I can put two and two together. You wanted to keep some locket a secret, and now you're

covering your chest . . . and I can see the chain around your neck."

Abby looked at Derick.

"I'm not sure how," Derick said, "but it sounds like she already knows about it. Let's step out into the hall so no one else in here gets curious. Once Abby and I see what's going on, we'll decide if you can know more." Carol agreed, and all three of them left the cafeteria and found an empty hall.

Carol brought her plate of fajitas and waited a good distance away.

Abby pulled at the chain until the locket emerged from under her shirt. The top of the locket had opened, the cover splitting into two pieces that had slid away from each other. "Did yours do this?" Abby asked Derick.

"I . . ." Derick stalled for a moment. "I left mine in my room. I didn't want to wear a necklace. It felt . . . weird."

The front of the locket was completely uncovered. Abby peered in, utterly confused. Inside were two items: a folded slip of paper and a small key held by two metal clasps.

"What does the paper say?" Derick asked.

Abby grabbed the small paper, which was folded into a square about the size of the tip of her index finger. She unfolded it and peered at the paper for a moment.

"It's a Bridge code." She pointed at the date and the numbers that followed: *Decision 08/13/2056—0005440543*.

"I guess he wants us to look at whatever is logged in under that number," Derick said.

"I guess so," Abby said.

"Wait," Derick said. "The Bridge can't show you things

unless they happened over fifty years ago. This date is less than twenty years old. That seems a little inconsistent, don't you think?"

"Yeah, that is strange," Abby said.

"I can't think of anything special that happened on that date," Derick said. He turned on his rings and began a quick search. "Looks like the Fryson virtual amusement park opened. Some place called Yikirotech launched a new system to preserve memories digitally. The pogoball made a comeback. DisneyUniverse opened in Texas. And Ezzie O'Neal was nominated for an award for her performance in *Drisdale's Conscience*."

"Doesn't sound like anything Grandpa would want us to know about," Abby said. "What about the key?"

"No idea," Derick said. "Maybe it's to some box in Grandpa's lab or something." They both looked at the small metal key for a few moments, trying to decide what it could go to.

"Have you guys decided if I can see yet?" Carol asked. "Or are you like looking at pictures of long-lost relatives, or staring at jewels . . . or. . . What else would be in a locket? Oh! Eating candy!"

Abby knew this was important and that her grandpa had asked her to keep it secret, but she couldn't bear to exclude Carol anymore. She was the only person other than Derick who had been nice to her, who had included her.

"She's too curious now. Maybe we should show her the key," Abby suggested. "That's pretty simple."

Derick was reluctant, but eventually agreed. Abby

tucked the paper into her pocket, motioning for Carol to join them.

"That is one tiny key," she said. "Do you know what it goes to?"

"No idea," Abby admitted.

"Maybe it's a jewelry box or something," Carol suggested. "Or one of those tiny doors in *Alice in Wonderland*. I always thought those books were kind of creepy, and maybe even drug-induced. I think it would be more accurate to call them *Alice in Drugland*, but it just doesn't have the same family-friendly feel to it."

"Those are some great ideas," Derick said, raising his eyebrows at Abby.

"I wasn't serious about the tiny door," Carol said. "But I do have some great ideas. Like, I think they should use avatars to bring in our luggage when we first get here, because my suitcases were really heavy. And I think some sort of milkshake bar in the hallways would really help me out after a couple classes in a row. Oh, and we should make a haunted house in this place using the projectors. That could be freaky!"

She looked at Derick. "We could go through it together. But I might get scared and have to hold your hand. Or you might get scared and have to hold mine. I'm fine with either way. I'm versatile."

"Um . . . ," Derick stalled, not knowing how to answer. "Keep thinking of more ideas," he finally managed.

"More like the first two, or more like the last one?" Carol asked.

Abby couldn't decide how she felt about Carol's flirting with Derick. It made her feel awkward, which she didn't enjoy. But it also made Derick feel even more awkward, which she *did* enjoy. "Derick and I have to go to the Bridge labs to do some homework. Want to come?"

•   •   •

Carol was going to do her homework in another Bridge, and had promised to sync up with a friend from home, so Abby closed the steel door to a Bridge with only Derick next to her.

Abby synced her rings, entered the date and code, and waited.

A message reading "seeking authorization" scrolled across the screen.

"That's new," Abby said.

"What?" Derick said.

"I need some sort of special authority to . . . oh, wait," Abby said.

A new message appeared.

Attachment recognized. Sync will continue momentarily.

"We needed my ring attachment to watch this," Abby said.

"That's different," Derick agreed.

What was going on? Grandpa said that they would need the attachment for unlogged entries, including his journal. Maybe that was it—something like a journal. In a moment, both she and Derick stared at the phantom image of

Grandpa Cragbridge. He stood only slightly hunched over in the center of the room. If Abby had to guess, he was at least fifteen years younger. She remembered the date she had entered. It was eighteen years ago. Her guess had been close.

"Hello," Oscar Cragbridge said, "to whoever you may be. But whoever you may be, chances are that you are a good friend of mine, and someone I respect very much." Abby smiled to think that what her grandpa said applied to her. She also realized there were probably more people with the lockets than just her and her brother—after all, she hadn't even been alive when he made this message.

"If your locket has opened," the ghost of Grandpa continued, "that means that something has happened to me. Every day before noon, I trigger the device that keeps the lockets closed. When the locket opened, it was the first day past my ability to keep it closed. This could mean that I have died of natural causes. Or it could mean that someone has . . ." Grandpa paused. It looked like he was choosing his words carefully. "That someone has sought me out with other intentions."

Abby's heart beat faster. Could Grandpa really have died? Abby imagined him in a long mahogany casket with friends and family gathered around. Her heart felt as though it would collapse on top of itself. No. He seemed fine yesterday. He was probably safe and sound, working hard on his next project, reading an old classic, or catapulting marshmallows as her parents tried to do their work.

And what did he mean that people would seek him out

with "other intentions"? Abby didn't like the sound of that; it seemed sinister or conniving, as though her grandfather actually had enemies. The thought made Abby sick. Could someone really have done something to her grandpa? Was he okay?

Grandpa cleared his throat. "Either way, I now bequeath a great secret to you—the beginning of it, anyway. You'll want to . . ." Abby couldn't handle it anymore. She shut off the Bridge and threw open the door. Derick followed quickly afterward.

"Hey, guys. Are you done?" Carol asked.

Abby didn't bother answering. She selected communications mode on her rings, then set them to her grandfather's number. She paced the lab as she waited for him to sync.

She waited longer than usual. Or did it just seem longer because she was under stress?

"Call Mom and Dad," Abby told Derick. "We need to make sure . . ." She had trouble saying the words. "We need to make sure Grandpa's okay." Her eyes welled up with tears.

"Already on it," Derick said, his trained fingers moving quickly.

Abby still waited. And waited. Grandpa wasn't syncing back. Why not? He always wore his rings. She disconnected and tried again. "I'm still not getting anything."

"Me, neither," Derick added.

"Try again," Abby ordered.

For once, Carol was silent.

Nearly a minute later, Derick reported that still no one answered.

Abby burst into a sprint down the hallway.

"Abby!" Derick ran after her, Carol close behind.

Abby didn't look back.

The three teenagers rushed down the hall and out of the building. Abby sprinted down the long sidewalk. She approached the looming outer walls of the school several yards ahead of the others. A large gate was surrounded by several guards. On her way inside yesterday, she'd noticed they were all armed.

A guard approached her. Abby slowed down, not wanting to excite him. She wiped her face with one sleeve.

The guard was muscular and well over six feet tall. "Where are you going in such a hurry?"

"I was told I could leave to visit my grandfather when . . ." Abby paused as a sleek robot with arms as thin as bamboo rods seemed to be scanning her. It rolled around on a single wheel.

Just like when they'd passed through the gates the first time, the guard explained that the scan was for both the safety of the students and the protection of the inventions inside.

"You see," the guard said, humdrum, "no one can leave without permission." He didn't seem interested in the rest of her explanation. "Especially when the next classes start in just a few—" A green light flashed on the side of his booth. The man stopped midsentence. "I've never seen that before. The man used his rings for a moment, obviously

103

double-checking the information. "Huh?" he grunted. "I've never."

"Please, sir, I really need to leave. It won't take long." Abby wiped her face again.

Derick arrived, and the thin robot scanned him. Carol followed behind, talking despite the run. "You know we aren't going to be able to leave. This place is like a prison. Don't take that the wrong way—I mean, it's an amazing *educational* prison with fantastic opportunities. It's just that we can't—"

"Oh," the guard said. "Looks like that last name of yours comes with some privileges." The man's all-business attitude broke a little as he looked at Abby again. "Are you sure you want to leave?"

"I'll be fine. I just need to check on something," Abby said.

"You can go, but lunch ends soon and classes will start, so you'd better hurry. If you're late, they'll mark you truant and track you through your rings—for your safety, of course. They want to take good care of you." He motioned with his hands, as the large gate opened. It had to be at least six inches thick and made of heavy metal. Abby walked forward through the open doors. When she heard the gates close behind her, she looked at another set of gates in front of her. The protective system let students out gradually; no one could rush out when the large gates opened. They had to get permission, step through one set of doors, and then another, before they reached the large front gate. Abby could hear the guard's voice reminding her to hurry.

The third and last set of doors opened, and Abby broke into a run. She raced up the street and turned left at the light. She passed a string of cars in recharging slots. She glanced over her shoulder; Derick followed after her, but not Carol—she wouldn't have the same privileges as a Cragbridge.

Abby ran with everything she had. Her sprint up the monk mountainside was a jog compared to this. Derick couldn't keep up. Soon Abby's legs felt rubbery, and her lungs half their normal size, but she pushed on.

She told herself to stay calm. Everything would be fine. Grandpa fell asleep or got too involved in another project. Mom and Dad would be there, working so hard that they didn't sync back. She was getting all worked up over nothing. Abby consciously lengthened her stride, trying to get a few more inches with each step.

No matter what she told herself, Abby didn't believe it. She felt like her heart had fallen into her stomach.

Abby reached the front porch of the 1997 rambler. She waved at the sensor, then waited for the security system to let her in. After what seemed like ages, the little green light shone, and she twisted the handle.

"*Grandpa!*" she shouted, entering the living room. "*Dad!*" There was no answer. "*Mom!*" She repeated the calls as she ran from room to room.

She passed Derick, who was calling out their names as well.

"*Grandpa!*" Abby repeated. Tears cascaded down her face and onto her shirt.

After racing out of the kitchen, Abby met up with Derick again in the middle of the living room. She swiveled her head in different directions, hoping to see her parents or her grandfather—hoping to feel the relief of finding out that they were okay.

"Grandpa's lab was open," Derick said. "And that massive door we aren't allowed through—where Grandpa, Mom, and Dad work—isn't locked anymore. And there are the scrapes on the walls. Someone was here and they took something out. I'm checking satellite pics." Derick turned on his rings.

"What for?" Abby asked, wiping her face.

"To see who came in," Derick said. "The satellites can show you any public place at any time, unless someone has sued for private air space."

"Someone . . . here?" Abby muttered. "Why would they?" Her mind skipped from one thought to another. She began pacing in a daze, walking to move, to do . . . something. Was this really happening? Her family was all fine yesterday. How could everything have changed so quickly?

Abby looked at her grandfather's chair. He should be sitting in it now. Where was he? She turned away and walked down the hall. The house felt so distant, empty. She walked through the open door into her grandpa's bedroom. She had seen the room before. There was the same bed, same side table, same closet, but no Grandpa. She opened the fold-out closet doors. She hoped he would be behind them waiting to surprise her. She even parted several groups of shirts, hoping to find him. She headed toward the bedroom door.

But before stepping out into the hall, she paused. Something was out of the ordinary. Grandpa's bed was made. Abby had heard her mother pester him over and over again to make his bed. When they visited, she would say things like, "You can make the world's most innovative inventions, but you can't make your own bed?"

Grandpa always replied with something like, "Why make a bed when you're just going to have to mess it up again in a few hours? I used to do it when Emma was alive, but that was just because I loved her and wanted to please her. I'd rather do things that matter."

So what did it mean? That Grandpa had started to make his bed all of a sudden? Or was someone trying to cover something up?

Curiously, Abby lifted the covers. Underneath was Grandpa's electronic reader. Why would that be in his bed? This was getting stranger all the time. She'd never seen him actually read from his e-reader. He always said he preferred "real books." She opened the reader. An array of book titles was available. She scanned through his reading history, which had a short list of titles. The latest book had been opened at 2:24 A.M. that morning—the only time the book had been selected, and the reading session had lasted less than a second.

The book was *Kidnapped* by Robert Louis Stevenson.

Abby gasped. This was definitely a message. Grandpa had selected this book, early this morning, for a reason. He'd hidden it in his bed, then made it, because he knew that those who loved him would know he didn't make his bed, and they'd find the clue.

Abby wanted to collapse to the floor.

"There's nothing visible on the satellite pics," Derick said from the living room. "All of the lights within a block went out for four hours. Whoever came here made sure nobody would see them."

Abby quickly raised her rings and selected communications mode. Moments later, she stared into the office of the nearest police force.

"Hello. BPD," a woman with a short haircut and high cheekbones said.

"I think . . . something's happened to my . . ." Abby broke up with emotion. "My grandpa and my parents. I think they were kidnapped."

INVESTIGATION

There was definitely someone here," the officer said. "And at your parents' house too. But the people who did this were professionals—could be the best I've ever seen. They must have disabled the security systems and then restarted them. I've never seen that happen."

His words didn't exactly console Abby.

"We believe they accosted your grandfather here, but that he was apparently awake enough to send you the message that he'd been kidnapped. The suspects stole something large from the basement. Nothing that we can tell is missing from your home other than your parents. I still don't understand why anyone would do this to the Cragbridges." The officer stopped for a moment to direct one of the other three officers as he placed a few hairs he found on the floor in a thin black container. "Does your family have any enemies that you know of?"

Abby looked at Derick. "Not that we know," she said. She took a deep breath. "But Grandpa did tell us that he had a secret that some people would do anything to get."

Derick's eyes flashed with panic.

"Really? What sort of secret?" The police officer's thick eyebrows stood in stark contrast to his light skin, but his eyes were intense, penetrating.

"We don't know. Just some secret."

"And how do you know?" the officer asked.

Abby looked at Derick, who motioned for her to keep her lips shut. But she couldn't. Speaking up may help them find their grandpa and parents.

She took a deep breath and grabbed the chain around her neck. Derick stepped forward to stop her, but she already had the locket out. She explained what had happened with the locket during lunch.

"This is interesting," the officer said typing a few notes with his fingers. "The locket must be special to you, but we're going to need it for our investigation." He held out his hand. "We'll return it to you as soon as we can."

Abby removed the chain from her neck and looked at Derick one more time. He closed his eyes. Abby dropped it into the policeman's hand.

"Thank you," the policeman said, placing the locket into another black container. He looked at Derick, "Do you have anything that would help the investigation?"

"No," Derick lied quickly. "We only got one locket between the two of us, and Abby wore it. It's kind of girly."

The policeman chuckled. "It is. Well, thank you. You've been very helpful. We'll have another officer escort you back to school." He looked first Abby and then Derick in the eyes. "We're going to have to insist that you stay at school. We'll give instructions to that effect to the guards. Security at Cragbridge is as good as anything we could provide you. So no more unlimited access to come and go. Do you understand?"

"Why?" Derick asked.

"Just in case," the police officer said.

"In case they come after us?" Abby asked.

"At this point, all we know is that we have a high-profile citizen and his son and daughter-in-law kidnapped. There are crazies out there . . . and, well, we don't know. We just want you to be safe." There was something about the officer that made Abby feel safe. She was glad he was on the case. She could picture him braving all sorts of dangers to find her parents and grandpa.

The twins turned to leave, when the officer called again. "Oh, Abby and Derick." They both stopped. "We're going to keep this case confidential. You won't see anything about it on the news or the net for a day or two. We want to make sure we know what we're dealing with first."

The twins nodded and then followed another officer out of Grandpa's house. They soon walked the long sidewalk inside Cragbridge Hall.

"Why didn't you tell them about your locket?" Abby asked.

"He took yours," Derick said. "I didn't want to give it up. Grandpa gave them to *us*, not to the police."

Abby didn't say anything.

"Why do you think Grandpa had to trigger a device every day to keep our lockets closed?" Derick asked.

"I don't know," Abby confessed, wiping her eyes and trying to stand up straight and tall. She wanted to be strong.

"And he gave lockets and rings to other people too?"

"Sounds like it," Abby said. "Do you think Mom and Dad have them?"

"Maybe," Derick said, and then looked at the floor. The lockets were a painful reminder that their parents were missing.

"Or maybe other teachers got them too," Abby suggested.

"I wonder what the big secret is," Derick said.

Abby had no idea. Why would anyone want to do something to her family? Was it because Grandpa was famous? Would they get a ransom note soon asking for billions of dollars? Or did he do something wrong? Did he actually have enemies? And what about her parents? How were they involved?

Abby couldn't help but think back to *The Strange Case of Dr. Jekyll and Mr. Hyde*. She imagined her grandpa turning into some sort of monster, hunched over, grimy, and decaying. She quickly shook the image from her mind. She was glad she wasn't sitting in the Chair right now, having her thoughts portrayed on a screen for others to see. She remembered how Ms. Entrese had caught a glimpse of the locket. Had she baited Abby on purpose?

Did her time in the Chair have anything to do with all this?

All Abby wanted to do was cry, but she couldn't let herself. She also couldn't let herself simply wait for the police to finish their investigation. There had to be something she could do. She looked at Derrick. "We've got to go back to see the message again."

• • •

Once again, Abby and Derick stood in the Bridge.

Abby tried to clear her mind, to get ready to listen and remember, but emotions kept creeping back. Tears waited to slide down her cheeks. She closed her eyes, took a deep breath, and turned on her rings to initiate the sync.

Access Denied.

Abby tried again.

Access Denied.

"What's taking so long?" Derick asked.

"It won't let me in," Abby said. "My access is denied. Give me a minute. I need to figure this out."

Abby came out of the room and walked straight to the desk where the lab supervisor sat. "I don't know what's going on, but it won't let me into the Bridge."

"What's your name?" the lab supervisor asked, a boy

with floppy blond hair that hung over his eyes. He must have been in eleventh or twelfth grade.

"Abby Cragbridge."

The boy in the lab raised an eyebrow.

"I'm his granddaughter," she said, not waiting for the question.

The boy looked at his screen for several seconds. "Sorry. Your Bridge privilege is temporarily revoked."

"What? Why?" Abby asked.

"Couldn't tell you if I wanted to," the boy said. "All I've got here is that the head honchos have suspended your privileges. Did you get caught cheating or ditching?"

"I missed some classes this afternoon, but it was an emergency," Abby said.

"That could be it," the boy said. "You might have to straighten things out with the attendance department." He gave her a half smile. "That's all the info I have."

Abby rejoined Derick in the Bridge, who had already synced with his rings. The image of Grandpa was paused and ready to go.

"He said I'm suspended from the Bridge," Abby said. "And he guessed it was because of missing a few classes."

"That doesn't make sense," Derick said. "I logged on while I was waiting for you. Why would they deny you but not me?"

"*Uuuugh!*" was all that came out. "I can't believe this."

"We'll straighten it out later," Derick said. "Right now, let's figure out what Grandpa was going to say."

In a moment, Grandpa began repeating his message.

Abby couldn't help but feel heartbroken as she saw him again.

"I have a secret that others would go to extreme measures to obtain. Therefore, I have given you this entry to tell you that I need your help. No police, no investigator, no government can solve the large problem that faces you." Abby immediately felt guilty for giving the police her locket. But should she have really done anything differently? What else could she have done when the officer asked for it?

"You see," Grandpa said, "I've opened a Pandora's box of sorts. I have kept it controlled, but others will not."

Abby remembered that Pandora was a Greek myth about a woman who opened a box full of plagues. She was pretty sure Grandpa meant that he'd invented something that could cause some serious problems.

"But I can't tell you everything about it here. The situation may not merit it, or this message may have been intercepted. If I have passed away by natural causes, I want you to know that I loved and trusted you, which is precisely why you are listening to this now. I must pass my secret to someone. Sooner or later, someone else will discover it, and I'd much rather it went to someone I trust."

He inhaled slowly, then closed his eyes as he exhaled. "If foul play is involved, whoever is against me will probably not be kind enough to leave much of a trail. They will most likely be professional and determined."

Abby remembered the police describing how proficient the criminals must have been.

"They may," Grandpa continued, "even be ruthless in their efforts to accomplish their goals. In that spirit, I feel that I must warn you. Be careful about who you trust. Some people would do absolutely anything to know my secret and use it for their own purposes."

Again Abby thought about Ms. Entrese.

"My secret cannot die with me. It is too dangerous. But it would be foolish and irresponsible of me to give it to you all at once. In a way, you must earn it and that process will help you be ready for what the secret is. And I need those I trust to be ready. To discover more about my secret, you'll have to decipher a clue and retrieve another key."

Abby grimaced and twisted her hair into a ponytail. Another key? The first had to be the key in her locket, which she'd given away. Hopefully the police would give it back soon. At least Derick still had his. "I have tried to make the clues something specific to you, so that if this information is intercepted, it will be burdensome for someone else to figure out. But I'm afraid I've had to make the clues a little difficult as well, to keep at bay those who seek my secret without the right intentions. Please insert your key into the small opening on the Bridge console."

So there was a need for the keyholes after all. Abby waited in the Bridge for Derick to retrieve his key from his room. She thought through everything again and again. A clue was coming, and it would be specific to them. But what was the secret? Why couldn't Grandpa just come out and say it?

Finally Derick returned, panting and holding a small

key. Abby could make out a glimpse of the chain under-neath his T-shirt. Apparently the locket wasn't too girly anymore. Derick put the key into the hole in the console and turned it. Grandpa appeared again, but this time he looked as he had yesterday. No longer was he young and stronger, but his normal elderly but happy self. He must have recorded it recently.

"Dear Derick and Abby, I decided years ago to give you both the same clue. If you are going to succeed, I be-lieve you'll have to work together. Here it is: When Derick turned twelve, I gave him a book. In books we often begin a journey to find freedom." Grandpa began to walk away, but stopped. "Oh, and check the top of the armoire."

"That's it?" Derick asked. "That doesn't make much sense."

"No, it doesn't," Abby agreed. "What do books and an armoire have to do with Grandpa's secret?"

DOUGLASS

Abby repeated Grandpa's clue. "'In books we often begin a journey to find freedom.' There is no way Grandpa is asking us to search for clues in every book in the world."

"No," Derick said. "It must have something to do with the book I got when I was twelve. He's given me quite a few—*Lord of the Flies*, *The Adventures of Huckleberry Finn*, biographies of Thomas Edison and Benjamin Franklin."

Abby tried to think through the clue. Grandpa always gave them old-style hardcover books for every birthday, holiday, and special occasion she could remember. Over the years, both of the twins had gained quite a collection. "Wait," Abby said. "When we turned twelve—that was when he gave us books about the people we're named after."

"You're right," Derick agreed. "You got a biography of Abigail Adams, and I got Frederick Douglass." He smiled.

"When I was really young, I couldn't figure out how Derick came from Frederick."

"Maybe you aren't such a genius," Abby suggested.

Derick ignored her. "And it fits. Douglass was a slave who escaped and became a famous speaker and writer against slavery during the Civil War—that might be why the clue has to do with freedom."

"Makes some sense," Abby admitted.

"'In books we often begin a journey to find freedom,'" Derick repeated.

"Maybe we're supposed to study how he got free," Abby suggested. She pictured a dark-skinned man running through the forest with barking dogs chasing him and men following behind with glowing lanterns.

"I guess so," Derick said. "But I remember that in his autobiography, Douglass didn't tell us how he became free. He didn't want to give away any secrets that would keep other slaves from being able to escape the same way. I'm sure the way he escaped is out there somewhere, but I never got around to researching it."

Abby activated her rings. She searched, her fingers moving quickly and sharply. She read over the bites of information presented in a series of three-dimensional windows. "Yeah. He wrote more than one autobiography. Eventually he wrote the whole story, but even better, I think it's logged on the Bridge. See if there is an entry for Frederick Douglass, September 3, 1838."

Derick moved his hands along the screen of the Bridge. "Here it is," he said and pushed the button.

The first thing Abby saw was a large steam-engine train. She'd seen them in pictures—and one old one in a museum—but never one that actually worked. It was a long mass of metal with a huge steel grate on the front and a series of long wheels attached by strong bars. It must have weighed tons. When a tuft of steam came out the top of a funnel, Abby wondered how the heat could really power such a heavy machine. Abby walked a few steps back and forth, inspecting the ghost of a train from the past.

Men in suits and women in dresses gathered in clumps on the platform. Wives hugged their husbands and business partners gave final advice. Every now and then one of them said good-bye and boarded the train. Several black men waited to board. They were all gathered near a back car, away from the others. It seemed strange to see them completely separated from everyone else. Derick searched them, hoping to find Frederick.

"Can you find him?" Abby asked.

"None of them look quite right," Derick said. His eyes wandered for a moment more, searching. "I think that's him," he said, pointing to a black man leaning against the wall of the train station. Derick moved the perspective of the Bridge to better see the man. He was tall and strong. Years as a slave must have built some decent muscle. His thick, wiry hair stood up several inches. Abby guessed he was in his late teens or early twenties. He wore a red shirt, a sailor hat, and a black scarf tied around his neck.

Abby eyed the group of black men waiting to board the train, then Douglass. "What's he doing here?"

"I think he's going to get on that train," Derick guessed.

"Then why is he waiting by the wall?" Abby asked. "And where are his bags?"

"I don't know," Derick said. "But this is the day he escapes from slavery, right? Maybe he's just nervous."

Abby tried to imagine what it would be like to try to escape from slavery. She'd read enough to know that when slaves were caught, they were whipped and beaten, sometimes to the point of being killed. They were valuable property, so they weren't usually beaten to death unless a master wanted to use a slave as an example to scare the others.

Abby saw determination in Frederick's eyes. He knew the risks, and he was trying to escape anyway. He looked calm and collected, but every now and then, Abby thought she caught a twitch in the leg, or shift of the eye that betrayed some nervousness. In his shoes, she would have been terrified.

Abby turned around to survey more of the situation. Her eye caught a different black man approaching a uniformed man at the ticket window.

"One ticket please, sir," the black man said. "Northbound to Wilmington."

"Papers," the man in uniform said gruffly, holding out a hand.

The black man quickly produced some folded papers. Abby guessed they were proof that he was free and not a slave. Papers like that were a precaution against escaping slaves. The train station employee read part of the papers, then said, "It says here you have a scar on your left leg."

The black man quickly lifted his pant leg, revealing a long, pink scar that ran from behind his knee to a few inches above his ankle.

"And another scar on your right arm, just above the elbow," the man in uniform said. The black man rolled up his sleeve. "And you have whipping scars on your back?" The man raised his shirt to show an array of grooves and lines.

Abby gasped. She could hardly imagine the whip and pain it would have taken to make such scars. The man had passed all the tests, so the worker finally took the black man's money.

As the worker leaned out of his window to give the man his ticket, he noticed Frederick. "Can I help you?"

"I don't know yet, sir," Frederick responded. "I have a friend delivering my bags. I'd better not buy a ticket until I know I can travel."

"The train leaves in minutes," the man said.

"Yessir. I hope he hurries," Frederick said.

Frederick waited for the man to leave his window and go back to his work station. Then he pulled a slip of paper from his pocket. Abby circled around to get a better look.

"Pause it here, Derick," Abby said. The image froze.

She looked closely at the document. It was a sailor's paper, which made sense with the way Frederick was dressed. The emblem of an American Eagle graced the top of the page, making the whole document look official.

"What's he looking at?" Derick asked.

"His identification papers, I think," Abby said.

"Are they really his? I mean, if he's escaping, there's no way he has his own papers, right?"

"They're definitely real," Abby said, reading over Frederick Douglass's shoulder. "But they aren't his. Look at this," she said, motioning for Derick to join her. "I don't think he fits this description." She pointed to a few lines on the page.

"No, he doesn't," Derick said. "Douglass was a mulatto—his mom was black, but his dad was white. That's why his skin isn't as dark as some of the others, but the papers describe someone with a lot darker skin. Definitely not Frederick's papers."

"If that conductor looks over his papers like he did that last guy's, he's busted," Abby added.

The whistle blew. More and more people hugged their relatives or shook hands with their business partners and said their good-byes. The lines at the entrances of the train grew longer. Frederick looked up at the clock on top of the train station.

"I still don't get it," Abby said. "Is he going to miss the train?"

"What, did I see this before you?" Derick snapped. "All we can do is watch and find out."

The train whistle blew again.

A horse and carriage pulled up to the side of the road beside the station. The driver leapt from the seat and tethered his horses. He pulled two bags out of his coach and ran toward the train station.

The train lurched forward, the huge heavy machine toiling to get any momentum.

The man from the carriage brought the bags to Frederick. "Perfect timing," Frederick whispered. He then looked at the man who sold tickets.

"You can buy a ticket on the train," the man said.

"Thank you sir," Frederick said and ran toward the train.

"Have a nice trip," the carriage driver said. "And you're welcome."

The last of the crowd waved to those at the station and jumped onto the train. Frederick hurried to catch it, his strong body moving quickly—Abby couldn't run that fast while carrying bags. As the train reached the end of the platform, Frederick jumped onto the train car. He had to lean on the handrail to keep from falling back off. A few other latecomers jumped on behind him.

Derick flicked his fingers, ordering the Bridge to follow Frederick. The runaway slave set down his bags and waited for his turn with the conductor, who was dealing with the last-minute rush. Frederick asked to buy a ticket. Busy, the man quickly glanced at his paper.

"Sailor, huh?" the conductor said, speaking loudly over the sound of the train.

"Yes sir," Frederick said. "I know ships from stem to stern, and from keelson to cross-trees." The man nodded and took Frederick's money.

A moment later, he handed over a ticket. "We appreciate our sailors and the free trade they encourage," the conductor said. There was no smile, no 'have a good trip,' from him, but Frederick was on the train.

"He did that on purpose," Abby said. "He waited until the train was moving so they wouldn't look as closely at his papers."

"Yeah," Derick said. "And the book Grandpa gave me said that Frederick worked repairing ships, so that's how he knew how to talk like a sailor. This guy is smart."

They watched as Frederick walked through the car filled with other dark-skinned travelers. They probably weren't allowed anywhere else on the train. She watched as Frederick stored his baggage and found a seat.

Frederick looked across the car, then immediately turned his head the other way. He must have seen someone he recognized. He turned slightly and tilted his sailor hat. Abby watched as a man farther down the railcar gazed at him for a few seconds, then looked away.

After several minutes, another conductor entered the car and moved up the aisle. Abby's heart skipped.

"Papers and ticket," the man said. Apparently, this would be a more thorough check. These train conductors did not take chances.

Abby's heart pounded just watching the incident. The passenger closest to the conductor quickly produced his ticket and papers. The next passenger had them out before the man asked for them. Everyone seemed eager to prove their freedom. As the conductor moved along, he scowled and asked to see scars or birthmarks, checking each passenger against his or her description.

When the conductor approached, Frederick did not produce his papers right away like the others had. He sat calmly. Abby wondered if she could ever act so calm under pressure. She saw something change in the conductor. His brow straightened, and he spoke coolly. Maybe the sailor uniform made the difference.

"I suppose you have your free papers," the man said.

"No, sir," Frederick responded.

What? Of *course* he had papers. Abby had seen them a few minutes ago. Frederick continued, "I never carry my free papers to sea with me."

The man said, "But you have something to show that you are a freeman, haven't you?" His voice sounded less condemning than when he'd asked the others.

"Yes, sir," Frederick answered. "I have a paper with the American eagle on it, and it will carry me around the world." Frederick reached inside his pocket and produced his paper.

The man glanced at the paper and then moved on.

Abby exhaled. She hadn't realized she'd been holding her breath.

"He's good," Derick said. "Cool under pressure."

"Yeah," Abby said, as she watched him situate himself again so the other man on the train couldn't recognize him.

Derick fast-forwarded the scene, making sure Douglass traveled safely.

"But I don't get it," Abby admitted. "That was amazing, and I'm glad he became free, but I didn't see any signs or clues to Grandpa's secret."

"Me, neither," Derick admitted.

TO THE OFFICE

I'd suggest we watch it again, but after as many times as we've seen it, I don't think it would do any good," Derick said, motioning to the image of Frederick Douglass riding a train to freedom.

"I know. We've watched it so many times, I think I almost have it memorized," Abby said. "We're not on the right track."

"Are you trying to make a train joke?" Derick asked.

"No. You know what I meant." Suddenly an image appeared in Abby's contact lens. *Abby Cragbridge, please report to the front office. Thank you.*

"Huh," Abby said. "I just got called to the office."

"Me, too," Derick said. "It's probably about missing class today."

The two of them followed their guidance systems to

the office. As soon as they stepped inside, they knew it was about something more than their missing class. The first thing they saw wasn't the secretaries busily typing and speaking on their syncs. It wasn't the student aides, filing digital documents and entering some sort of reminder on the bulletin screen—something about the lunch menu switching.

Instead, they saw police officers, who stood as Derick and Abby came in. One was a husky woman dressed in a navy blue uniform, hair pulled back into a tight ponytail. The other, a thin, but athletically built man, his hair buzzed short.

"Are you Abby and Derick Cragbridge?" the female officer asked. Her voice was smooth and professional. She logged onto her rings and flicked her fingers. Abby guessed she was recording their conversation.

"Yes," Derick said. Abby nodded.

"Please come with us," she said, and pointed toward a door along the back wall of the office. She led the way, the twins walking behind. The man with the buzz followed. When they were all inside, he closed the door.

"We have a few questions to ask you," the man with the short hair said. Abby mentally nicknamed him Buzz.

"Have you found our grandpa and parents?" Abby asked.

The police officers looked at each other for a moment. "Where were you at 12:30 today?" the woman asked.

"We were either here, or we were at my grandfather's house," Derick said. "I didn't look at the clock. Why?"

The woman typed something—maybe making a few

notes. "And what were you doing at your grandfather's house?"

"We were looking for him," Abby responded.

"Why did you think that he was missing?" Buzz asked.

"We already told you all of this," Derick said. "Well, not you, but some other police officers."

The man and woman glanced at each other again. "And how did you meet up with these other officers?" the woman asked.

"I synced up with BPD," Abby said, "and they met us at the house."

Buzz took a step closer. "Can I sync up with you and see your log?"

"Sure," Abby said, turning on her rings. In a moment, she checked the list of her previous syncs with the officers watching. "Here it is," she said, highlighting an entry.

"The time matches up," Buzz said, reading the log from the side. "Sync up with the BPD again, would you?"

Abby obeyed, and a moment later, viewed a man with short, spiky hair. "BPD," the man said. "How can I help you?"

"Hello, Dave," Buzz said. "We're just asking someone here a quick question." He turned to Abby. "Was this the man who you spoke to?"

"No," Abby said. "It was a woman."

The husky woman officer made a few additional notes with her fingers. "Would you describe her and the other officers you met at your grandfather's house?" she asked.

"No offense," Derick said, "But these seem to be really

weird questions. Shouldn't we be focusing on our missing parents and grandpa?"

Buzz lifted a hand. "We'll need to know all about that in a moment, but first please describe these people you spoke with at your grandfather's house."

"I don't understand," Abby said.

The woman exhaled slowly. "They weren't police officers. Whoever they were, they put up an elaborate façade to fool you. We didn't hear from you at all. Our guess is that someone intercepted the call because they were expecting it. They must have some pretty state-of-the-art gear to do that. We didn't hear about your grandfather's disappearance until a neighbor called it in. They just wanted to know why the police—who apparently weren't police—had been there."

Abby's mind was swimming. Who had she spoken to?

Buzz stepped in. "We've studied the public satellite footage of your grandfather's house, and we were able to identify you, but not the officers. They were all very good at keeping their heads covered and never looking up."

"Then who was the big guy with thick eyebrows and a flat nose that took my locket?" Abby asked. "He wore the same kind of uniform as the rest. He promised they'd find my family. He said they'd keep the whole thing quiet, and I wasn't going to hear about it on the news. Who were they?"

"That is a very good question," Buzz said.

"And you're definitely going to hear about this on the news," the woman added.

THE ARMOIRE

I can't believe this!" Derick said, walking slowly down the hall to nowhere in particular. "This thing just keeps getting bigger and bigger. Grandpa's secret has to be a pretty big deal if someone has kidnapped him and our parents, and pretended to be police officers."

"They wanted our lockets," Abby said, following her brother. "And I gave mine to them." She knew she had made a mistake.

Derick didn't speak for a moment. "It's over now," he finally said. "With the info we just gave the police, they'll nail them."

Abby wanted to believe him. She wanted to think that all they'd have to do was hold tight and everything would work out, but something inside her knew it wasn't true.

"No," she said. "We can't depend on them at all.

Remember how Grandpa said that no police or government was going to solve this? We have to do it. Now that they have my locket, I think we need to move faster. They'll be trying to find the secret too."

"It's like a race," Derick said.

"And if Grandpa's right, the stakes are pretty high."

"But we have no idea what to do next."

Abby logged onto her rings and began a search.

"What are you looking for?" Derick asked.

"I'm not sure, but I thought it wouldn't hurt to look for references about Frederick Douglass and freedom." She searched the results for a minute. "But there are tons of hits. He wrote a lot of antislavery stuff and gave lots of speeches."

"Wait a second," Derick said, his eyes going wide. "Let's go back to the Bridge." He changed direction and walked quickly. Abby was only two steps behind. "I just remembered something. I think Frederick Douglass once talked about a different kind of freedom—one that had to do with books."

"Books? That would certainly fit Grandpa's clue, but I still don't get it," Abby confessed.

They arrived at a Bridge lab, opened the metal door, and stepped inside. Derick searched through the Bridge's logged events. "I feel dumb for not remembering it before. Watch this." With a quick flick of the finger, he started another scene.

A woman sat writing on a small chalkboard, with a black boy standing a few feet away. She turned the board around to reveal the word *ant*. The black boy struggled but eventually sounded the word out. They repeated the process over and over with words *sun*, *fall*, *work*, and the hardest: *plant*.

"That's Mrs. Auld," Derick said. "And the boy is Frederick. This was years before he became free. Mrs. Auld and her husband took on Frederick mostly to play with their boy."

They heard the sound of a door opening and closing. A large man with dark hair and a receding hairline entered the room. The hair on the sides of his head was matted with sweat, and he rubbed his eyes with one hand. He looked like he was about to speak to his wife, but then he watched as young Frederick learned small words.

It only took a moment before he interrupted her. "You do not teach him," the man said, his voice shrill and commanding. Derick and Abby both winced at the man's tone.

"Why not dear?" Mrs. Auld asked. "He is doing quite well."

"It is foolish—even wrong—to teach a slave to read," the man said. "The only thing a slave needs to know is to obey his master—to do as he is told. Learning would spoil the best slave in the world. He would be no good to me, and no good to himself. He'd become discontented and unhappy."

Abby took in the man's speech, analyzing as he went. "That's terrible," she said. "How could he think slaves are better off not knowing how to read?"

"I don't know," Derick said, pausing the scene. "But Douglass didn't see education that way. Reading changed his life. Frederick believed that keeping him from learning was how they kept him a slave. He thought if he could learn to read, then he would be free—free to learn and experience other things outside of slavery. Mr. Auld made him even more determined."

"But how would he learn?" Abby asked, gesturing toward the image of young Frederick. "It doesn't look like Mrs. Auld was able to teach him anymore."

"He grabbed sections of newspapers to read. He tricked people into spelling words for him. He was resourceful. It took years, but he learned."

The whole thing felt like something Grandpa would want them to think about—one of his preachy lessons. "'Freedom in books,'" Abby said. "I think it fits."

"And there's an armoire," Derick said, pointing to a large hickory cabinet behind Mrs. Auld. He walked over to it in the paused scene. Grandpa said that they should check the top of an armoire. "Come on over, and I'll give you a boost. Check the top."

Derick lifted Abby up the best he could. She stood on his clasped hands, and steadied herself by grabbing the back of his head. It was awkward; he wouldn't be able to hold her for long. On top of the ghost of an armoire was nothing but a piece of paper.

Something was written on the paper—a sentence or two. After reading only the first few words, Abby gasped; the note was in her grandfather's handwriting.

How?

"It's a message from Grandpa," Abby blurted out and

quickly read it aloud. "*Remember the first clue. And remember how you used to play Jonathan Code and Kimberly Spy.*"

"What?" Derick asked.

"Put me down," Abby instructed, tapping Derick on the shoulder. He lowered her, and Abby stepped to the ground. "Grandpa wrote it. It's definitely his handwriting, but somehow it's on the armoire."

"But how?"

"I don't know," Abby said.

Derick reached for the armoire, but his hand passed right through it. Same with the table and the painting on the wall. "This doesn't make any sense."

"I know," Abby agreed. "Plus, I wasn't expecting him to refer to our old games." Growing up, she and Derick used to try to sneak past Grandpa without him noticing. They planted old smart phones to record conversations, and left each other secret messages that they had to piece together. She once cut up a bunch of letters from a newspaper, and Derick had to put them in the right order—back when one newspaper was actually printed on paper to try to bring back the old days. "Our spy names were terrible."

"Kimberly Spy is a terrible name," Derick agreed, "but Jonathan Code is . . . I was going to say *awesome*, but it's really just as bad."

"Alright, Jonathan Code," Abby said. "Get to work on this one."

"Let's see," Derick said. "He told us to remember the first clue—'In books we often begin a journey to find freedom.' But then the second part of the clue has to do with the two of us pretending to be spies. What do they have to do with each other?"

"I don't know," Abby admitted. "Do you think there's some sort of code we're supposed to put together from this scene with Frederick Douglass?"

"I don't know," Derick said. "It couldn't hurt to check."

The twins spent the next twenty minutes scanning the scene again and again. Of course, they started with the armoire. Then they reread the note countless times and looked for any clues in the note, but they couldn't find anything. They looked through the rest of the armoire, which held several vases and decorative cups, but nothing to give them any hints. They watched the scene three more times just to be sure. Abby typed notes about everything they thought might be some sort of a message—the words Frederick Douglass repeated, the headlines on the one-page paper near the chair in the living room, even the names of Frederick and the Aulds. As they left, they were filled with information, but felt no closer to solving the clue.

"I don't get it," Abby said, sitting down and putting her head in her hands.

Derick looked at his watch. "We've already missed dinner, and we've only got a few minutes to get back to our dorms before curfew. We can use the Bridges there, but we'll have to split up."

Abby nodded.

"Let's see what we can do on our own tonight, then meet right here an hour before breakfast," Derick said.

The two walked along the pathway. Abby thought

about their insane day. Her parents and her grandfather were missing, and she'd learned that there was some sort of great secret she needed to find. She wanted to collapse and cry.

"Sleep on it," Derick said, and turned toward the boys' dorm.

Abby stopped cold, only now realizing that she still had nowhere to sleep.

ROOMMATE

Abby walked back to her dorm, figuring she'd have to sleep in the linen closet. At least that way, no one would yell at her. She had a lot to think about. But when she came up the elevator chute, there was a crowd of girls in the hall.

"There she is," a girl whispered as Abby approached.

"I'm not changing rooms for her," another added.

"Alright, alright," a voice at the front of the room said. "We need to resolve a certain problem before you can go to bed." Abby had heard the voice before—articulate and confident—but couldn't quite place it. "Is Abby Cragbridge here?"

Couldn't the day just end? Couldn't she just sleep with the linens and disappear? Abby raised her hand and started passing through the crowd of girls. She was only halfway through when she recognized the voice—Ms. Entrese.

"Hello, dear," Ms. Entrese said. She turned to the crowd of girls. "I don't think there is a more tactful way to say this. I believe everyone is aware that Abby was kicked out of her dorm room last night. Jacqueline refused to sleep in the same room with her when she discovered that Abby was admitted to this institution largely on the reputation of her grandfather."

The words stung. It hurt for Jacqueline to kick her out because she'd gotten accepted because of her grandfather, but to hear a teacher state it just as matter-of-factly as she would facts for an upcoming test, cut deep. If Abby hadn't had much bigger things on her mind, she might have broken down.

"I've arranged," Ms. Entrese continued, "for someone to take Abby's place in Jacqueline's room, but what we need to discuss is whether anyone of you would voluntarily take Abby into your room."

Abby went from depressed to embarrassed. She couldn't have felt more awkward. Was she on auction? The only thing worse than Ms. Entrese's words was the silence that followed. No one moved. Abby looked at the girls, but they all avoided her gaze—except for Jacqueline, who looked her in the eyes, beaming.

"I will," a voice came from the back, breaking the silence. "Sorry, I would have spoken up earlier, but I was in the bathroom. You know you just can't wait about some things. And, by the way, I don't know about you girls, but

Jacqueline pulled me aside and tried to convince me not to room with Abby. Though she was really friendly and even kind of persuasive, I mean, she offered me a new wardrobe, and she's got some really cute stuff—especially this pink V-neck that kind of gathers on the sides. But despite the cuteness, I just don't feel good about that. Don't you think that's low?"

Abby didn't need to see her face. She knew who it was.

"I like Abby," Carol continued. "I think she's fun to talk to. Well, maybe I do most of the talking. That's what my mom tells me all the time, but my mom talks a lot too. I mean I probably get it from her, but anyway, Abby is great. Plus her twin brother is hot. I mean like lava-burning-into-gas-in-the-center-of-the-sun hot. So you know, this might lead to a friendship or something more. You know, good friendships. Good networking."

Relief swept over Abby. Someone had stood up for her. And she'd finally have a place to sleep.

Then again, the way Carol talked, maybe Abby wouldn't get much sleep. Abby didn't care, though she couldn't help but wonder if Carol's former roommate was relieved.

"Alright, alright," Ms. Entrese said. "Bless you for taking in this poor thing. We may have to shift around a few more room assignments to make this happen, but we'll get it done. You'll only have an extra half hour to get your things moved, then into bed."

• • •

"So, what happened?" Carol asked, helping Abby carry one of her suitcases. "I've been worried about you all day. I haven't been this worried since I lost my rings at a party, and the boy who was throwing it—Garrett Shaw—I think he was kind of into me, and I had to go back over to his house to look for them, but I was worried he thought I left them there on purpose just to have an excuse to see him again. And he's nice, but you know . . . I wasn't interested. So anyway, what did you find out?"

It felt wonderful for Abby to have someone ask about her, to wonder about her. The whole day felt like a huge load Abby had carried by herself ever since she'd said good-night to Derick, but somehow the burden seemed a little lighter. But how should she answer Carol's question? Carol didn't know about the clue or the note, but she knew about the locket.

"Oh, I had to check up on my grandpa," Abby said, purposely being vague.

"Next time, let me know, because I'd love to meet him. I'm not becoming your friend just so I can meet him—that would be extremely shallow, like when this girl named Stephanie was really nice to me, until I brought her on set for *Halvishem's Eve*. Turned out, she just wanted to get in front of the director. After she met him and got an audition for another web series he was doing, she never talked to me again. At least, when I tried talking to her again, she said I talk too much, and that I was annoying, which isn't the first time I've heard it. And I don't think it's entirely true—at least not all the time. Anyway, that's not why I'm friends with you."

"Okay," Abby said, as she bent down to pull her last case into their room. It was three times as heavy as the others.

"Let me help," Carol said and grabbed the handle. She grunted with her first pull. "What the Valhalla is in this thing, rocks?" She struggled to pull the last case into the room.

"Books," Abby said.

"Really?" Carol asked. "Like *real* books? You do know that you can read billions of them just by using your rings, right?"

"Yeah," Abby said, "It's just that my grandpa . . ." Abby didn't finish her thought. Something suddenly made sense. "Remember the first clue," she whispered to herself. "'In books we often begin a journey to find freedom.'"

"What the heck? Are you like woozy in the brain?" Carol asked. "Because there was this one time that I met this insane—"

"No," Abby interrupted. "I have to figure out something, and I think it has to do with the books my grandfather gave me." Abby blinked away a few tears. She was surprised she had any left.

"Okay," Carol said. "Just don't go crazy on me, or I'm going to seriously reconsider being roommates. I mean, crazy people are okay, even entertaining, in their little crazy-people hospitals, and sometimes on public transportation, but I don't want to room with one."

"I'm not crazy," Abby said. "My grandpa trusted me to figure something out, and I think it has to do with the books he gave me. It's the only way I can think of that he could possibly control where we'd look for clues."

"I have no idea what you're talking about," Carol said.

The first clue was about a book that he gave Derick, so maybe the rest of it is in actual books too, ones Grandpa gave them. *Books*—plural—lead to freedom. It would make sense. If Grandpa knew he was going to give them clues, he could put them in books he knew they would have. And that way, he would know that if someone intercepted his messages, they wouldn't be able to figure out the entire thing. Abby opened her case and found her copy of *To Kill a Mockingbird*. She handed it to Carol. "Would you mind looking through this for . . . anything unusual?"

"Okay." Carol grabbed the book. "You realize that this is strange. I thought you were going to prove that you *weren't* crazy."

Abby didn't say anything, so Carol leafed through the pages.

"Boo Radley is a weird name," Carol said, pointing at a page. "But I kind of like it. Maybe I should name one of my kids Boo Radley." Carol looked up from the book. "Ichabod Crane is also a fun name to say. Oh, and . . ."

Abby pulled out a copy of a biography on George Washington. "I'll take this one."

"Do you have any idea what I might be looking for?" Carol asked.

"I'm not sure . . ." Abby said. She looked at the words

carefully. "If Grandpa really wanted us to catch something, he'd have to give us a hint. These books are *filled* with information."

Both of them thumbed through the pages for several minutes.

"Huh. That's strange," Carol said. "The *a* in this sentence is circled." She pointed to a specific spot on the page. "Is that what I'm supposed to find?"

"Maybe," Abby said, "but what kind of a clue is a circled *a?*"

"It doesn't tell us much, does it?" Carol said. "The whole sentence says, '*Most people are when you really see them.*' And the *a* in *are* is circled. It's on the very last page. I think someone is saying that most people are really nice, even though they misunderstand and do really hurtful things."

"Sounds like something Grandpa would like," Abby said. "Look through again; see if there are any other circled letters."

A minute later, Abby cried out, "Found one!" She pointed to a page. "Check this out!" she said, and pointed to an *l* with a box drawn around it. "But that one has a box, not a circle," Carol said. "What does it mean?"

Abby didn't answer, but she began unloading her books. For the next hour, the two of them leafed through them all, looking for any letter that had been marked. Some had boxes, some circles, some were underlined, and some had been double underlined. They made a chart of each of the letters and how they were highlighted.

Circled	In a box	Underlined	Double underlined
D	L	T	F
E	A	W	
R	H	A	
C		A	
		N	

Had these markings always been there? They must have been. Abby hadn't read all of these books, but had she just glossed over the markings in the others? They did seem familiar. Maybe she had seen them, but had been lost enough in the story she hadn't really noticed them.

"Is it a scrambled message?" Carol asked.

"Just like Derick and I used to play. That was what he meant by 'Jonathan Code and Kimberly Spy,'" Abby said. "The way Grandpa marked the letters could mean that they're separate words. But then, what would D, E, R, and C spell?"

"Cerd. Ercd. Recd," Carol tried.

"Those aren't words," Abby said. "Maybe Red C."

"But that's two words. Why would they be circled like that?"

Abby thought about it. "And the boxed ones don't spell anything either. Lah? Ahl? Hal?

"Hal? Who do we know named Hal? It doesn't exactly sound mysterious. There was a guy named Hal back home who owned the QuickPit. They had really good slushies! Oh, I'm really hungry all of a sudden."

The two logged onto their rings and looked for anyone with any connection to Grandpa named Hal. They couldn't find anyone who had a close relationship. There were a couple of bloggers posting pictures and talking about Grandpa's work, but that was it.

"Even if we find a connection," Abby said, "the other letters don't make any sense. The double underlined column has only one letter."

Carol proposed that maybe the way Grandpa marked them in the books didn't matter, and that the message was just one long, scrambled phrase, but they couldn't unscramble it, nor could any of the net applications they accessed.

Finally, both girls fell asleep on the floor, surrounded by open books.

THE DEBATE

Derick sat in the Bridge in his dorm. He stared at the armoire behind the young Frederick Douglass. No way was he going to sleep. He couldn't forget about the paper in his grandfather's handwriting they'd found on top of the armoire. How was it possible? There seemed to be absolutely no explanation for it.

He paced the room, stealing occasional glances at the wardrobe. Could there be some sort of connection between watching something in the Bridge and the past itself?

Derick changed screens with his rings. He searched for the words *Oscar Cragbridge* and *time*. Immediately several articles and videos appeared about the Bridge, explaining how it merely portrayed images from the past, but did not actually go into the past. Another article made a big deal about how the plans weren't public and how no other scientist had been able to replicate the Bridge. Derick looked at the bottom corner of his view—over 200,000 search results. He could imagine that most of the entries were more of the same. The Bridge had always been big news.

He knew it seemed crazy, but after a day like the one he'd had, anything was worth trying. He added a word so his search read *Oscar Cragbridge time travel*. He glanced through the first hundred results—more of the same. He moved the screen to show the last results. On the last page, he found a reference to a university newspaper from nearly thirty-five years ago. He scanned the summary.

Back then, some people had theorized that time travel could really be possible. The university had held debates, and among those who spoke was Oscar Cragbridge.

Derick looked at the year and did the math. His grandfather must have still been a professor then. Derick read the synopsis. The writer quoted Grandpa only once: "We shouldn't waste our time trying to change the past," Grandpa was quoted as saying. "But learn from it and move ahead."

Derick wished he could see his grandfather debate. He'd bet his grandfather did rather well. He was always so smart and passionate. Suddenly a thought occurred to Derrick: maybe he could see the time-travel debate.

Turning back to the Bridge, Derick selected his grandfather's journal, hoping for an entry about the same date listed in the article. There was. Derick selected it and watched.

His grandpa was much younger. He stood behind a table in a buttoned-up shirt and shabby blazer—typical Grandpa.

Across from him at a different table was another man, who, in contrast, wore a finely pressed suit.

A moderator stood and began. "Welcome to our debate on the ethics of time travel."

The subject still sounded absurd—like discussing the pros and cons of the boogie man—totally out of place at a university.

The moderator continued, "As we have determined that it is theoretically possible to travel through time, though no one has ever achieved it, we have scheduled this debate to explore the ramifications of time travel. It may prepare us for the day when the theory becomes possible in practical terms."

Derick smiled to himself. This was over thirty years ago and time travel still wasn't possible.

"And of course, we have selected the heads of the two teams," the moderator went on. "Both are pursuing research on the subject and hope to be the first to discover how to time travel."

Derick had no idea his grandfather had researched *that*. Maybe those studies had led to the discovery of the Bridge. "First, the valedictorian of Stanford University's college of science, Oscar Cragbridge. He is the leading scientist sponsored by ITT University." A decent amount of clapping sounded throughout the hall. Derick moved the perspective of the Bridge to see a full house of viewers waiting to hear the speakers.

"And of course, we would also like to welcome Charles Muns, an independent businessman and owner of Muns

Industries. He has been involved in several scientific discoveries and is funding the other team."

"Thank you for having me," Muns said calmly. Derick looked at him closely. The man was slender, with flawlessly styled blond hair. He had piercing blue eyes and a thin face with a sharp chin.

"Let's get right to it," the moderator said. "Dr. Cragbridge, if we ever discover the ability to travel through time, what ethical dilemmas do you anticipate?"

Derick watched as his grandfather rose and ran his fingers through his hair. He had hair! It had thinned quite a bit, but it did exist at one time, "I believe that if time travel becomes possible, it should be pursued with every degree of caution. Playing with time would be, at the very least, very delicate. If misused, or even ignorantly used, it could prove fatal. We must take every precaution not to interact with the past or the future, but only to observe it."

"And why is that?" the moderator asked.

"Because we do not understand the characteristics of time. If we change something in the past, it could have huge ramifications on the present and the future."

"Of course we could change things," Muns said, a genuine smile on his face. "What is the use of time travel if we cannot change the past? We could eliminate entire tragedies and save thousands—millions—of lives. It would be an utter waste to not use this tool to help our fellow human beings." Every word seemed well chosen, like he'd read it from a teleprompter.

"What is the use? What is the *use*?" Grandpa's tone was

incredulous. "Correct me if I'm wrong, but did you just ask what is the use of time travel if we do not change the past?"

"Yes," Muns responded calmly.

"The use is the same benefit history always has had—we *learn* from it. The past is not something we wallow in. We should not change what has happened, but learn from it—become better."

"But the wars," Muns protested. "We could stop Hitler before his first invasion. There would be no Third Reich, no concentration camps, no slaughter of millions of Jews."

Grandpa's head bowed. "The Holocaust was truly a tragedy, but we have learned from it. And how many great heroes came of that tragedy? Think of those who risked their lives, those who learned how to forgive, boys who left home to fight a tyrant, families who hid Jews because they believed in the importance of humanity. How many millions of students have read about those events in history books and vowed in their own hearts and minds that they would never let such a thing happen again?"

"But if we do not change those events, it would be like sentencing them to die all over again," Muns said.

"No!" Grandpa hit his podium. "Their deaths have already happened. It is the supreme disregard and disrespect to make those deaths mean nothing. We must *learn* from the past."

"Let me give you another example," Muns said, moving from behind his podium. "What about the *Titanic*? What if you had the power to warn the captain and prevent more than fifteen hundred people from dying in the icy waters of the Atlantic? What would you do?"

Derick watched as his grandfather once again bowed his head. "Even if I could prevent the tragedy," he said slowly, "I would not change it. I would sit in this room and cry all over again for the victims." He raised his head. "We cannot change the past. We can learn from it and then look ahead. We make our own futures, building on the foundations of our past."

"No!" Muns said. "If my team discovers the secrets to time travel—and we will—we will right all wrongs. We will correct the mistakes of history." He looked at Cragbridge for a reply.

Derick watched his grandpa stand silently for a moment. Then he slowly licked his lips and spoke. "Then heaven help us that you never discover time travel."

THE WATCHMAN

Abby woke up, her sore muscles screaming. She'd slept in an awkward position with a Florence Nightingale biography as a pillow. When she looked at Carol, asleep atop *Pride and Prejudice*, it all came rushing back.

Abby blinked long and hard. The few hours of sleep definitely weren't enough, but she had no desire to sleep anymore. She checked the clock—5:30 A.M. She still had half an hour before she had to meet Derick. She turned on her rings and looked at a page with the columns of letters. In the process, she accidentally bumped Carol's arm, who snorted and changed her position. Abby looked over the letters they'd found in the books last night. She and Carol had to be on to something. There had to be a message in the letter, and it had to be from Grandpa—she just couldn't figure out what it said. Maybe when she showed Derick . . .

Abby had a flash of inspiration. "Wait a second," she said to herself. "We probably only have half of the letters. I bet Derick has the other half." Why hadn't she thought of that before? She must have been really tired. In a moment, she was contacting Derick with her rings.

"What?" Derick asked. He'd synced up, but the picture showed the ceiling of his room. He hadn't bothered to turn and lift his hand so the camera in his rings could show his face.

"Derick. Wake up," she commanded. "I need you to do something."

She heard a groan, then saw his half-open eyes and tousled hair. "Did you figure it out?" he asked, sounding more awake.

"We've found something," Abby answered. She told him about the books and highlighted letters. "But they don't make sense as they are; I'm pretty sure the message is incomplete."

"Because the other half of the letters are in my books," he said.

"Wish I'd figured it out that fast," Abby admitted.

"I'll go through them all and meet you at breakfast," he promised.

"Make sure you log them like I did." She sent him the file of the columns and letters. "Chart them by how they're marked. I think that's important somehow."

"Agreed," he said. "It will probably take a while. Let's

just meet at breakfast. Oh, and I have something else to tell you. See ya then." Derick logged off.

Abby looked down to see Carol still fast asleep. She hadn't even flinched.

• • •

Abby pushed her sausages around her plate with her fork. She'd forced herself to eat her eggs, but her stomach was too unsettled for sausage.

"Are you going to eat that?" Carol asked. She'd cleaned her plate and was motioning toward Abby's sausage.

"No. Go ahead," Abby said, and slid her plate closer to Carol.

"Thanks," Carol said, stabbing one sausage and then the other. "When is your brother going to get here? Not that I'm eager or anything. You barely gave me any time to get ready; good thing I'm naturally beautiful. That's what my mom always told me anyway. Makeup just finishes the beauty. Then again, my dad says that even a barn looks better painted."

Five minutes after Carol had finished both of Abby's sausages, Derick ran in.

"Finished," he said. "Sync up."

In a moment, all three students looked at the chart with Derick's additions.

Circled	In a box	Underlined	Double underlined
D	L	T	F
E	A	W	O
R	H	A	
C		A	
G		N	
G		C	
A		M	
I			

"Can you make any sense of it?" Derick asked.

"Not really," Abby admitted. "With your letters, we have more information, but it doesn't look complete. We don't have any more groups, though—still four. And the double-underlined row has to be 'of.'" Abby switched her rings to the web and began punching in letters.

"So," Carol interrupted, "Is this when you guys tell me what this is all about?"

"No," Abby and Derick said at the same time.

"Okay, okay," Carol said, her hands in the air.

Abby sighed. "I've put it into that logarithm on the web twice now and it still doesn't come up with anything."

"Wait," Derick said. "Do you remember that time we went to London for a family vacation?"

"Yeah," Abby said.

"I forgot my bag on the subway. It had some of my books in it—*The Jungle Book, Uncle Tom's Cabin*, and I think two more. Grandpa gave them to me."

"So we could be missing letters from those four books," Carol realized.

"Most of the books only had one marked letter in them," Abby said. "So let's see if I can program in four blanks. Here we go." She watched her screen intently. Still nothing.

"Wait," Carol said. "Put them in a column at a time, like just the boxed letters."

"Okay," Abby said moving her fingers. "If the code has one blank in the word that the boxed letters is supposed to spell, then there are a few possibilities: hail, haul, hall."

"Wait. Hall! Would *Cragbridge* fit for the circled group?" Carol asked. They both studied the letters. It was missing an R and a B, but it fit.

"Let me try the underlined letters with a blank. It came up with *Watchman*," Abby said.

"Watchman of Cragbridge Hall," Derick said. "That's the name of the tower, right?"

"Yeah. It's basically the logo for the place," Carol said.

Abby immediately thought of the blazer her grandpa wore with the tower embroidered beside the lapel. The same symbol was on the netsites. But the real thing stood proudly atop Cragbridge Hall, the center building of campus, and rose at least two stories taller than the rest of the roof; its stone walls were capped with a round room and a spire. Thin windows circled it. The style was old, but the building looked new and strong.

"Alright," Derick said, glancing at his watch. "We have twenty minutes before class. Let's go find a way in."

• • •

The three made their way to the center of Cragbridge Hall and up to the third floor. Abby tried to picture the tower in her mind and approximate where it would be.

"This is the highest floor," Derick said. "I think the tower comes off somewhere around here."

Abby thought they needed to move a bit farther down the hall, but she wasn't sure.

Carol grabbed the shoulder of a boy walking by. "Excuse me," she said, and looked at the tall boy with short, black hair and dark brown eyes. "You look like you're older than me. Not a *lot* older, but at least a little. I mean, if you wanted to hang out with me sometime, I think I'd be okay with that—just thought I'd clarify. Unless you're just a good-looking shell with a shallow, unfeeling core. Then never mind. But the reason I stopped you is that I need to ask a question of someone who has been at Cragbridge longer than I have."

After taking a moment to process what Carol said, the boy responded, "Okay."

"'Okay' as in you want to hang out with me, or 'okay,' you'll answer my question?"

"The question," the boy said.

"How can I go up to the top of the Watchman?"

The boy laughed. "You must be a seventh grader. You can't. You can go down this hall, and up the spiral stairs, but it ends. You can't go all the way up. Rumor is that kids used to ditch class up there, and one even fell from the tower, so they closed it off."

"Okay, thanks," Carol said. "And you were right. I am a seventh grader. I just don't know these things. Maybe I need a friend. Maybe a friend with short, black hair, a cute face, a decent build, maybe he's wearing a green T-shirt." She eyed the boy carefully. "Someone like that to help me find my way in this strange new world."

"Uh . . . you're strange," the boy said.

"That's not really very nice. I mean, you're probably strange too, but I don't go around saying it to your face." The boy smirked and continued down the hall. Carol called after him. "But if you ever want to hang out and be strange together, like over dinner or something, let me know. My name is Carol Reese. Look me up."

The boy didn't turn around.

"Thanks for finding out the info," Derick said. "And thanks for hitting on him. It's good to see someone else completely uncomfortable."

"Sure," Carol said. "But I wasn't hitting on him. I just wanted to make you feel jealous." She raised both her eyebrows and grinned.

"Can't you two stop to think how awkward this must be for me?" Abby asked.

"I don't stop to think about *awkward* much," Carol admitted. "I'm too excited."

Abby returned to the subject at hand. "That boy said we can't go inside the Watchman, but we might as well try."

Derick led the girls down the hall and up the stairs.

Abby followed behind Derick, figuring that if she didn't, Carol would take advantage of the stairs and watch his backside for much of the way.

After a few more minutes, Abby rounded a bend to see Derick with his head touching a rock ceiling.

"Looks like this is as far as we go," he said.

Abby looked at the ceiling. "Maybe you used to be able to get to the top back when Grandpa made the message."

"I doubt it," Derick said. "By the feel of this whole thing, nothing about discovering the secret is going to be easy." He pressed his hands against the bricks.

"Are you looking for a secret passage?" Abby asked.

"I guess," he said.

Carol giggled. "That's so cute."

"Do you have any better ideas?" Derick asked.

"I guess it's worth a try," Abby said. Over the next few minutes, they pushed and pulled on every brick in the ceiling and the walls surrounding it. They tried the tiles on the steps. They even tried all standing on one stair at a time, and in different combinations, hoping something would open a way up to the Watchman. Finally, they came back down the stairs.

They walked out of the front doors and onto the grass outside, then looked up at Watchman, standing tall and picturesque at the very heart of the academy.

"Maybe we can get there from the outside," Abby suggested.

"We'd need a really, really tall ladder," Carol said.

Derick snorted. "I'm sure three kids holding a five-story

ladder wouldn't look conspicuous at all," he said sarcastically. "Everyone would let us do our thing without asking any questions, especially the guards."

Abby had to agree. "Besides, does anyone know where we can get a five-story ladder?"

"Have Carol ask the next boy who passes," Derick said.

"Oh, it worked," Carol said. "You're *jealous*."

Derick rolled his eyes.

"Even if we could get up there," Abby said, pointing to the tower, "we couldn't get through those windows. They can't be more than five inches across."

"If we somehow got up that high, maybe we could reach in and grab what we needed," Carol suggested. "Hey, maybe we could climb up there."

Abby approached the wall and tried to gain a foothold. She managed to get about eight inches off the ground before falling. "There's no way. Maybe a monkey could do it, but none of us could."

Derick gasped. Both Carol and Abby turned to look at him. He smiled. "Thanks, sis. I think I know how we can get in. Meet me at the east side of the biology hall before lunch."

A LIMP AND
A JAGGED WOUND

Hello again, Oscar," Charles said, walking across the stage-type podium.

Oscar didn't respond. He didn't even sit up in his bed, which guards watched carefully. He glared at Charles.

"Oh, a bit uncivil today huh?" Charles asked.

"Excuse me," Oscar said. "I don't believe I'm the one threatening innocent lives or holding an old man captive against his will." Oscar rolled over, facing away from Charles.

Charles walked slowly toward the bed. "Of course, it's understandable that you are upset. Indeed, a lot is on the line, but I had to put you in this position to make you realize how much we could do together if you would just share your secret."

Oscar didn't respond.

Charles motioned toward the scene portrayed by a Bridge across the lecture hall. The ghost of a giant ship cut its way through the ocean. "And you aren't even watching what I've provided for you. It may help you come to a quicker decision. You could end this at any moment."

"You are heartless," Oscar said, a bite in his voice. The guard who stood next to him poised himself to restrain the old man if necessary.

"No," said Charles. "I'm a visionary. There is a difference, though it may be slight."

Oscar slowly turned and sat up. "Oh, do tell Charles. When has pride or vainglory become 'visionary'?"

"You are trying to upset me," Charles said, his tone even.

"No, I'm trying to help you see who you really are. You are threatening murder. Do you see the animal you have become?"

"And you are threatening to let tragedies remain when you have the power to reverse them."

"You have not learned from the past. You cannot buy or bully your way to greatness."

"We can change the world," Charles said.

"You should worry about changing yourself," Oscar said back, pointing his finger. "I would worry about *that* tragedy before any others."

Charles stood silently, lips tightened. After several moments, he said, "You know you only have two more days. You are the one who decides if they live or die. The responsibility is yours. And if you let them die, perhaps it is you who should reexamine himself."

• • •

Mr. Hendricks's eyes drooped, and he blinked slower than normal. "Go ahead, Andrew." He nodded at the boy with his hand raised.

The boy in the back row had red hair and freckles. "Did you read the news this morning?"

"I did." Mr. Hendricks took a few tired steps, much slower than the day before, and sat upon his desk with a wince.

"And what's your opinion about it?" Andrew asked.

"Overall, I never think the news is adequate, but it does serve a purpose."

"No, I mean, I watched the vid that said Oscar Cragbridge is missing," Andrew said. "They haven't ruled out foul play."

All the feelings Abby had been trying to suppress, to forget for a few moments, came rushing back. She could feel the stares of the class, but she didn't want to look back. She did *not* want to break down.

"I'll tell you what I know," Mr. Hendricks said. "But this will be the only question about the situation today. As you can probably tell, I have had a rather long night. I'm not feeling one hundred percent well today." He gave them a tired smile. "Also, I need to announce that I will not be in my office during lab hours today. If there is any reason you need to meet with me, please see me afterward. We can try to schedule a time. However, with the way I feel, please see if it can't wait a day or two." He didn't pace in front of the room as usual.

"Now as far as your question goes," Mr. Hendricks said, giving a subtle nod to Andrew, "I suspected someone may bring that up." He cleared his throat. "It's terrible news. Of course, Oscar Cragbridge is very much the reason this school exists. He founded it. Paid to build it. I've even heard that he designed this building we meet in. He was a pioneer in science, history, and other areas. I cannot see why anyone would bear him ill will—he is a remarkable, visionary man." He stood and took a few steps, but then stopped. "I know Oscar reasonably well. He is likely to get an idea and go after it with speed and zeal. I hope he's simply gone doing some research somewhere."

"I don't think so," Derick interjected. "My parents are gone too, and we can't get a hold of them."

"Yes," Mr. Hendricks said, and bowed his head, genuine sadness on his face. "I'm still hoping for the best regarding your parents. I worked with Oscar Cragbridge, testing some of the early Bridge prototypes to be used in history classes. We used to spend quite a lot of time together."

"Really?" Abby asked.

"Yes, we did," Mr. Hendricks said.

"Wait. Did you finish testing those early prototypes?" Derick asked.

"I wanted to," Mr. Hendricks started, "but something . . ." He paused and took a deep breath. "Something happened. Something in my personal life, but that is neither here nor there. All I would like to say about Andrew's question is that I am optimistic that they'll find all of the missing Cragbridges soon, healthy and happy. Now," he said in a commanding, we're-not-going-back-to-that-subject tone, "for today's lesson, I'm going to ask you all to study the beginning of the Revolutionary War. Your Bridge labs are already prepared. If you sync to my class page, you'll find a series of questions to answer."

Abby didn't move. She waited for most people to file into the Bridges and then made her way to Mr. Hendricks at his desk.

"Excuse me, Mr. Hendricks," she said. "I have a question."

"I'm so sorry to hear about your family," Mr. Hendricks said. "Your grandfather is truly a great man, and I expect your parents are no less. I hope everything is well."

"Thank . . . you," Abby said, choking back her emotions. She wanted to ask if he knew about the lockets, or about the secret and the possibility of a kidnapping. It would be so nice to ask someone older and more experienced for help—someone who knew Grandpa personally. Though she opened her mouth to speak, she decided against it. She would respect her grandpa's wishes.

"Now what was your question?" Mr. Hendricks asked.

"For some reason, my Bridge access has been blocked," Abby said, changing the subject. "Could you tell me why?"

"Hmmm," Mr. Hendricks said. "That's very unusual so early in the school year." He turned on his rings and began moving his fingers. "What have you been trying to see?"

Abby swallowed. She didn't want to tell him, but then again, for all she knew, he was looking at the information as she spoke. "My grandpa gave me access to some of his journals."

"And after you watched some of them, your access was denied," Mr. Hendricks suggested.

"Yeah," Abby said.

Mr. Hendricks moved his fingers again. "I see the block. You had rights to whatever you were watching, I must assume, or else you wouldn't be on a private file. But someone thought you shouldn't. I cannot overrule the block, as it comes from another teacher. You can imagine the trouble that would cause if one teacher kept overruling another. I can submit a request to have your access restored after a probationary period. In two days, if all goes well, you should be able to log on again."

"Thanks," Abby said, but her stomach tightened. Two days was too long. Who knew what could happen to her parents and grandpa in two days? She had to find out more. Derick still had access, but she may need her own. She'd need the Bridge. "I don't want to be ungrateful, but is there any way I can get access sooner? I mean, I have homework to do." Homework was really the last thing on her mind.

Mr. Hendricks shook his head. "Not really. Like I said on the first day, the Bridge is a privilege that can be revoked. I'm not in a position to overrule that."

"Could you tell me who blocked me?" Abby asked. "Maybe I could explain what happened."

"Sorry," Mr. Hendricks said. "Revealing that

information is against school policy. For today, I will give you the assignment from a textbook." He turned on his rings and flicked his fingers. Abby turned her rings on as well and found a message with a textbook chapter attached. Opening it felt like failure, like she had left behind all the wonderful inventions of Cragbridge Hall and returned to regular school.

Abby went back to her desk and began to read, but she couldn't focus. Before the end of the period, someone would see her sitting in her desk reading on her rings because she couldn't use the Bridge—yet another reason she wasn't as good as everyone else. Even more upsetting was the question of who had blocked her access. Abby thought about Ms. Entrese and her fascination with Grandpa's locket. She seemed to be the leading suspect.

Abby hadn't even looked up the first question on the homework sheet when Mr. Hendricks walked to her side.

"My wife died," he said. "That was the reason I quit working with your grandfather. I . . . I . . . gave up my work for months—actually, for over a year if I'm honest."

Abby had no idea what to say. "I'm sorry."

Mr. Hendricks met her eyes. "I thought you should know. Under normal circumstances, I would never pass up a chance to work with Oscar Cragbridge. He is a great man. I hope he returns safe and sound soon."

Abby forced a smile. Her emotions swirled together as she thought about what Mr. Hendricks had said—he knew tragedy. She wanted to ask if his wife went missing before she died. Had he experienced anything like she was going through now? But then she realized she didn't want to know. She didn't want a story that ended in death to be anything like her situation with her missing parents and grandpa. They would not die. She refused to believe they would die. Abby watched as Mr. Hendricks slowly walked back to his desk.

• • •

Before English class could begin, Abby quickly approached Ms. Entrese at her desk.

"Abby Cragbridge." Ms. Entrese wore a gray shirt with her black pants and a thin, black sweater—her version of variety. "I hope your new accommodations are suitable."

"They are. Thank you," Abby said.

"I have never had to switch roommates so early in the semester," Ms. Entrese said. "Of course, we've never had a student admitted to this academy . . . quite like . . ." Her voice went flat. "You."

Had she been insulted? "I guess not," Abby managed to respond.

"I was very sorry to hear about your parents and your grandfather," Ms. Entrese continued. "I hope you're doing okay." The words were nice, but there was no indication that she meant them. Her eyes even looked around at others in the room while she was speaking.

"Thank you." Abby wanted to quickly move on to the subject of her denied Bridge access, but she wasn't fast enough.

"The police came. They asked me questions about your grandfather," Ms. Entrese said. "I guess they'd heard that he and I had our share of disagreements in the past. Did you know that, Abby?" Her words felt like an accusation—like Abby had sent the police to question her.

"No," Abby said. "I didn't even know that you knew him."

Ms. Entrese eyed Abby carefully. "If class weren't about to start, maybe we could discuss this while you sat in the Chair. Of course, I'd take my turn in it too." Abby had no desire to sit in the Chair any time soon. "Of course, I'd never seek to harm your grandfather, but I definitely disagreed with him."

"What did you disagree about?" Abby asked, feeling suddenly brave.

Ms. Entrese raised an eyebrow. "That's no concern of yours. Now, why have you come to talk with me?"

"My access to the Bridge has been denied, and I . . . I was wondering if you knew anything about it," Abby sputtered out. The plea sounded awkward, so Abby tried to correct it. "I'm just checking with all of my teachers. I don't want to fall behind on my homework."

"Your access has been denied?" Ms. Entrese asked louder than necessary. Abby wanted to shush her. Ms. Entrese had glanced around again, and out of the corner of her eye, Abby had noticed several students listening in. Jacqueline laughed. "I didn't do it," Ms. Entrese said.

Abby wasn't sure whether to believe her. "Do you know what I can do to get my access back?"

The bell hummed, signaling the beginning of class. Ms. Entrese promptly stood. "I did you a great kindness by arranging a new dorm room for you. I don't think you're in a position to ask for any more favors." She moved to the center of the room to address the class.

• • •

Abby watched as a leather soccer ball balanced on the edge of a peach basket before falling in. The basket hung from a balcony in an old school gym.

"This is the beginning of basketball," Coach Horne explained, gesturing toward the Bridge image. "In the late 1890s, James Naismith, the man in the corner"—Coach Horne pointed in the direction of the man with a mustache and hair parted down the middle—"was looking for a game to keep the boys at a school in Springfield, Massachusetts, physically fit on rainy days and during long winters. He wanted something that would require skill rather than strength. With the help of the janitor, he mounted peach baskets to the balconies, and the students tried out his new game. They had no idea they were making history."

Coach Horne chuckled and then continued. "Eventually they thought to take the bottom out of the baskets." The class laughed, watching as a couple of students used a ladder to retrieve the ball. Abby imagined how inconvenient it would have been to have to retrieve the ball every time someone scored. "Of course, many of the rules have changed. For example, dribbling wasn't part of the original game. That came later, with better balls. Since we'll play by modern rules, and some of you may be unfamiliar with them, I'll do a little overview."

As Coach Horne spoke, Carol whispered, "Kind of weird to see them trying to throw a ball into a peach basket. I mean, now we're used to like eight-foot-tall barbarian men crashing into each other, and dunking. Which, of course, I'm not complaining about. In fact, I think the muscles and shorts make modern basketball far superior to the original."

Once again, Abby was at a loss for words.

Soon the two coaches had everyone divided into teams. Carol played on the other side of the gym, while Abby found herself on a team of four facing another team of four.

"We're short two people," Coach Horne said. "If it's alright with you guys, I'd suggest Coach Adonavich and I join you. What do you think?"

Abby and the others thought for a moment. Did they want to play ball against someone as big and burly as Coach Horne?

"Okay," one of the boys said. "Sure."

"Are you okay with that?" Coach Horne asked Coach Adonavich. "You could politely withdraw if you don't feel up to the challenge."

"I never withdraw from anything," the Russian said. "But that was a nice try."

"Even with that limp you have?" Coach Horne said.

"It's nothing," she countered.

Abby could feel their competitive spirits kicking in.

Somehow the atmosphere had changed from a scrimmage in gym class to a world-class rivalry.

Soon, Abby found herself playing one of the most competitive games of basketball she had ever seen, let alone experienced. She could keep up with many of the boys; she scored on them twice. But she stayed out of the middle—that was where Coach Horne ruled. He seemed to swat every shot that got close and grabbed nearly every rebound.

Coach Horne was definitely bigger and stronger, but Adonavich was quicker and more agile, and passed the ball well. Though she couldn't stop Coach Horne under the basket, she managed to steal it from him several times.

Abby's team maintained a slight lead for most of the game, but Coach Horne's team battled back. With only a minute to go, a boy passed to Abby. She faked like she was going to make a move toward the basket, drawing Coach Horne toward the top of the key. Abby dished the ball off to Coach Adonavich, who drove to the hoop. Coach Horne tried to get in position to stop her. They collided, and Ms. Adonovich came crashing to the ground.

"Sorry," Coach Horne said, quickly offering his hand to help her up.

Ms. Adonavich raised her arm to accept the offering. Her workout pants had slid up above one knee, revealing a jagged red wound that went up her leg. Abby watched as Coach Horne noticed the wound too. Ms. Adonovich quickly pulled down her pant leg. "I cut myself yesterday," she explained. "I caught the inside of a door frame."

"Are you okay?" Coach Horne asked.

"Yes, I'm fine. Lucky for you, it has made me slower than before. Otherwise, the game wouldn't have been this close."

Coach Horne helped her up.

A small beep sounded.

"Time," Coach Horne said, and dismissed the class for the showers.

As Abby walked to the locker room, she wondered how Coach Adonavich had really been cut—doorframes didn't make jagged wounds like that.

Just before Abby entered the locker room, she looked back at Coach Horne. She caught him glancing at Coach Adonavich's leg as she returned a basketball to the equipment box.

RISKING IT ALL

Derick leapt from one tree branch onto another. He tried to use his tail, but it still felt foreign. A monkey dangling from a branch several feet above him waved.

"Show off," Derick mumbled. The other monkey was Rafa, the prodigy teacher's assistant.

Derick's monkey avatar leapt to the next branch and clung tight. He heard his teacher's voice through his earpieces.

"Careful, Derick. You have shown enough promise that working with Rafael today can be a great help. But remember, though the avatar is dexterous and durable, it is also very expensive. Take it little by little. Don't push yourself too far like last time."

Derick took the advice and practiced clinging to the branch he was on, swinging beneath it and back up the other side. He repeated the drill over and over until it felt natural, but he was thinking about something else—a tower he needed to climb. He had tried to watch closely as Dr. Mackleprank opened the lab, but there was no way to see the code. Plus, it took a fingerprint read, and only the teacher and Rafa had clearance for that. No way could he possibly break in.

"Alright, let's bring it in," Dr. Mackleprank said.

Derick jumped to a lower branch, and then another. He had much more confidence than before. While most others in his class were trying to progress from walking to running, he was learning to scale trees.

Rafa's monkey passed by, gliding downward a second or two slower than falling. He hopped from branch to branch with such agility that he seemed as at home in the tree as a human walking.

After joining Rafael's avatar on the ground, Derick walked his monkey to the corner storage center. Then he pushed the button on the back of his neck to log off.

He felt dizzy and nauseated as he came back to reality in the lab room. Derick took a few moments to reorient himself before trying to take off the harness.

Then it came to him. He had an idea. He remembered Frederick Douglass, how waiting until the last minute had helped him. Sometimes that was when people paid the least attention. Derick would have to be as cool and calm as his namesake had been.

He walked down the hall toward the issue room, where they received their equipment and lab room assignment for the day, and where they returned their gear after labs. Derick planned quickly, pushing toward the front of the group. He wanted to be one of the first to turn in his sensors.

"Here you go," Derick said, handing his gear to Rafa, who'd beat him to the issue room.

"You're learning quickly, *rapaz*," Rafael said. "Just don't try to go too fast. If you keep practicing, you'll join the real monkeys by the end of the semester." Rafa didn't seem as rigid and unfriendly as he had before. Perhaps he was warming up. Of course, that didn't make Derick feel any better about what he was about to do. Rafa logged the gear back in and placed it on its rack. He pressed the button that made the hooks that held the sensors clamp shut.

"Thanks," Derick said. "How did you get so good?"

"Oh, I've been practicing for a long time," Rafael said.

"Makes sense. See you tomorrow," Derick said.

Rafa nodded, and Derick moved out of the way. Rafa had many more students to help. But instead of going out into the classroom to wait for class to end, Derick paused in the issue room. He checked the clock on his rings. Rafa only had three minutes to finish checking in the equipment. Derick watched as the long-haired Brazilian worked quickly to log in all of the visors and black straps. When he was too busy, he didn't always push the hooks closed. He was probably planning on closing them as soon as all the students left.

Derick tried to estimate his timing carefully. Like Douglass, he needed the rush to make those in charge less observant. He could tell that the other students were becoming a little more anxious as time wore on. They'd be late to class if they didn't get done soon.

Only a minute left. Looking at Rafa one more time, and seeing him moving in a flurry, Derick decided it was now or never.

Making sure his backpack was open, Derick walked toward the door. Along the way, he passed close by the avatar sensors on the wall. He didn't slow down or look back as he slipped a sensor off its hanger and dropped it into his pack. With any luck, no one would even notice that one was missing. Since his first day in the lab, Derrick had noticed that there were more hooks than sensors—perhaps some sensors were out for repair. Derick walked out of the room and toward the exit.

"Derick Cragbridge," a voice said, "let's talk."

. . .

"Wait up, Abby," Carol called. She ran to catch up. "Do you have your math assignment ready?"

"Yeah. Story problems are a lot better when I get to see the train leaving St. Louis traveling at sixty miles per hour," Abby said, "but I'm still not that fond of them."

"Math isn't my favorite either," Carol said. "But gym was alright. And I thought English was pretty good, as far as the Chair goes. I mean, some people's imaginations of *Old Man and the Sea* are much better than others'."

They approached the biology hall.

"So where do you think your brother is?" Carol said,

looking around. They were supposed to meet him now. "Not that I'm excited to see him, I'm just . . . *really* excited to see him."

"I'm not sure," Abby admitted. "He said he'd be here."

"Sorry I'm late," Derick said, coming out of the avatar lab. "Dr. Mackleprank wanted to tell me about some extra lab time for those at the head of the class. Scared me to death. Thought I was busted."

"Busted? For what?" Abby asked.

Derick raised an eyebrow. "You said you'd have to be a monkey to get to the top of the tower."

"No . . ." Abby said, realizing what her brother was thinking.

"Yes," Derick answered.

"But how could you get an avatar out of the room?" Abby asked.

"Yeah," Carol agreed. "I have that class, and unless you have the codes and fingerprints of Dr. Mackleprank, I think you're stuck."

"At first, I thought the same thing," Derick said. "I tried to look over Dr. Mackleprank's shoulder and stuff to figure out the keycode, but then I thought the secret might be in getting info from the teacher's aide. That didn't work either. He seemed even more careful than Dr. Mackleprank. And then I had a genius idea."

"Of course you did," Carol said with a dreamy sigh.

"Focus, Carol," Abby said. "What was your idea?"

"We'll unlock it from the inside," Derick said.

"That's . . . brilliant," Abby said with a fake smile that quickly faded. "But we're all out here."

Derick didn't answer. He lifted a set of sensors from inside his pack. "I've got a little part of me in there dying to get out."

Carol gasped. "You are brilliant. We can get married whenever you want. You've proven yourself." A thought occurred to her. "But how did you get the sensors out?"

Derick told the story. Carol leaned in. "Oh, I could just kiss you over and over again," she said. Abby pulled her back by her ponytail. "Ouch. It was just for congratulations."

"We haven't done anything yet," Derick said. "Let's duck in here."

The three of them stepped into an empty zoology room. All of the other students had gone to lunch. Derick sat down and put on his sensors.

"Wait," Carol said. "Wait. Wait. Wait. Wait. I just realized what we're doing. We're trying to figure out this puzzle or whatever that your grandfather gave you, and that's fun and everything, and of course Derick has eyes that make me melt like snow in Waikiki, but . . . but . . . but we could get into some seriously serious trouble for messing with an avatar. I mean, we could be thrown into jail and forced to eat terrible food, and end up talking to ourselves for hours and hours at a time, in a cell with no windows, or posters, or anything to look at. And we'd finally get out when we're old and wrinkled and all we can do is input boring data onto huge sites about the sizes that certain loafers are available in, and about the different flavors of Chapstick people can buy."

"Carol," Abby started, "You have to understand that—"

"No, *you* have to understand that this isn't okay," Carol said. "I mean, I tried to be nice to you. I've been picked on too. I've been underestimated too, but this is too much." She started walking toward the door.

"Wait, Carol," Derick said.

She stopped and turned to face Derick. "Don't even ask me to stay. I know you're gorgeous, but I won't risk all of my hard work for this, or for you. There are other amazing, knee-weakening boys in this school. I can think of three off the top of my head, maybe even four. No, wait—five."

"I wasn't going to ask you to stay," Derick said.

"You were going to say that I'm right, and then you'd join me for a nice lunch for two in the cafeteria?" she asked hopefully. "I've forgotten the other five boys already. And no offense, Abby, but we could meet up later."

"No," Derick said. "We can't tell you what this is all about, but I can tell you that it is important enough for us to take this risk." Derick paused, choosing his words carefully. "People we love . . ." He stopped and started again. "Listen, you don't have to help us, but please don't tell anyone about what we're doing."

Carol looked at him, then at Abby. "I won't," she said. "Unless I get busted walking out this door. Then you'd better run." Carol opened the door and disappeared down the hall.

"Should we go through with it?" Abby asked. She

couldn't help but remember Mr. Hendricks's lecture on Blackbeard and the price for breaking the rules. Plus, the punishments were much more severe for stealing an avatar than for breaking the rules to use the Bridge. "We won't be any good to Mom, Dad, or Grandpa if we're kicked out of here, sitting in jail."

"Too late," Derick said. "I've already got the sensors. There's no turning back. You could leave, and if I'm busted, I'll just tell them I did it on my own."

Abby looked back at her brother. "No. I'm staying. I've been thinking about why my access was denied. I think it's because whoever we're up against knew that I had a locket, and somehow they knew I'd logged into Grandpa's journals. They were trying to stop me—to stop us. We've got to do this. We'd better get started."

• • •

Derick looked through small monkey eyes. The past two times he had logged on, he'd taken several moments to get used to his small body, but in this case, he knew he didn't have a lot of time. He got up and stumbled over the top of the other monkey bodies, knowing they weren't alive to feel any of it.

Derick felt pain in his shin.

"You just hit a desk," Abby said. "I'm not sure what the avatar is doing, but out here, your real body is in a biology room, and you can crash into things. Try to remember that we don't have the same equipment out here as you do in the lab. Your body is moving all over this room." Derick could hear her moving desks out of the way to give him more space. He moved gingerly over the last few monkeys.

"I need a running start—that way." He pointed toward the wall. "Am I clear?"

"Yeah," Abby said. "But you only have about twelve feet until you hit the wall."

"That should be enough," Derick said. The monkey ran and jumped onto the railing at the same time Derick's body nearly jumped right into the wall. The monkey shimmied across the metal bar until he reached the door. Derick imagined Abby was working hard to keep desks out of his way.

He pulled down on the handle and it opened from the inside. Yes!

He walked through a second door and out into a hallway. He was out.

"Very impressive, *rapaz*, but your little joyride is over."

Derick recognized the voice of the last person he wanted to hear: Rafa.

MONKEY ON
THE RUN

Derick pushed the button on the back of his neck and let the monkey go limp. He blinked several times to see Rafa standing in front of the door.

"*Sem vergonha*," Rafa said and shook his head. "I hope you liked your time here at Cragbridge. Don't know why you wasted it."

"Wait," Derick said as Rafa activated his rings—surely to call a teacher or guards or someone who would make sure that the Cragbridge twins would be expelled.

"My grandpa is missing," Derick blurted. "Someone kidnapped him and my parents, and we're trying to find them."

"I've heard about their disappearance, but . . ." Rafa looked confused. "How would stealing a monkey avatar help you find them?"

Derick looked over at Abby.

"We might as well tell him everything," Abby said. "Or else we're gone, and then we won't be able to help at all."

Derick nodded in agreement. He began to tell Rafa about the last twenty-four hours. He told him about the locket, the message from their grandfather, and how they visited his house, but he wasn't there, and neither were their parents. Abby told him about the clues and the message to check the Watchman.

Rafa listened closely. "How do I know that you didn't just make up that entire story?"

"Why else would we do this?" Abby asked. "Why else would we risk our grandfather's reputation?"

"I'm not convinced," Rafa said. "You seem like the type of kids who would think it would be funny to send a monkey running through the commons."

If Carol had been there, Derick was sure she would have laughed, and then apologized for laughing. Then she'd say something like, "But it *would* really be funny."

Rafa eyed them. "There is only one way to know," he said. "Follow me." He turned and opened the door. "And don't bother running. I have enough evidence against you."

The twins followed Rafa across the hall and back into the avatar lab. They went up into a large room with several log-in stations that had suspension systems and several large monitors. Rafa locked the door behind them.

"Let's hook you up," Rafa said, motioning toward one of the stations. As Derick approached, Rafa turned on one of the monitors. "Send your monkey in, and we'll watch and see what happens in the tower. If there is something there

to do with your grandfather's secret, then I'll know you're telling the truth. If not, this is your last day at Cragbridge, and perhaps your last day of freedom for a while."

Derick nodded.

"Now you must know as you begin," Rafa added, "that you are the only one on the register. If something happens to that avatar, *you* are responsible. I am only here as an observer, and perhaps as an enforcer, depending on what we find."

Rafa double-checked Derick's connections. "Whenever you're ready, I'll open the door."

Once again, the monkey came alive. This time, Derick heard sounds through the speakers. Life was in stereo. He imagined that Rafa and Abby could see what he saw through the monkey eyes on their monitors.

Derick's avatar ran through the open door and into the room they were in. Through his monkey eyes, he looked at his own body moving in the suspension system. The sight was completely surreal. He looked ridiculous moving without going anywhere. He also looked like a giant—*fee fi fo fum* huge.

He ran the avatar, scampering across the room, then jumped onto a seat, a desk, and finally onto the long windowsill along the far wall. Derick heard his little monkey breathing over the speakers. He rapped on the glass and looked back at his sister.

Abby looked at Rafa, who nodded. She unlatched the window. "Good luck," she said. The monkey responded by sticking one thumb up in the air.

Derick's avatar ran along the edge of the roof and around the corner. Rafa and Abby could only watch on the monitor now.

Derick moved across the shingles and up toward the peak of the roof. Once there, he had to stop to get his bearings. He soon spied Watchman Tower and began to run toward it. He moved his monkey legs as fast as he could. He needed to get this over with before someone else discovered them and things got worse.

The monkey skidded to a halt at the edge of the roof. He looked down at a forty-foot drop to the ground below.

Derick could hear Abby back in the lab. "Oh, we didn't even think he'd have to cross there. At least, I didn't think about it."

The monkey turned back the way he had come.

"Are you going to go back down and across the ground?" Derick heard Abby ask. "It seems like someone would see you that way."

No sooner had she asked that than Derick turned the monkey again, sprinting toward the edge. If his skills had been more advanced, maybe he could have used both his arms and legs to push his body forward, but he didn't know how to. He could simply run, and he needed as much speed as he could get for that. He had to get onto the roof of the next building over.

"*Don't!*" Rafa shouted.

But Derick leapt into the air, spreading himself out and reaching toward the neighboring roof.

He heard Abby's whisper, "Please make it. Please make it. Please make it. Please make it."

Derick hit the edge of the other roof, pain surging through his chest. His monkey hands managed to grab the overhang. Derick struggled to breathe, the wind knocked out of him as he dangled forty feet in the air. He could hear the monkey's grunting and gasping echo through the room.

In a few moments, he had his breath back, and he managed to scramble onto the roof.

Abby exhaled long and hard.

"If you hurt that avatar, Derick, you're as good as gone from this academy," Rafa warned. "They're each worth more than all of our educations combined."

Derick acted as though he couldn't hear Rafa. Sure, the monkey may have cost a fortune, but it wasn't worth more than the lives of his parents and grandpa. The monkey moved across the other roof and approached the bottom of the tower. He began to slowly climb, putting his little fingers into the edges of mortar between bricks. He felt less sturdy than he thought he would with each grab.

"Remember," Rafa said into his microphone, "your body weighs less, so you don't have to hold up as much. And you can use your tail for balance."

Derick had to concentrate hard to curl his tail beneath him, against the wall, but with a little practice, it felt like a third leg. He climbed slightly faster.

"I'm impressed," Rafa said. "Using a tail isn't easy. That isn't what I was thinking of, but it seems to work."

Derick lost his grip on his left hand and groped madly to

keep from falling. He managed to stabilize himself at the last moment. A few more feet, and he reached one of the small windows. His slim frame easily slipped through the opening.

"Good work, Derick," Rafa said. "And now we find out if your talent is wasted."

Derick's eyes took a moment to adjust to the darker room. It was small, only about six feet wide, and the inside walls were made of the same stone as the outside. It was easy to picture a watchman looking out over the entire area. Derick couldn't help but imagine that if he were in the tower when someone attacked, he could probably get off some pretty good shots—like a sniper.

"I don't see anything," Rafa said through the speakers.

"Give him a few minutes," Abby pleaded.

As Derick moved the monkey to the center of the tower, metal blinds slid down over the windows. Darkness swallowed the room. Derick heard a voice.

"I'm sorry that it was so difficult for you to get here, but it was for a calculated purpose. This secret is important enough that I must take precautions. The secret must go only to those with determination and the right intentions, and under the right circumstances."

It was Grandpa Cragbridge's voice. Abby sighed in relief. Derick didn't hear Rafa say anything.

"And I must stress my point again," Grandpa's voice said, echoing in the tower. "This is Watchman's Tower. There is a reason I brought you here. The tower is symbolic of a place empires used to view their enemies coming. It could be a great help in defending those they loved and everything they worked for."

Suddenly the walls filled with color. "For example," Grandpa said.

The walls served as a screen to show a view of a great valley with mountains in the distance. An army marched over the horizon. Silhouette after silhouette moved toward the tower. Derick looked down and saw an entire city below him. Women took their goods to market, children following close behind. Men moved their horses from the stables to prepare them for travel. Merchants set up their shops.

Derick looked back at the army in the distance and realized that someone was on the tower with him—a man, dressed in simple skins. A cloth was draped over his head and tied with a string of leather. He picked up a drum and began to pound it. The city below changed. The women grabbed their children and rushed out of the streets. Men ran to get their swords and spears. The walls of the city filled with archers. The enemy was coming, and by the time they arrived, the city would be ready.

The scene changed. Derick was still on a tower, but the war wasn't far away, and it was no longer a time of simple skin clothing, but of armor and long, shiny swords and shields. Arrows rained down from the sky. Soldiers dumped a huge pot of boiling oil onto the attackers below.

"They're moving the siege tower to the south wall!" a voice cried beside Derick—another watchman calling out warnings. Derick saw a messenger at the bottom of the tower rush into the fray. He bolted across the castle walls, reaching a general who guided his men from atop the wall.

After a few orders, a new squad of soldiers rushed to the south wall. The siege tower, large, mobile and made of wood, steadily pressed closer to the wall. The enemy could use it to get inside the city. The men on the walls shot arrows and threw spears at those on the battlement. Enemy soldiers fell from the wooden tower to the ground below, but there were plenty remaining to press forward.

One man on the castle wall dipped his arrow in fire, then shot it into the wood. He repeated the action several more times. In less than a minute, the entire war machine was engulfed in flames. Men ran out from inside it, as it would soon burn to the ground.

"Another battering ram is coming!" the watchman on the tower shouted. Beneath him, a group of enemy soldiers held their shields above their heads as they approached the front gate. Derick could barely make out that beneath all their shields, they carried a large trunk of wood. They were going to burst through the gate. Men of the city quickly moved reinforcements to the tower. Some moved another pot of burning oil into position.

"Watch the east!" the watchman yelled again. "Archers from the east!"

To the east, a group of archers climbed a hill, where they could better launch their arrows in at the wall. And then the image faded out.

Derick heard his grandfather's voice again. "I cannot stress enough that unless your situation looks to be as life-threatening and significant as these, do not continue further. Unless you suspect an enemy, unless there are signs that something has happened to me, and that someone or some group is in hot pursuit of the same secret you seek, stop at once. What you will find through your journey is only to be known under the direst of circumstances."

Rafa asked, "Do you think this qualifies?"

"Yes," Derick heard Abby say without hesitation. "Both my grandpa and my parents are missing. A group of people questioned us, pretending to be police, and they took my locket. Someone has denied my Bridge access. I suspect some of the teachers are involved. Whoever took my parents and my grandpa is probably after the same information we are."

Grandpa's voice returned. "If you are determined to continue, you will need this." A stone in the wall moved outward. From the monkey's perspective, Derick couldn't see anything but the hard underside. "If there is any doubt at all, leave now, and the stone will return to its place."

There was no doubt in Derick's mind about going forward. As he climbed the wall, he realized that the stone had been hollowed out. It contained a small, white cube big enough to fit a golf ball inside, but nothing more. The avatar monkey grabbed it and jumped back to the ground, where Derick could examine it. It appeared to be solid. There were no handles or buttons to open it.

Once the cube was removed, the blinds on the tower windows opened again.

"To open the cube," Grandpa said as Derick blinked

against the light. "You must know what saying was carved on the mantelpiece in my study."

Back in the lab, Abby's voice spoke up. "Derick knows what it is, but he can't say it as a monkey. He has to bring the cube back."

Derick nodded his monkey head, knowing Abby and Rafa would see it on-screen. He approached the wall below a thin window and began to climb up.

His head was just high enough to see out when Rafa yelled, "*Get down!*"

Derick dropped to the floor.

"What just happened?" Abby asked.

Derick heard Rafa pushing buttons.

"Derick," Rafa said, "I'm showing Abby what I saw when you looked out the window." Several seconds of silence passed, and then Rafa said, "Look there."

"It's Ms. Entrese," Abby said. "She's on the grounds below you, and at least a few seconds ago, she was there looking right at the tower."

Rafa spoke, "Don't try to come out of the window again until I give the word."

Derick heard more movement from the lab.

"Don't go near the window, Abby!" Rafa commanded. "If she suspects an avatar is in the Watchman, she may also be watching this lab. In fact, she might have someone coming to check it out right now."

THE WHITE CUBE

W hat are we going to do?" Abby asked.

"You've convinced me, Derick," Rafa said. "Unless you feel confident coming down the other side while carrying the cube and staying out of view, I suggest you come out of the avatar and let me take it from here."

Derick was stunned. Rafa had suddenly changed from someone who was going to turn them in, to someone who was going to help them.

The monkey went limp, and Derick opened his eyes. Rafa helped him unlatch the sensors, and Derick handed them over.

Before Rafa began to control the monkey, he said, "Grab your things. I would suggest you leave, but I doubt you will without the white box. When I get back in, we may need to leave in a hurry."

Derick watched the screen as the monkey Rafa controlled picked up the cube from the floor and peeked out the window. He saw nothing. He moved quickly and smoothly, shimmying down the tower with surprising speed. He ran across the roof, then jumped the divide, landing on his feet on the other side.

"Yeah, yeah," Derick mumbled flatly.

Soon the avatar was back, through the window, and it handed Abby the cube. Rafa logged off, put the monkey away, and within a minute, all three of them had their packs and were gathered around the door.

"Let me look out first," Rafa said. "It will be much less suspicious for the avatar TA to be seen leaving the lab."

Abby and Derick waited for his all-clear signal, then followed after. They walked down the hall and into the commons area, moving quickly, but trying not to draw extra attention to themselves.

Rafa looked over his shoulder. "Some private study rooms are down this hall. Duck in there and look at the box." He led them through the masses of students. Abby felt better being with a large group—less chance of being caught—but something about Rafa leading them made her nervous.

Rafa looked into two of the rooms before finding an empty one. He opened the door, and they all went inside. They surrounded a small table with several screens lining the top for student use. Five simple chairs circled the table. No one sat.

Rafa raised his hands and spoke. "I realize that this is

none of my business, and you probably aren't sure you can trust me. But if you'll let me help, I'd like to."

An awkward silence lasted for several seconds.

"He really helped us out," Abby said tentatively.

"He hasn't tattled on us yet," Derick countered.

"All you have is my word," Rafa said, "but I promise to tell no one. I won't take the time to explain here, but your grandfather was once very kind to my family. We owe him a great debt of gratitude. If I can do something to repay that debt, it is worth risking my hard work here."

"Thanks, Rafa," Derick said. "We'll let you know."

Rafa nodded. "I'll leave now, but if you need any more help, I promise that I can be trusted. *Com certeza.*" Rafa stepped out of the door and closed it behind him.

Abby and Derick waited a moment to make sure Rafa was gone. "Do you think he's sincere?" she asked.

"I'm not sure," Derick admitted.

Abby held up the white cube and changed the subject. "I think this is like the locket. It doesn't seem to have any way to open it from the outside."

"Grandpa got pretty good at that," Derick said. "He said we had to know what was carved on the mantelpiece in his study. That means only people who knew him well could open it."

"So do we say the quote?" Abby asked. "I don't see what else we could do."

"Give it a try," Derick said.

Abby remembered the words easily. Grandpa had forced both her and Derick to memorize them, probably in preparation for this very moment. "'Those who cannot remember the past are condemned to repeat it.'"

The small box opened, and a three-dimensional image was projected onto the table, almost a foot tall and two feet wide. Thank goodness Rafa had brought them to a private place. This would be awfully difficult to conceal in the commons.

The image showed someone walking down a dark hallway, like watching a miniature reality. Both Abby and Derick leaned forward to get a closer look. The hallway was so poorly lit that it was hard to tell what the walls were made of. Occasional dim lighting showed only splotches of gray that looked like hard cement.

"Where is that?" Abby asked.

"Oh, I know," Derick said with a sarcastic grunt. "Grandpa told me all of the secrets he wanted to keep from everybody else. He happened to tell me the location of the creepy secret hallway one day while we were sipping root beer and watching old movies."

"Not funny," Abby said.

The person in the image continued down the virtual hallway until he came to two large double doors. The metal plating and complicated handles made the doors look impenetrable, but they opened, and the journey continued for a few steps before fading away.

"Okay," Abby said, straightening. "So we need to find some creepy hallway that leads to a set of huge doors."

"So easy," Derick said sarcastically.

Each side of the cube unhinged from another, so it fell

flat against the table. What had been a box was now a collection of flat little squares on the table. Both Abby and Derick leaned in for a closer look. On five of the squares were intricate pictures, like the smallest murals they had ever seen. On the sixth, little metal clasps held another small key like the ones in the lockets, plus a rolled piece of paper.

Derick removed the key and put it on a metal ring with the others. "It feels so strange to have real metal keys," Derick said. "What does the paper say?"

Abby removed the paper and unfolded it. Written in her grandfather's handwriting was one phrase—*By Endurance We Conquer*. She showed it to her brother.

"Cryptic," Derick said. "You'd think Grandpa would be a little more straightforward for once. He is a scientist after all."

Abby leaned farther forward and examined the minipaintings on the inside of the cube. She tried to identify what was going on in each: a ship completely surrounded by ice, two armies—maybe from the Civil War—clashing in battle, a small boy on a bed surrounded by doctors, a young lady with a neck wound fighting in a battle, and a man dangling from a rope beside a ship.

"I don't get it," Derick admitted. "Are these all supposed to be related? I don't see a connection."

"Me, neither," Abby said. "Maybe we need to study."

"Where do we start?" Derick asked.

Abby turned on her rings and began typing. "I'm

searching about the phrase Grandpa wrote," she said. "'By endurance we conquer.'"

"That's just a saying," Derick said. "He might just be telling us not to give up."

Abby scanned the results. "It was the family motto of Ernest Shackleton."

"Who?"

"Ernest Shackleton. I'm not sure who he is," Abby admitted, "But it says here that he named a ship *Endurance* after the motto and sailed to Antarctica." Abby pointed to the picture of a ship surrounded by ice.

"You're brilliant," Derick said. "Let's go check it out on the Bridge." Abby gathered all the little squares and stored them in her pocket. Derick opened the door to leave, but stepped back into the room. "Oh no," he said. "Look." He pointed down the hall.

Rafa was talking to Ms. Entrese.

SHACKLETON

Derick and Abby decided to go different ways and meet up at the Bridge lab. That way, hopefully, at least one of them wouldn't get busted. Abby waited several uncomfortable minutes outside the lab, waiting for her brother. Then the thought occurred to her that if Ms. Entrese wanted to, she could summon both her and Derick to the office at any moment.

Derick finally showed up. "Sorry," he apologized, approaching his sister. "I bumped into Dothan, a kid from music class. I didn't want to look suspicious, so I had to chat for a minute."

"It's fine," Abby lied. "I was here, all by myself, worrying about how everything could collapse around us at any moment."

"Good to hear you could handle it." Derick turned on his rings and synced up to the Bridge. "Dang it!"

"What?" Abby asked.

"I'm blocked too."

"Oh no," Abby said, running her fingers through her hair. "It'll take days to get your access back."

Derick paced for a moment. "But we need this. We could try studying it on our rings, but maybe a clue is in the actual Bridge entry."

Abby stood there in silence as her brother still walked back and forth.

"What are we going to do?" Derick asked.

After a moment, Abby smiled. "We have to ask someone else to let us use their Bridge code."

"We're in too deep," Derick protested. "We can't tell anybody else about this."

"Precisely," Abby said. "Someone else already knows quite a bit."

"Rafa?" Derick asked.

"No," Abby said. "I'm not sure we can trust Rafa. I was thinking of someone blonder."

"Carol," Derick said. "Do you think she'll help us after she freaked out in the avatar lab?"

Abby smiled again. "I think we have a good chance if *you* ask her."

• • •

Carol opened the door to her dorm, and her eyes immediately went wide.

"Hey, Carol," Derick said.

"Derick!" she blurted out and hugged him like a long-lost friend. "I'm glad you're not kicked out of school. That would be terrible. It would be a waste of a great mind and a great face. I guess neither would really be *wasted*, but I wouldn't get to see your face, so that really would be a waste, at least to me."

Derick awkwardly hugged her back. "I'm glad I'm not kicked out too, and that my face isn't . . . wasted. So far, no one has said a thing."

"Good," Carol said, letting go of him, "but I couldn't be involved. I hope you understand. That was just crazy."

"Yes, it was. And I'm sorry," Derick apologized.

"I mean, I guess you guys must have your reasons, but I don't know what they are, so to me it just didn't make any sense. I was thinking that—"

"I'm going to tell you those reasons," Derick said.

"You're opening up to me? That's awesome!" Carol said, grabbing his hand. Derick had to fight his reflexes not to pull away. "I didn't think we were at that stage in our relationship. After you, I'll be sharing something super personal, like how when I was nine, I . . . Oh, I almost told you. That would have been embarrassing, especially if it was worse than—"

Derick pulled back his hand and pretended he needed it to pick an eyelash out of his eye. "My grandpa and parents have been kidnapped."

"I heard they were missing, but kidnapped? That's super terrible, awful stuff. Are you okay? I'm here for you," Carol said. "I've been really worried about you and Abby. Speaking of Abby, where is she? Not that I don't love this alone time with just me and you."

"My grandpa had some sort of secret," Derick said. "And we think some people have kidnapped him for it. We still haven't figured out how my parents fit in. Maybe they knew the secret."

"I'm so sorry," Carol said, and hugged him again. "That's scary." She squeezed him tightly and then settled back.

Derick shuffled uncomfortably. "I need to ask a favor."

"You need a girlfriend to get you through this difficult time. We're probably too young to start dating, but I'm really good at comforting. I've learned a lot about that. I had a dog, and her name was Cleopatra. She was part-poodle, part-Maltese, which made her a short, black thing with curly fur. But anyway, when I was sad, she used to be able to just tell—like dog sense or something—and she'd snuggle up close to me and—"

"I was wondering if we could use your Bridge code," Derick interrupted.

Carol let go of him. "You came here to ask if you could use my code?"

"Yes," Derick said. "Both mine and Abby's have been blocked, and we think we're on the trail to helping our parents and our grandpa, but we really need to use the Bridge to figure it out."

Carol opened her mouth. Derick could tell she was

poised to say yes, but she stopped and said something else. "I know you're in a really difficult situation, but it does sound crazy that looking at the Bridge is somehow going to help your family. Aren't the police already on it?"

"Yes, but the bad guys posed as the police before we got to the real ones, so they know more than they should. And I don't think the real police will be helpful. This is beyond them. That's why my grandpa left *us* the clues. We need to follow the clues to find him. But we can't go any further without your code."

"Hmmm," Carol said. "That sounds crazy. Which, don't get me wrong, you're very cute when you're crazy, and I know that you're in quite the emotional state right now, which also makes you a mopey kind of attractive. I'll do it, if—"

"If what?"

"If . . ." Carol got up and walked to her closet. She pulled out a rolled-up white T-shirt. "If you wear this," she said. "For a whole day." She tossed it to Derick.

"Uh . . ." Derick floundered. He was about to quickly accept but decided he'd better look at the shirt first. He unfolded it and gazed at big, bold red letters that said, "I'm in love." Beneath the words was Carol's face, smiling, her blonde hair in pigtails. He flipped the shirt over. *Popuhilarity.com* was printed on the back.

Derick had no idea what to say. Carol apparently did.

"They made them up for a promo for this web series pilot I was in—Popuhilarity. It's the words *popular* and *hilarity* mixed together. I think they were trying to be clever, but most people didn't get it. Anyway, I was this love-crazy girl. They said I was a natural. I was always saying 'I'm in love.' The pilot never got picked up by any of the prime networks, so they gave me the extra T-shirts. For some reason, I've never been able to persuade anyone to wear them except my mom."

"Okay," Derick agreed quickly, trying not to imagine what people might say. He started to put the shirt on.

"You can wear it right now if you want, but the deal is for a whole day, to classes and everything. Which shouldn't be a big deal, because it's such a good-looking shirt. Since today's almost over, if you wear it now, you'll have to wear it another day too."

Derick froze. "I'll just wait until I can do it all at once," he said, then realized it could hurt her feelings and tried to recover. "Just because it doesn't really go with my . . . shoes."

Carol looked down in thought. "You're right. I should get you some bright red shoelaces to go with the shirt."

"Don't worry about it. I'll figure it out," Derick said. "So we have a deal?" He offered his hand to shake and seal the agreement.

"Definitely," Carol said, and shifted to his side to hold his hand, not to shake it. She intertwined her fingers in his.

Derick couldn't believe he'd left himself so open. They walked out of her room a few steps hand in hand before Derick pretended he had to look something up on his rings and wriggled his hand free.

• • •

By Endurance We Conquer. That was the motto. And it was put to the test.

Shackleton drove screws through the bottoms of his boots to make them into improvised ice-climbing shoes. Two other men did the same; their thick clothes, covered in dirt and grime, weren't enough to keep out the cold as they completed their task.

From the Bridge, Abby, Derick, and Carol watched them shiver in the arctic air.

One of the men looked up at the frozen mountains, then at their only map. "It only shows the coast. We have no idea what's ahead," he said.

"Whatever is there," Shackleton said, "we have to cross it." He had a full beard and wore some sort of hat wrapped around his head. "We'll make it. We'll wait until the middle of the night when the snow is frozen and easier to walk across. We'll travel light. No sleeping bags. Nothing we don't need. We have to make it by the following night."

Carol fast-forwarded the Bridge event to get through the long wait. She slowed it down again about 3 A.M., when the men grabbed some rope and a few rations and began to hike across the first ice field. A plateau, then a series of snow-covered peaks lay ahead of them. It was one giant frozen obstacle.

"I don't know if I could do that," Abby confessed.

"Me neither," Carol added. "I get cold when the air conditioner is on too high. I don't think I'd last a day in

Antarctica, let alone with only a rope and a little food. These guys haven't eaten a good meal in forever. I wouldn't want to even try a day hike on an empty stomach."

"But they have to, or their friends are going to die," Derick said.

Sick and freezing comrades were depending on Shackleton to reach them. The three men hiked the wind-raked, icy ground, their feet crunching in the frozen snow.

"This doesn't look safe at all," Abby said.

"It isn't," Derick agreed. "They have no idea where hidden crevasses are under the snow. With any step, they could fall to their deaths."

Carol giggled.

"I didn't think any of that was funny," Derick said.

"You . . ." Carol giggled again. "You said *crevasses*. I used to think that was a swear word, so now every time I hear it, I laugh."

Abby smiled, welcoming a break in the tension. She couldn't believe this whole ordeal. They'd watched Shackleton's expedition for over two hours now, and still had no clues.

First Shackleton and his crew of twenty-six adventurers, plus one stowaway, launched for Antarctica. They traveled through ice-riddled waters until, during the night, the water had frozen around their ship, trapping them in the middle of a huge ice sheet. Abby heard the cracks and groans of the ship as ice grew, expanded, and eventually crushed the boat. It sounded like a war, with explosions and counter fire. The broken masts and sunken hull left the men stranded on a huge slab of ice hundreds of miles from land and without a way home.

The men salvaged three small lifeboats and supplies and marched across the ice. At one point, the ice became too thin, and a man fell through. Shackleton reached into the frigid waters and pulled the man back to safety.

Then they rowed in their lifeboats for seven days straight. Sometimes huge waves crashed over them. They were soaked through with freezing arctic water. Abby felt cold just watching it. When the men traded rowing shifts, their hands were often frozen to the oars—they had to chip them free from the wood. Their ears were covered in frost-bite.

Finally, they found land—Elephant Island. Abby had thought that was the end—the ordeal had already lasted months—but it was a desolate island. Other boats never visited it, so there was no hope for rescue without moving on. By then, most of the men were freezing and sick.

Shackleton handpicked a few of the best sailors, and together they headed out eight hundred miles to South Georgia Island, to a whaler's station. Abby could hardly believe it—traveling eight hundred miles in a makeshift sailboat. The men talked about their chances, knowing they wouldn't be able to see much over the waves to chart their course, and if they were even a degree off, they could miss the island by sixty miles, and sail out into the open ocean. If that happened, all of them—on the boat and back on the island—would either starve or freeze to death, whichever came first. Carol fast-forwarded through their chilling journey. Abby saw blowholes of killer whales nearby as they struggled through the icy ocean.

The men barely managed to land on the other island, but their boat could no longer sail, and the whaler's station was on the other side of the frozen land.

Abby watched the three men take step after step into unknown terrain, moving forward and upward—the same repetitive motion over and over, their breath escaping in little clouds. They talked little.

"How long have they been lost now?" Carol asked.

"Looks like"—Derick flicked his fingers, searching the net for a few moments—"whoa . . . about a year and a half."

"You're kidding me," Carol said. "And I think I have it rough when I have to wait in a long line to get French fries. Don't get me wrong, that's still a pain, but it's nothing compared to this."

Abby had never really thought about how much some people had gone through to survive.

Carol moved the image forward until the next evening. The party had been hiking since three in the morning, walked all day long, and yet they still moved forward as it neared midnight. Abby calculated the time in her head—twenty-one hours of straight hiking—hard hiking, trekking up and down mountains without trails. They were nearing the top of another peak, with wind whipping at their faces.

"We've got to get down soon," one man said, panting.

"You're right," Shackleton answered. "We can't be caught up here during the night."

"We've got no sleeping bags to fight this cold off," the other answered. "Not that we planned on sleeping."

"We'll get down," Shackleton said and approached the peak. As soon as the view down was visible, none of them spoke. The mountain dropped so steeply, it was impossible to walk down. The men paced along the top, looking for a safer way down—nothing. They met back together.

Shackleton looked at the other two. "We've got to take a risk. Are you game?" The men didn't answer. "We'll slide," Shackleton said. He took their rope and coiled it up so they could sit on it, kind of like a saucer-type sled.

After a few moments, the men agreed.

"They have no idea what's down there," Carol said. "I mean, there could be, like, sharp rocks, or huge cracks in the ice, or a giant cliff. They don't know."

"They have to try something," Derick said. "Or they're all dead."

The men sat on the rope, latched to one another, and slid off the top of the mountain. They tried to brace themselves against the snow to slow themselves down, but they rushed down the mountainside. The wind pulled at their clothes and faces. They leaned and twisted, trying to stay together to keep the rope sled beneath them. A bump nearly sent them sprawling, but they regrouped as they continued to career out of control down the slope. Finally, they crashed into a snow bank. A moment later, all three men stood and brushed themselves off. There were no screams of delight; there was no celebration. The nearly broken men solemnly shook hands. Their gamble had paid off.

Finally, at about 5 A.M., they were at the base of another hill and sat down to rest. Abby did the math. They had been hiking for twenty-six hours. Within moments, both of Shackleton's companions were asleep. Shackleton himself blinked hard and struggled to stay awake.

"If he falls asleep," Derick whispered to himself, "all three of them will probably never wake up—they'll freeze to death."

After about five minutes, Shackleton shook the other two back to consciousness. "It's been a half an hour," he lied. "Time for a fresh start."

Carol fast-forwarded the image. An hour and a half later, they could see the bay, and by three in the afternoon, they'd arrived at the whaler's home. They had successfully finished a thirty-six-hour, nearly nonstop hike over a frozen island.

But that wasn't the most moving part for Abby. Shackleton and the other two men were rescued quickly, but those on Elephant Island had to wait. Shackleton tried to reach them four times before getting through the packed ice. When he finally succeeded, and Shackleton counted the silhouettes that emerged from a small hut the men had made from the two remaining boats, Abby had to blink away tears.

At last Shackleton said, "They're all here."

Abby couldn't believe it. Stranded for nearly two years in Antarctica, and they had all survived. Maybe part of why Grandpa wanted them to study this expedition was to see the power of endurance, the power of hope. Maybe he wanted them to know what people could overcome if they kept trying, going on when they had no more reason to hope. Maybe Grandpa and her parents were okay, and more importantly, maybe they were going to be back soon.

"We have to figure this out," Abby said, with new determination. "How does knowing about Shackleton lead us to the next clue?"

SIMULATOR

Grandpa had written Shackleton's motto on the slip of paper, and Shackleton's ship was portrayed on one of the little squares from the inner side of the cube, but Derick, Abby, and Carol still had no idea what Shackleton had to do with Oscar Cragbridge. They turned to the other small pictures from the cube, hoping those might have some answers.

The next miniature painting was of a Civil War battle; the blue and gray uniforms gave that part away. A boy in the next picture must have been about to have some sort of surgery, but there was no figuring out who the boy was.

Carol suggested that the girl with the wounded neck in another picture may have been Joan of Arc, and after some research, they felt it was probable. But what did she have to do with the Civil War? With Shackleton? With the boy having surgery? How were they related? They found a lot of information, but they still couldn't put the pieces together to make any sense of them.

The three students didn't stop for dinner. They took turns sneaking down to the cafeteria one by one to eat while the other two worked.

Abby insisted she take the last turn. She couldn't help but think of her parents and grandfather and wonder where they were and how they were doing—if they were still alive at all. A lump stuck to the sides of her throat as she thought about the possibilities.

She eventually stepped out of the Bridge to eat, leaving Derick and Carol to continue without her. As she closed the door, she was glad they had a clear goal, or leaving Derick alone with Carol would have been downright cruel.

Many questions reeled through her mind as she walked down the hall. So what if Shackleton and his men survived a horrendous journey? What if the battle they were looking at was really during the Civil War? Where did any of it lead? They had gained another key, but what was it for? None of it seemed to bring her any closer to her parents or grandfather.

As she walked, she looked at the walls of Cragbridge Hall, not wanting to make any eye contact with anyone who passed. If she couldn't be alone physically, she'd be alone with her thoughts. She looked at the patterns in the bricks. She watched the lockers. She glanced at a painting—a picture of two armies facing off with a field between them.

Abby slowed as she passed the painting. It definitely wasn't the same picture as the one in the cube, but there were some striking similarities. It could have been another artist's version of one of many Civil War battles. The questions and answers haunted her. Abby wanted to scream. The picture hung there silently as a testament that she couldn't figure out the next clue.

"It's called a painting," a voice said.

Abby turned to see Jacqueline flanked by two of her friends.

"Leave me alone, Jacqueline," Abby said.

"I was just trying to help," Jacqueline said. "It starts with a canvas, and then someone dips a brush into paint. With little bristles on a brush, they put the paint onto the canvas. That's why we call it a *painting*."

Abby closed her eyes and bit her bottom lip. She wanted to say so many things to Jacqueline, but refused. The words wanting to come out definitely weren't nice, and they wouldn't help her situation. She started to walk away.

"Maybe," Jacqueline called after her, "at a different school you could take a class where you'd learn something . . ."

Maybe the pressure had built up in Abby for too long. Maybe she couldn't take the teasing anymore. Or maybe Jacqueline was too rude at the wrong time. Regardless of the reason, Abby cracked.

"*Stop it!*" she yelled. "Don't you read the news? Don't you know that my grandpa and my parents are missing? Do you think I'm worried about your little clique or some upcoming test—or a stupid painting? I thought you had an

217

exceptional mind. I don't think it takes a genius to figure out that it's not the stress of school that has me worried."

Jacqueline took a step back, a look of surprise on her face.

"I'm . . . I'm sorry," Abby said, calming down. "I just . . ."

Jacqueline looked at her friends. One stepped away from her and toward Abby. "I'm sorry about your grandpa and your parents," Jacqueline said quickly. "I really am. And I hope the police find them soon." Her voice chilled a bit. "But that still doesn't change the fact that you don't deserve to be here. In fact, this might be the perfect time—"

"To quit talking to you," Abby said, finishing Jacqueline's sentence. "I couldn't agree more." And Abby turned and walked away.

"I wasn't done," Jacqueline called out after her.

"I was," Abby said, surprised at her tone. She didn't turn around; she simply put one foot in front of the other and continued down the hall. She thought she heard Jacqueline say something else, but she couldn't hear. More importantly, she didn't care.

Abby walked for another minute before noticing another painting on a wall—a boy on a bed, surrounded by doctors. Abby nearly passed it before turning back. This was also similar to one from the cube. Abby read the note about it. It was a boy named Joseph Smith. He was seven years old when doctors cut open his leg and chipped away fourteen pieces of infected bone—all without anesthesia. Abby shuddered just reading about it. The surgery had saved the boy's leg, but afterward, he walked on crutches for three years, and had a slight limp for the rest of his life. Joseph Smith grew up to be the founder of a new American religion.

Excited now, Abby rushed down the hall until she found another painting, this one of a ship with a man dangling from the rope beside it. The plaque said the man was John Howland and that the ship was the *Mayflower*. He was being pulled back to safety after falling overboard. The paintings all matched those from the cube. Abby touched the frame. This painting certainly looked old enough to have been there since the founding of Cragbridge Hall. She tried to pull it from the wall to see if anything was behind it, but it was mounted fast against the bricks. It was meant to stay put—maybe even be there permanently.

Abby walked past the cafeteria but couldn't find any other framed pictures. She retraced her steps and turned down a hall going the other direction.

There was a painting of Joan of Arc engaged in battle despite her wounds. The pictures were leading Abby somewhere. She passed a smaller hallway as she continued her search, but when she found no more matched paintings, she backtracked.

The hallway she walked back to was empty. It had shorter ceilings, and no classrooms, just storage closets. It was probably for the janitors. More importantly, it had no paintings. It ended in a brick wall.

Abby stared at the brick—a dead end. Maybe there was another picture before the Civil War painting. Abby ran back where she started, but couldn't find anything. Before allowing herself to get too frustrated, she ran back to the Bridge to get Derick and Carol to help.

Within a few minutes, she, Derick, and Carol searched the halls for the fifth painting.

"The other one has to be here close by, doesn't it?" Abby asked. "Or is this all a coincidence?"

"I really think you're onto something," Derick said. "We just have to keep looking."

"What's missing?" Carol asked.

"The *Endurance*," Abby said. "And based on Grandpa's message, that painting seems to be the key."

After ten minutes of searching without success, they regrouped. "Alright," Abby led off. "We're missing something."

She thought it out as best she could. "The paintings have been evenly spaced, so the next one should either be down the large hall, or at the dead end brick wall."

Knowing that it all had to do with a secret, Abby guessed that the next clue would be in the smaller hallway where no one ever went.

She walked down the small hall, looking at the molding along the edge of the floor, hoping for any sort of clue. Nothing but whitewashed baseboard. It was the same above on the crown molding, except that it was broken up with an occasional block with an ornate picture on it. The ceilings were low enough for Abby to see the blocks. She glanced at the closest one. It had the insignia of Cragbridge Hall—the Watchman. The block before was the same, but near the spot where the next painting should be, the picture was different. It was a small impression of a boat trapped in ice.

"Carol! Derick!" Abby called out. Within moments they were beside Abby, and Derick had boosted her up for a closer look.

The detail was amazing. The phrase *By Endurance We Conquer* was written in tiny letters above the ship. Not knowing what else to do, Abby pushed on the block. After a deep click, a panel of bricks shifted from the wall like a door on hinges. It moved slowly and heavily, but revealed a gap barely wide enough for one person to slide through.

Derick peered in. "There is a whole hallway back here."

"Don't wait around. Go in," Carol commanded. "No way could this be the wrong way. Little blocks don't just open up strange hallways for no reason."

Derick took a deep breath, then stepped through the opening. The other two followed.

As soon as they entered the hallway, dim lights along the walls cast a dull glow. Several feet of darkness stretched between the lights, but they illuminated just enough for the three students to see the general path. Abby smelled a musty odor as she continued down the corridor. All at once, she realized it was the same hallway she'd seen when they first tried to open the cube—the image of someone walking down a dark hall. They were on the right track.

"This is so mysterious," Carol said. "Secret passageways. People in danger. I feel like I'm in a movie. Oh, but if I were, who would play me? They'd have to get someone blonde and really pretty—maybe Chloe Xander—but then, I don't know if she could be as funny as I am."

"Aren't you an actress?" Derick asked. "Couldn't you just play yourself?"

"Yeah, I guess I could," Carol said. "I'd do a really good job."

"I'm sure you would," Derick said.

"But my question is, is this an action-adventure or a romantic comedy?" Carol asked, walking behind Abby and in front of Derick. "It feels more like an action-adventure movie right now, but we'll have to wait to see how it ends." She looked over her shoulder at Derick, who was walking with one hand in his pocket and the other against the wall, safely away from Carol.

Abby rolled her eyes. They walked for over a hundred yards before Derick stopped and cried out. "Ouch!"

"What's wrong?" Abby asked.

"I walked into something. I think I got cut," Derick said. He stepped away from the wall. His pants were torn just above the shin. Derick lifted up his pant leg. Droplets of blood began to surface.

Carol looked closely at the wall. "It was a piece of metal," she said. "Nasty, jagged thing."

Abby moved over to get a closer look. "It looks like another door. Maybe there's a painting or a mirror on the other side, but someone tried to use the metal to weld it closed. I'd guess that when someone managed to open it, the metal ripped away, and the jagged edge left behind is what cut you." She looked over at Derick.

"Whatever it was, it hurt." Derick limped a few paces, favoring his leg.

Then it hit Abby. "Coach Adonavich," she said, her eyes going wide. "She had a mark on her leg—a jagged wound."

"Really?" Carol asked.

"Yeah, I saw it when we were playing basketball. Do you think she's already been here?"

"It sounds like she has," Carol said.

"I guess now the question is if she's on our side, or the other," Derick said.

"I don't know," Abby said.

Carol hurried on. "And if the metal cut her, who was the one who tried to weld the door shut? They'd have been here before she was. And that means we have at least two other people looking for the same thing we are."

"Why couldn't Grandpa have just left us a list of all the people he really trusted?" Abby said.

"If we have as much at stake as Grandpa made it seem," Derick said, "he probably couldn't be sure of who would stay loyal to him anyway."

"No matter who else has been here," Abby said, "we still have to help. We don't know if they can be trusted, and Grandpa and Mom and Dad could be counting on us."

The three friends walked several more yards before the hall turned. Around the corner, they faced two large double doors—just like they'd seen from the cube before it fell into flat squares. Abby stared for a moment, taking them in. The doors looked more like they belonged on a safe than an entrance to a room. They were made of metal, with bars

223

crossing each other for the entire width and height of the doors. About waist high ran a long, thick bar with what looked like plate-sized gears behind it.

Derick stepped forward, and after a few moments found a small keyhole in the bar. He inserted the key from the cube. It looked incongruently small, but the lock clicked. Several gears slowly began to turn, grinding under the load of the heavy doors. Whatever was behind them was meant to be kept safe. The doors gradually swung open.

The three friends walked through the opening—and nearly fell off a ledge. The passage opened into a dark shaft that went straight down. In the darkness, they couldn't see the bottom. A metal ladder descended into the black. As the three friends peered down, they heard another clicking sound, and the gears worked the door back closed.

"I hope we don't need to get out of here in a hurry," Carol said. "But if something down here makes us upset, and we could manage to slam that door on the way out, I think the whole school would shake."

Neither Derick nor Abby responded.

"So who's going first?" Carol asked.

They all stared over the edge of the dark descent.

"C'mon," Derick said and began climbing down the ladder.

"He's so brave," Carol said. "Thirty-one percent hotter than before."

As Abby climbed down, the steel rungs chilled her hands as if she were grabbing icicles. She must have descended more than three stories before she finally reached a floor.

They had no sooner dropped to the ground than the image of Grandpa appeared again, glowing in the darkness.

"Hello, whoever you may be," he said. He looked younger again. Abby guessed that Grandpa had prepared the image about the same time as the first journal entry. "Many trials led here, and I must congratulate you on getting this far. You are almost to your goal. I must also recognize that because you are doing this, something terrible must be at stake. I hope that your heart is honest and your courage strong, or I doubt you will proceed any further.

"You see, I have developed some technology that one day I may release in schools, but as for now, I've decided against it. It is a simulator unlike any other you have experienced. From inside it, you become as if you were a figure from history."

Grandpa's eyes smiled at the corners; he was very proud of this invention.

"However," Grandpa continued, "through technology I will not explain—for it begs questions that are not to be answered yet—this simulator can make you feel what someone in history actually felt." He cleared his throat. "Or what they may have felt. You use a suit that hangs inside the lockers. Your key from the cube will only open one such door. I apologize if the suit is not your exact size." Grandpa continued, pointing his finger. "Do not be afraid. The simulator will not hurt you, but it may seem as though it can. If you are to proceed, you must complete a challenge that someone from history has passed. The question is, will you? Doing so will take more than curiosity or knowledge. You must have a cause so important that, like these people in history, you absolutely refuse to give up. If not, you will not pass.

"You have already heard me say throughout these challenges that I've tried to allow only those I trust to successfully discover the secret. Only those with integrity, intelligence, and strength of character should uncover it. Knowing how to use it—or not use it—requires much wisdom. This is my final attempt to ensure that you have such a character.

"You may try as many times as you like, but each situation will be different, and each will try your mettle. If you're on my side, if you are someone worthy of my trust, I wish you good luck."

And Grandpa was gone. Just hearing his voice helped Abby remember her cause, the reason she had for going on, but she could not help but feel intimidated by what her grandfather had said—that this would test their mettle. Abby just hoped she had enough courage to make it.

• • •

A second after Grandpa's image disappeared, a few sets of simple lights illuminated the space at the bottom of the ladder. Derick could make out a wall full of thin doors—the lockers Grandpa referred to.

Derick couldn't believe what he'd heard. A simulator? And he would feel what historical figures had felt? Part of him was thrilled. He might be one of the first to try out this invention. Then again, Grandpa had said it would test him. Maybe he didn't want to feel what others had felt. Derick looked at both his sister and Carol. "He said only the key from the cube will open this door, so only one of us can do it at a time," he said.

"I can do it," Abby offered.

Derick knew she would volunteer. She was always willing to try, but could she do it? He loved Abby, but there were many things she struggled with. She wouldn't have even made it into Cragbridge if Grandpa hadn't pulled some strings.

"Or I could try, if you want me to," Carol offered. "Don't get me wrong, I can't say that I'm leaping at the chance. I mean, some people in history have gone through some pretty crazy stuff."

Could Carol pass whatever test waited for them? She was fun, bright, and flirty, but this challenge was bound to require more than that. They didn't have time to waste. Derick thought about his accomplishments, his grades, honors, and athletics. No matter what challenge awaited, he was probably the most likely of the three to make it. This was his responsibility.

"No," Derick said. "I should do it." No one argued further. Derick was pretty sure he saw relief on Abby's face.

"That's pretty heroic," Carol said, and fanned her face with her hand.

Derick stepped forward and pressed the key into one of the lockers. It wouldn't budge. He tried two more times before one opened. From inside, he pulled out a suit and put it on. It was similar to the avatar sensors; perhaps Grandpa had used some of the same technology. Of course, the suit was several sizes too big. Maybe Grandpa hadn't expected to send his grandkids down to the basement of Cragbridge Hall when he originally planned all this out.

Along the wall furthest away were two more doors, separated by ten feet or so. They both looked similar to the previous doors—the thick frame, crossbeams, and several gears along the front. The other door looked just as thick and solid. Derick surveyed them both and realized the difference: the keyhole to one was larger. His key would fit only one door. What was the other door for?

Derick inserted his key into the thick door. After another series of clicks and turns, it swung open. Derick took a deep breath. "Wish me luck."

"Good luck," Abby said.

"I would, but I don't believe in luck," Carol said. "I think life is more about skill, intellect, and striving to make your own opportunities."

"Alright," Derick said, "Wish me skill, intellect, and the chance to be successful in this opportunity—but that isn't nearly as catchy."

Carol laughed. "Do you need a good-luck kiss?"

Derick didn't turn around.

"Wait a second," Abby said. "I just thought of something. What if the pictures in the cube, and the paintings, are clues as to what you're about to go through? What if you have to go through a battle, or a surgery with those old tools, or be part of the *Endurance* crew?"

Derick paused. Any one of those experiences would try him to the core.

No one spoke for a moment. Finally, Derick broke the silence. "It can't really hurt me, right? I might as well give it a try." He blew out a gust of air and stepped into the doorway. As soon as he was in, the large door automatically closed.

Derick stood in complete darkness. What had he gotten himself into? No time to think about that now. He had to focus. He had to succeed. He took a step forward.

MAUL

Grandpa's voice echoed through the simulator. "If at any time you decide you can't continue, press the button on the back of your neck. You must remember it's there, for it will only be there on your real body, not the one you see in the simulator." So this was just like the avatar. "If you go unconscious, the equipment will automatically terminate the simulation. Remember, you have to complete the task to move on."

Derick's heartbeat raced. He had no idea what to expect.

A breeze. He felt a breeze. And he could smell . . . brush and pine and dirt—mountain air. He knew his body was in the basement of Cragbridge Hall, but his senses were completely deceived. In a moment, Derick saw green and trees, dirt, and rocks. It was absolutely amazing. He had somehow stepped into the great outdoors, and it was larger than life. Huge mountains jutted up at the sky. Trees stood tall and strong almost everywhere he looked. He turned all the way around, taking in the scene. He could even hear the sound of a river nearby.

He stepped forward through the brush and noticed a weight in his hand. He looked down to find a rifle. Good. If there was anything dangerous in these woods, he'd be ready. He looked at his clothes—mostly animal skins. He had a pouch of water slung around his neck and a large knife at his belt. He was some sort of mountain man.

Derick looked around again. He still couldn't get over the beauty of this place. He had been expecting absolute horror, but got this. A bird chirped in the distance. Bushes were laden with berries, and trees with fruit—maybe plums.

Derick lifted his arm to move a branch out of the way and stepped into a clearing.

Less than ten yards away, two bear cubs stood by the berries. There was something beautiful about seeing the wild creatures paw their food off the brush and onto the ground or bite it off the bush.

Oh no. Panic rushed through Derick. Wherever there were cubs, there would also be . . . Derick saw the mother bear rise up on her hind legs and roar.

He took several steps back, his eyes riveted on the beast. She had to be at least seven feet tall, and her bellow seemed to vibrate his bones.

The bear came down onto her front paws with a thud. She had to weigh hundreds of pounds.

This wasn't good. The mother grizzly surely felt that he was a threat to her cubs. Derick remembered hearing somewhere that he should stand as tall as possible, raise his hands in the air, roar back, and try to appear bigger than the bear. The theory was that the bear would respect him and back down. But in the situation, he thought that was the dumbest theory ever suggested. It would be like a baby squirrel trying to intimidate a wolf.

The bear lumbered forward, teeth bared.

Derick turned and ran, the bear less than twenty feet away. He sprinted through the brush in sheer terror.

Climb a tree. Run downhill. Zigzag.

All of the things he'd heard about surviving a bear attack rushed into his mind. In a split second, he decided to run a zigzag pattern. Derick veered left past a bush and then cut back to the right past a tree. He could hear the bear gaining on him. He thought he could feel its breath against him. He rounded a boulder, and turned—

A giant paw knocked his body to the ground. It felt like being hit by a baseball bat. Derick skidded across the dirt. His rifle fell from his hand to the ground. He had forgotten he had the gun.

Derick shuffled to the rifle and turned to face the bear. He only had a second. He pulled the trigger. The kickback from firing the rifle pounded Derick's ribs, but the bear stopped cold for a moment. Derick had shot the beast in the shoulder.

The bear roared and bore down on Derick again. With new confidence, Derick pulled the trigger again—nothing.

What? One bullet? Derick registered that it was an old-time powder rifle that had to be loaded after each shot at the same time that the bear's heavy arm collided with the side of his body. He felt claws rip through his skin. The bear hit him again on the other side. And on the head. Derick saw blood. It was getting hard to breathe. Maybe the bear had broken a few of his ribs. Maybe worse.

He had to get out of there.

Between blows, Derick managed to scramble across the ground for a few feet before being hit again. He could see blurry images of fur, teeth, and claws. Pain surged through his body over and over. The bear was on top of him. Someone went through this—and lived? Someone was mauled like this and . . . Derick couldn't think. Another blow. The pain crushed out any thought. Teeth dug into him. Derick screamed. The only clear idea he could manage was *Get out*. He felt as if someone had dropped bricks on his shoulders, like his body was being pushed farther into the ground with every strike. He tried to keep his eyes open, but everything blended together.

He knew he would be clawed and hit again, and again. How much longer would he have to take this? How much longer until he was dead? Just because someone in history survived it didn't mean Derick would. What if Grandpa was wrong? What if Derick died in the simulator? Would he die in real life?

The bear's jaws gaped wide and she raised her paw.

• • •

Abby and Carol waited outside the simulator, hoping Derick was doing okay. They thought they heard screams, but listening from the other side of the steel door, it was hard to tell. They had no idea how long he had been in there or how long it would take.

Finally the door opened. Derick stumbled out and collapsed onto the floor.

"Derick!" Abby yelled and ran to his side. Carol was only a step behind.

"What happened?" Abby asked.

Derick breathed heavily, his face soaked in sweat and his eyes bloodshot. Several times he looked like he was going to try to speak, but couldn't.

"It's okay," Abby consoled. "You're here. We're with you." Her imagination went wild with what could have possibly happened inside the simulator.

Derick checked his body with his hands, passing them along his face and torso. "Am I okay? Am I bleeding? Am I still . . ." He didn't finish.

"You're fine," Carol said. "You're okay. You're back with us, and you're fine. You look like you've been through something terrible—I mean, really terrible—but you're fine now."

Derick lay down on the hard floor, still gasping. He closed his eyes hard and then covered his face with one of his arms. His chest rose up and down with heavy breaths.

Abby wanted to ask questions. What happened? But she stopped herself. She'd hear about it when Derick was ready.

Finally, Derick spoke. "I couldn't . . . I couldn't do it. I backed out."

"What happened?" Carol asked. "It must have been awful. Tell me before my imagination takes over, and I get overly freaked out."

Derick spoke again, his eyes still covered. "The simulator is amazing. I could smell the air, feel the breeze, everything. It completely tricks your mind. But I could also feel the pain."

"What pain?" Abby asked.

"I was in the mountains somewhere, and a bear attacked me. It came out of nowhere. I tried to run away, but it was fast. Really fast. And it pounded me. Each time, I thought it broke more bones. It was so powerful. I . . . was . . . completely mauled."

Abby shuddered.

"I couldn't find a way out." Derick told them about surprising the bear and running for his life. "I had an old-time gun and shot it once. The bear got to me before I could reload. It was going to kill me." He looked up at the two girls. "I never felt pain like that. . . . I knew I was going to die. There was no way out."

"There *had* to be a way out," Carol said. "Don't get me wrong, I'm sure it was absolutely, affirmatively, without a doubt horrendous, but your grandpa said that someone in history survived it. That means there had to be the possibility that you could too."

"She's right," Abby said. "Whoever went through this survived it."

"I don't know how," Derick admitted.

Abby had already turned on her rings and began

searching the net. Good thing that years ago technology had been developed to provide reception throughout the entire earth and miles under the ground. She found many bear attacks and she quickly narrowed them down. This attack had to be at a time with single-shot rifles, and the person survived.

"Hugh Glass," Abby said, reading her screen. "I think you experienced what Hugh Glass went through. He lived in the 1800s—sounds like the right period for the gun." She scanned the screen again. "While he was on an expedition, a bear attacked. I guess he must have rushed in quicker than you did, because it sounds like he might have had less time than you to react. And instead of running at first, he tried to shoot the bear, but didn't get a bullet off before the bear had him. It's pretty gross stuff. The bear nearly scalped him, and it even tore off some of his flesh and gave it to her cubs."

Abby grimaced. She couldn't believe Derick had been in the same situation. "Glass eventually stabbed the bear several times with his knife. Then his companions came running in and shot it."

Derick listened in silence. He'd forgotten about the knife. Maybe "friends" would have come in to save him at any moment.

"I guess Glass was so badly injured," Abby said, "that it was just a matter of time before he was going to die from his injuries. So the expedition leader told Jim Bridger, and someone Fitzgerald, to stay behind and wait for him to die, and then bury his body. They waited for days, but somehow Hugh Glass hung on. Eventually they left him."

"They just left him there, while he was still alive?" Carol asked. "That is so rude."

"They did," Abby said. "Glass tried to crawl to the next fort. He pulled leeches from the river to stop his bleeding. It's all pretty crazy survival stuff, but he made it. He traveled for miles but came out okay."

"I wonder how much of that I was going to have to take," Derick said.

"I don't know," Abby said, "but Grandpa wasn't kidding when he said that we would have to really need to get past this step."

The three friends stood in silence for a moment. Abby thought it all through. Derick had failed, and he never failed at anything. If he couldn't do it . . . Abby didn't want to finish the thought. Her grandfather and dad and mom were still missing. She and Derick needed to find out how to help. "I . . . guess it's my turn." Abby opened her hand. "Let me have the key."

Derick looked up at his sister. "You're not going in there. *I'm* not going back in there. No one is."

"We have to," Abby said. "Mom and Dad—"

"*No!*" Derick shouted. "You don't understand." Abby saw terror in his eyes. "You . . . you . . . don't want to go in there. And I won't let you."

"I have to," Abby argued. "We have to help Grandpa and our parents. Even if it is terrifying, I have to try."

"Don't go," Carol said. "At least, not tonight. No way you'll succeed right now. We've been awake for nearly two days. No way will any of us make it past the simulator in the shape we're in. We need to sleep, eat a good breakfast and then maybe, if you're still determined, you can give it a try. Besides, it's almost curfew."

"But my mom and dad—" Abby started.

"She's right," Derick interrupted.

"After curfew," Carol added, "someone will come looking for us, and we can't be discovered down here. And we can't go missing, either."

Abby tried three more times to convince them to let her try, but finally she surrendered, and all three of them climbed up the ladder.

• • •

"Aren't you going to sleep?" Abby's mother asked.

"Not now," Abby's father responded. His breath came out in small clouds as he spoke, steaming in the freezing air. He stared over the railing at the stern of the ship, the same view he had looked at all day. "I'm sorry you're in this danger with me. I guess you didn't know what a hazardous family you married into."

She hugged him and shared more of a blanket, which one of the staff members had offered them. "I'd do it again," she said. "But I never thought it would end this way."

"It hasn't ended yet," he said.

"I know. We have to hold on to hope as long as possible, but how much longer do we have?"

"Only until tomorrow night."

INFORMANT

Derick dreamed that he found his grandpa and parents on the top of a large mountain. He scaled it as best he could, but they seemed forever away. After hours and hours, just when they were within reach, he couldn't go any farther. He couldn't take the final steps. Then a bear appeared, and Derick turned and slid back down the mountain. He looked back, and behind the bear, he saw his father's disappointed face. His grandpa wouldn't make eye contact. His mother cried. Derick awoke in a night sweat.

Sunlight came in through the curtains. It was morning. Derick glanced at the screen on the side of his wall—6:45. It felt like he'd only napped. His muscles were sore, and his head pounded.

Why had he given up with the bear? Why couldn't he have toughed it out? Yet the thought of going back in the simulator terrified him. He didn't want to feel those things again. He couldn't forget the pain, the helplessness. He could try the same situation over and over and still fail. He rolled over in bed, and then rolled over again, unable to get comfortable.

He eventually punched his pillow, then buried his face in it. His grandfather and his parents were counting on him. His mind soaked in regret.

After several minutes, Derick logged onto his rings and synced up to the Cragbridge site. He entered his information and a sick code, which would go to the administration and all of his teachers. No one would expect him today. He fell back into bed and closed his eyes. He wanted to keep them closed for a very long time.

• • •

Abby and Carol sat facing each other in the cafeteria.

"I wonder if your brother's okay," Carol said. "I haven't seen him all day." She took a bite of lasagna, followed by a bite of breadstick from her other hand.

"Me, neither," Abby said, toying with her enchilada. She twisted the cheese into circles but didn't lift the food from her plate. "I tried to call him a few times, but the computer says he's sick in bed."

"I don't believe that," Carol said. "I think he's 'sick' because of yesterday. If I had to face a bear, I'd never want to get out of bed again—and he was nearly killed by one. Well, sort of. *Virtually* almost killed by one."

"I think it might be the failure bothering him," Abby said.

"What?" Carol asked. "I think it's the bear."

"That too, but Derick has succeeded in everything he's ever tried," Abby said. "He's had minor setbacks, but this was big. This whole thing must be really important if Grandpa is willing to put us through that."

"Are you ready to go through it?" Carol asked.

Abby paused, allowing herself a moment to imagine what horrendous challenge lay ahead of her. "Yeah. I've got to do it."

Abby was as ready as she'd ever be. She wanted to go down to the simulator before school, but Carol persuaded her that there wasn't time. They had no idea how long it would take, and if they didn't show up to class, the school would track them—and the last thing they needed was to have Cragbridge Administration discovering the passage-way under the school.

Abby wanted to go to the simulator instead of eating lunch, but Carol brought up the same arguments. They finally decided to go after school. They'd wait until after class when the halls were nearly vacant.

"And what if you don't do so hot?" Carol asked. "I mean like, fail miserably?"

"Then I'll try again," Abby said.

"And if you fail again?" Carol asked.

"Thanks for being so optimistic," Abby said.

"Sorry. I mean, it was pretty intense down there last night, and Derick . . . I thought he'd be able to do it, and he couldn't. I don't know that this is going to be anything close to easy. I mean a bear mauling—really? I wonder if any of us could succeed."

"Grandpa liked to say, 'You never fail until you quit trying.'"

Carol smiled. "That's cheesy, but I guess it's true. But do you think Derick will be okay? Do you think I need to send him a special message? Like a video on the net confessing my love? Maybe it would cheer him up. And if it went viral, I'd split all publicity revenue with him."

"Something tells me we'd better just let him—" Abby didn't finish. She felt a shadow cross over her. Someone stood behind her.

"Hey, Rafa," Carol said.

Abby turned to look at the Brazilian, his hair pulled back into a ponytail as always.

"*Com Licença,*" he said. "Sorry to interrupt, *meninas,* but I really need to talk to you."

"About what?" Carol said. "About you talking to Ms. Entrese in the hall after you pretended that she was watching the avatar go up the Watchman? Yeah. Derick told me about it. We're that close. And I think you're a double agent."

Rafa looked surprised at first. Then he rubbed his eyes with his hands and answered. "I was covering up for you."

"I'm not sure we can trust you," Abby admitted.

"I can understand that," Rafa said. "The more I know about your situation, the more I see its seriousness, but I have to tell you something. Then you can choose whether or not you believe me."

Abby could feel Carol's eyes on her, waiting to see what she'd say. "Go ahead."

Rafa motioned toward a chair. "Do you mind if I sit down? I think it would look less conspicuous that way."

Abby shook her head.

"I have learned something," Rafa began. "Someone I cannot reveal has given me information. I'm not certain you can trust it, but I need to tell you just the same."

"Okay," Abby said.

"Someone knows that you have been searching for the clues from your grandfather."

"We know that," Abby said. "Remember, Ms. Entrese was watching us."

"Let me restate that," Rafa said. "I believe that more than one person, or maybe even more than one group of people, knows that you have been searching for clues."

Carol swallowed a bite of lunch. "So what do you mean that more than one person knows?"

"I'm not completely sure," Rafa admitted. "But one person believes they know who is behind the kidnapping."

"Who?" Abby leaned forward.

"His name is Charles Muns," Rafa said.

"And where, Mr. Mysterious Ponytail Man, are you getting all of this supposedly secret information we're supposed to believe?" Carol asked.

"The person who told me also said that if I revealed them, their life could be on the line," Rafa said solemnly.

"Really?" Abby said, measuring Rafa's response. "And why did they tell you but not me or Derick?"

"I can't tell you that; it would implicate them," Rafa said. "I've done some research on Muns but can't tell if my source is correct. Muns is a self-serving businessman. He owns a movie studio, several digicommunications corporations, and a lot of real estate, among many other things. He has several hobbies, but the one of interest to you is that he hires scientists to do research for him."

"Did he hire my grandpa?" Abby asked.

"I couldn't find a record of it, but they do know each other."

Abby exhaled slowly. "Alright, but I don't know what to do with that information. Tell the police? Maybe it couldn't hurt, but nothing about this seems like something the police can solve."

"It's nice to have a name," Carol agreed. "But it sounds like Muns is everywhere and has too many resources. He could have hired a dojo of ninjas to kidnap your parents, put them on a private plane, and send them to the other side of the world—or hide them on the moon. He could be hiding them around the corner. That doesn't really matter, because it's not enough for a warrant. All he is now is a 'person of interest'—that's what they call them on the news."

"The person who has contacted me is sure that it is Muns," Rafa said. "But what to do from here, I don't know."

Abby closed her eyes for a moment. "I need Derick," she said. "He's the genius in our family. He'll know what to do."

"I already tried to tell him," Rafa said. "But he wouldn't answer a sync or his door. The computer says he's sick."

Abby and Carol shared a knowing look.

"But he's got to help," Abby said, turning on her rings. She tried to sync up to Derick. He didn't answer. She tried again. Again, he didn't answer. She stood up from her chair and left the cafeteria. With Rafa and Carol behind her, Abby walked out of Cragbridge Hall, across the lawn of bush sculptures, to the boy's dorm.

"Let me try to talk to him by myself," Abby said. "You guys come over in a few minutes if it's not working." Carol and Rafa agreed. After getting permission to visit her brother for twenty minutes, she walked to his door and knocked on it.

"Go away."

"Derick," Abby said. "I can't figure this out without you." She paused, glancing around to make sure no one else was in the hall to overhear. "Rafa says that someone he can't name informed him that a man named Charles Muns is behind the kidnapping. He's a powerful man. If Rafa's source is right . . . well . . . even if they're wrong, I don't know what to do. I need your help."

"I . . . can't. I messed it all up."

"No, you didn't," Abby responded. "You tried once and failed. All that means is that *one* time it didn't work out— just one time."

"Yeah, I failed when it was the most important—more important than anything else I've done so far."

"You've got to try to help us, Derick," Abby pleaded. "You've got to try—"

"I can't," he said louder. "I can't."

"Ple—"

"*I can't!*"

There was a long moment of silence. Abby's emotions rose within her. She couldn't stand it. She needed her brother—she desperately needed him. He couldn't give up.

"Do you have any idea . . ." Abby choked on the last word. "Do you have any idea how often *I* fail? Do you know how many times I try something and it doesn't work, or I'm left in the crowd? Once again, I'm mediocre Abby. Every time report cards come out, I want to bury myself in a hole. I try and I try, but I still never come close to what you can do. Whenever we come to a place like this, it takes you two seconds to make new friends, but I . . ." Tears were welling up in Abby's eyes. "I try to be nice, I try to talk to people, and I don't know if I get too nervous, or if I'm trying too hard, but it just doesn't work. Or when you invent something, or when one of your theories blows some teacher's mind, and someone finds out about it, I'm happy for you, I really am, but it's also just one more reminder that even though I was only born two minutes after you, I'm years behind. And what's worse, it feels like I'll never, ever catch up. Do you know what that feels like? Do you know how many times I've wanted to quit? Do you have any idea how many times I've wanted to use the excuse that I'm just not as good as you to not try anymore?" Abby paused, surprised at how intensely she had come after her brother.

No response.

Abby looked back and saw both Carol and Rafa. How long had they been there? Long enough. Rafa looked away and Carol's eyes were wide.

"Look," Abby said to the door. "I need you. I can keep trying, and I won't quit, but I need you on this one. I need . . ." She couldn't finish. "Please, just open the door."

Abby waited for several minutes.

"At least give me the key," she said. "I have to try."

The door never opened, but the key slid out from beneath it.

SHOCK

Abby sat through her last classes, fingering the key in her pocket. She couldn't concentrate at all. She could think only about facing the simulator and wondering what to do with the information Rafa had given her about Charles Muns. Worse, she had to wait more than two hours for the halls to clear out enough that she could trigger the brick wall without being seen.

Now Abby stood at the dead-end hallway. It was time.

"Are you ready?" Carol asked. She had come from behind and startled Abby.

"Yes," she said, after regaining her composure. "At least as ready as I'm going to get."

"Wait!" a voice yelled from down the hall. Abby turned to see Rafa coming toward them. "You have to come with me."

"No," Abby said, "I have to do this."

"Not yet," Rafa said. "We have something to show you."

"'We'?" Abby asked.

"Yes," Rafa said with a smile. "We—Derick and I."

Abby felt a wave of relief. Derick had helped. She followed Rafa down to the Bridge booths with Carol not far behind. Rafa pointed to a booth where a group could use the Bridge. Abby stepped inside, and there was Derick, still in his clothes from the day before and his hair wildly messed up. Abby threw her arms around him.

"Hey, sis," he said.

"Thanks for helping," Abby said. "I was so worried. You—"

"Don't worry about it," he said. "I shouldn't have . . . and I'm sorry I never stopped to realize how hard things must be for you too—"

"Oh, never mind about that," Abby said, not wanting to cry again. "Just . . . thanks."

"Sure," Derick said. "But I don't know if you want to hear this. It's bad." He bit his bottom lip and rubbed the stress from the back of his neck. "It's worse than you've ever imagined."

Abby and Carol looked at each other, then back at Derick.

"After you left, and I decided to quit sulking and actually do something, I looked up Muns. I did all the research I could before school got out. I found something I think might help us—a long list of complaints against Muns. He has fired his fair share of people, and he always does it with a certain style. Once, one of his communications men was caught secretly filming decision meetings and posting them in chat rooms for people who paid to see them. So Muns secretly filmed himself firing that same man and streamed the video over the same channel. Another time, one of his financial advisors got a small website business for the company out in South Africa. The deal was a front to embezzle money. Muns had his advisor relocated to South Africa, and then he sold the company. He prosecuted the man internationally to keep the guy in South Africa for seven years. It wasted a ton of money. Sounds like Muns doesn't cut corners on revenge."

"So what's the point?" Carol asked. "Other than Muns really wanting to get even when he fires people. What's he going to do with your grandpa? Hire him to fire him? That seems stupid."

"No," Derick said. "Worse. The point is that Muns likes to do things in his own style, and we should study it. If he did something to Grandpa and our parents, then—"

"Then it might fit with something—a meeting or a relationship—they had in the past," Abby finished.

"Right. I figured out why his name was so familiar to me," Derick said. "I couldn't believe I didn't remember before."

"It didn't sound familiar to me," Abby said.

"Rafa, will you show them?" Derick said. Then to Abby and Carol, he added, "I found this out by watching Grandpa's journal. I'm not sure you can find it anywhere else."

Rafa found the date of the debate between Oscar Cragbridge and Charles Muns.

Seeing her grandfather's face again was hard for Abby.

"One time, Grandpa and Charles Muns debated on the ethics of time travel," Derick said.

"Really?" Carol asked. "Time travel? That seems a bit out there. They've made some pretty good movies over the years, but it's all fiction. Except for the one with Joey Noel—I wish that one were real. I'd let myself get trapped any time with him. But, I mean, your grandpa is the best inventor ever—why talk about something so crazy?"

"At the time," Derick said, "Both he and Muns believed that time travel was possible, but Grandpa was a bit wary of it. Just watch. This is the part I couldn't stop thinking about."

All four students watched as the smooth billionaire and the inventor exchanged arguments. Clearly, they saw the issue completely differently.

"Let me give you another example," Muns said, moving from behind his podium. "What about the *Titanic*? What if you had the power to warn the captain and prevent more than fifteen hundred people from dying in the icy waters of the Atlantic? What would you do?"

Cragbridge bowed his head. "Even if I could prevent the tragedy," he said slowly, "I would not change it. I would sit in this room and cry all over again for the victims." He raised his head. "We cannot change the past. We can learn from it and then look ahead. We make our own futures, building on the foundations of our past."

"No!" Muns said. "If my team discovers the secrets to time travel—and we will—we will right all wrongs. We will correct the mistakes of history." He looked at Cragbridge for a reply.

Cragbridge stood silently for a moment. Then he slowly licked his lips and spoke. "Then heaven help us that you never discover time travel."

Rafa paused the image.

"Do you think *this* is the great secret?" Abby asked, twisting her hair into a temporary ponytail. "Did Grandpa discover time travel?"

Derick looked somber. "This is all we had to go on. I asked myself, if Grandpa did discover time travel, and Muns wanted the secret to it, or if Muns discovered the secret and was afraid that Grandpa would get in the way, what would he do?"

"It might have something to do with the *Titanic*," Abby said. "Maybe he'd trap them in a museum or a submarine down in the depths of the ocean, where the ship sank."

"Remember," Derick said. "This may involve time travel."

"Right," Carol said incredulously. "Wow."

Derick turned to Rafa and nodded. Rafa moved his fingers back and forth.

A massive ship appeared, gliding over the dark ocean. The lamps on deck and in the hundreds of rooms lit up a portion of the night. It was larger than Abby's apartment building, longer than Cragbridge Hall. It was more than a ship. It seemed like a town on the ocean.

"Get ready for the shock," Derick warned.

Rafa moved the point of view onto the massive deck. Abby moved nearer, looking at the passengers.

"This is the back of the boat, the part farthest from the side that hits the iceberg," Derick said.

Couples talked at tables, while other people lined the railings staring off into the darkness, listening to the ocean below. Abby looked from face to face while Rafa moved them through the crowd.

Abby gasped, and she started to tremble.

"What?" Carol asked. "What's wrong? Sure, these people are heading for tragedy, but what?"

Abby pointed to a man and woman leaning against the railing. "That's my mom and dad."

The whole moment was entirely too surreal. She gazed over the span of a hundred and fifty years into history and saw her own mother and father.

"But how did they get there?" Abby asked. "And why are they wearing the same kind of clothes as everybody else?"

Carol chimed in. "Yeah, maybe you're mistaken. Maybe they just look like—"

"It's them," Derick said flatly. "Rewind the timeframe, Rafa."

Rafa nodded and rewound the image. For nearly two days, the twins' parents had stood on the stern of the boat, taking only short breaks to eat and sleep. It was as though they *wanted* to be found—hoped to be found. Two bundles of clothes flew up from the ocean below into their father's hand—they were watching this backward after all. Their parents walked backward into a cabin and changed clothes. They appeared a moment later in their modern clothes. Abby and Carol watched as the twins' dad tried various door handles.

Abby had to think back through the Bridge image. Her dad had found a cabin with clothes of the time in it. They snuck in and changed, and then they threw their modern clothes over the edge.

Abby watched her parents as they walked backward down to one of the boiler rooms. Rafa zoomed in; there were fewer people down there. Her parents wandered in circles, sat and held their heads in their hands, paced back and forth and hugged. Then there was a low thud, and a circle of space seemed to deform. It was as if a portion of the air bulged and Derick's parents were sucked into the bubble.

"What was that?" Abby asked.

"I think it's how they got there," Derick said. "Show it from the beginning."

Rafa stopped the footage and played it forward. Again the spot bulged, and Derick's parents flew in, like someone had thrown them into a room.

"Look," Carol said, pointing to the screen on the Bridge. "They disappeared three days ago, in the middle of the night. It would have been our first night at Cragbridge."

"It all fits," Abby said. "The next day is when we figured out that they were missing."

"Are they . . ." Carol cleared her throat. "Are they going to be on it when it sinks?"

"Fast-forward the image," Derick said.

As the people moved, talked, and ate in fast motion, Abby's eyes grew wide. She kept track of her parents. She followed them to the cabin and then followed them back up to the end of the ship. Part of her didn't want to watch anymore. Was she about to witness her own parents' deaths on a ship that sank decades ago?

Abby's and Derick's parents suddenly vanished from the scene.

"What happened?" Abby asked.

"Rewind it," Derick commanded.

Rafa rewound again. One second their parents were on the ship, and the next, they weren't. He repeated the process a few more times, and each time Abby and Derick's parents stayed in the picture a few seconds before vanishing.

"That must be where they are in time," Abby said.

"Yeah," Derick agreed. They're moving along in time there, while we move forward here. Which means they haven't sunk yet, but they *will* be on the *Titanic* when it sinks if we can't find out how to get them out."

"When does it sink?" Abby asked.

"For everyone else, 1912. For Mom and Dad, tonight," Derick said.

Abby felt a chill in her spine at the words. Her parents would die tonight unless she found a way to stop one of the greatest tragedies from happening over a century ago.

"The ship runs into the iceberg at 11:40 tonight,"

Derick said. "It's sunk by 2:20 in the morning." He let them ponder that for a moment. "It's nearly six o'clock now, but where my parents are in time it is ten o'clock. We have a little over four hours to get them out before the ship is under water and it's too late."

Silence. Abby didn't know what to say. Not only had her parents been kidnapped, but they were about to die, and she didn't know how to stop it.

"But why would Muns do this?" Carol asked.

"We don't know," Derick said. "We've been putting this together as we went. I can think of two options. Either Muns discovered time travel on his own and wants anyone who knows anything about it out of the way—which includes Grandpa, or he hasn't mastered time travel yet, and he's threatening our parents so Grandpa will give him the technology."

"Grandpa!" Abby burst out. "Is Grandpa on the *Titanic* too?"

"I don't think so," Derick said. "At least, we couldn't find him. But I have a theory about where he is."

"Where?" Abby asked.

"Remember when Muns asked Grandpa what he would do if he had the power to warn the passengers on the *Titanic*?"

"He said he would watch it and cry."

"Right," Derick said. "But more specifically, he'd sit in *that room* and cry. If Muns is the terrible man I think he is, he is holding Grandpa there—in that very room they debated in, and making him watch his own son and daughter-in-law die, unless he gives Muns more information about time travel."

"But where is the room?" Carol asked.

"A few hours away by car. It's at the university where my grandpa taught. I found out that Muns donated a lot of money to renovate it two months ago. Right now, it's closed to the public. I think that fits. I think Muns wants the room available just to hold Grandpa."

Abby's mind spun. "So how are we going to save them?"

Derick shrugged. "I have no idea. All I know is that we have to."

"If this isn't presuming too much," Rafa said, "I'd propose that Abby and Carol continue to follow your grandfather's clues. That may be the only hope of saving your parents. Derick and I will go after your grandfather."

"But how could you get off campus?" Carol asked. "Let alone travel all the way there in time?"

Derick smiled. "Maybe we can use the avatars again. We could fly there. Can we control them from here and go that far."

"The connection is strong enough that we could take the avatars halfway around the world, maybe all the way," Rafa said. "But there are other reasons we can't. There is no way you could learn to fly that fast, and besides, I believe that if Muns had help to kidnap your grandfather, then he won't be left alone. There will probably be guards. Muns probably has a lot of people working for him, watching over him. I don't think we'll be able to do much good with bird avatars."

"I guess you're right," Derick said.

"I know what we can try," Rafa said. "But you're going to have to trust me."

"Okay," Derick agreed.

"Meet me at the avatar lab in ten minutes."

COLTER

Derick waited outside the avatar lab for Rafa, wondering what the TA could possibly be thinking of. Rafa came down the hall with someone—Ms. Entrese.

Derick wanted to run.

"Calm down," Rafa said. "It isn't what you think. Let's step into the lab, and I'll explain."

Derick was still wary, but he followed Rafa and Ms. Entrese inside.

"I'm the one who told Rafa about Charles Muns," Ms. Entrese said after they were behind locked doors. Derick gaped. *She* was Rafa's source?

"I . . ." Ms. Entrese bowed her head, then inhaled and raised it again. "I used to work for Muns."

"I thought he hired scientists," Derick said.

"He does. English was one of my degrees, but I have a

PhD in physics," Ms. Entrese explained. "Muns was on a mission to discover the secret to time travel. It was all very exciting. I loved the science; we all did."

Derick could see the excitement in her expression.

"We tried everything," she said. "Sometimes we felt we were near a breakthrough, but each time, we came up short. Then one of his scientists discovered something. It was all kept very hush-hush, but I stumbled onto some information that led me to believe that because of the discovery he had dangerous intentions toward your grandfather." The excitement was gone, her tone serious.

Derick wanted to ask if they had discovered that Grandpa invented time travel, but he didn't know how much Ms. Entrese knew, and he wasn't going to tell her anything he didn't have to. Ms. Entrese continued, "Muns wanted something from your grandfather. He was soon taking the most elite of our scientists. Several secret projects started. But I saw fear in one of the scientists I knew. Muns is a shrewd man, and he won't stop until he gets what he wants. He would break people and completely ruin their careers if they got in his way."

Derick's heart beat faster. He thought about the burst that sent his parents back in time onto the *Titanic*. Was that one of the secret projects?

"When I sensed that things were getting dicey," Ms. Entrese continued, "I made up an excuse to quit. I was a lower member of the team, not essential. He let me go without question, but I believe I am still being watched, especially since I ended up teaching here."

"Have you told my grandfather any of this?" Derick asked.

"Yes," she said. "But I had no evidence, just suspicions. When Mr. Cragbridge hired me, he advised me to be cautious. In fact, it was his idea that I teach English so it would look like I was no longer interested in science. And he suggested that I put on an act—that I be distant and even critical of him and those most supportive of him."

"That's why you were mean to my sister," Derick suggested.

"Yes. My actions and attitude would keep anyone from thinking that I consorted with those who may oppose Muns. And yes, I believe Muns has people who report to him, even here."

That was nothing new. Derick knew someone had been trying to stop them—someone working for Muns—but he had thought it was Ms. Entrese. "But when your sister was in the Chair in my class, I saw her picture a locket. I had seen one before; I noticed it on someone here at the school that I'm sure your grandfather trusts. I knew that they must be important somehow, part of some sort of contingency plan. But I thought Abby had only mistakenly seen one while with your grandfather.

"I became extra vigilant, walking the grounds, looking for anything suspicious. I don't want Muns to succeed in whatever he is planning. I started working for him to discover something amazing, not to hurt people or steal secrets."

Was she telling the truth? All her information seemed to fit. And she had tipped them off to Muns.

"Then I saw the avatar climb into Watchman Tower," Ms. Entrese continued. "Knowing Rafa was the teacher's assistant, I confronted him." She looked over at Rafa. "He was very loyal to you. In fact, he covered up quite well. But I hounded him. Eventually, I told him that if this had anything to do with the lockets that whoever was behind it needed to know about Muns. I told him of my suspicions that Muns was behind the kidnappings, and I asked him to warn whoever he needed to that Muns would oppose whatever they were planning. I had already warned the other professor I had seen, and sent an anonymous tip to the police. But I expected Rafa would be warning another teacher, not kids."

No one ever expected kids. But Grandpa was different. Derick thought back to how Grandpa had trusted him with a locket. He felt stronger, almost bigger somehow, thinking of the amount of trust his grandfather had in him. But he was still confused. He looked at Rafa. "So, why is she here?"

"We need a way off campus, and teachers can come and go as they please," Rafa said.

"Are you willing to help us?" Derick asked.

Ms. Entrese covered her eyes with her palms then rubbed her temples. "Doing so will show my hand to any of Muns's men watching me. It will be clear that I've sided against him—very dangerous. But if he has threatened the lives of Oscar Cragbridge's son and daughter-in-law, and is holding him captive, I don't see how I can turn a blind eye and live with myself."

"You can get us off campus, but how are we going to

take care of any men guarding my grandpa?" Derick asked. "And that's assuming we find the right place."

For one of the first times, Derick saw Rafa smile.

• • •

Abby stepped into the simulator determined and terrified. She had to do this, and she had to do it soon. She just hoped it wouldn't be a bear. She wanted to close her eyes, but was too scared.

In an instant, she was sitting in a canoe, floating down a river. Grassy mounds surrounded the water, with wildflowers scattering color through the view. Rocky mountains weren't far away, and trees poked out of the ground in groups.

She floated for a while, staring at the beautiful countryside. How could such a place be the environment for a trying situation? Was this what Derick had seen before the bear attacked him? Probably not. Unless a bear caught her by surprise, she would probably be able to get away.

Abby heard someone close by clear their throat. She whirled around to see someone else in the canoe with her! She almost sprang into the water before she realized that the man was gazing at the surroundings too. He must be her traveling companion.

"Falling asleep up there, Colter?" he asked.

Colter? Who was he talking to? It took a second for Abby to realize that in the simulator, she must be standing in as someone named Colter.

"Yeah," she said, sure he'd be surprised by her girl voice.

But the man didn't seem to even notice. Maybe that was part of the simulator. Abby tried to think of something a mountain man would say. "Fatigue got the best of me. Won't happen again."

The man laughed. "You act like we haven't been traveling together since Lewis and Clark." He cleared his throat. "Now let's check for more beaver."

Abby looked at the floor of the canoe, where several dead beavers lay. Apparently, she and her friend were checking their traps.

A noise echoed along the river. It sounded like hundreds of animals trampling through the wild. This had to be it—her terrifying moment. Abby looked in every direction, but she couldn't see anything other than the tall banks beside the water.

"Let's get out of here," she said, knowing that something terrible was coming, or she wouldn't be there.

"Why? Because of a few animals? If I didn't know better, I'd think you were a coward," the man said.

"I'm not a coward, but sometimes it's wise to get away." Abby looked around carefully, her heart beating faster. She craned her neck, trying to survey the land. She noticed every tree that swayed, every shrub that shook. In only moments, she saw an arrow pointed at her through the trees— and a Native American behind it.

Abby pointed at the Native American as if to warn her companion, but she didn't need to. She saw another native and another. They came out of hiding and lined the banks, all at the ready to attack.

Her companion cursed and then mumbled, "Blackfeet. Been wanting to get them back since our injuries at Fort Raymond. But it looks like today is not my day."

The tall banks gradually leveled out to a landing where grassy mounds and rocks approached the river. Brave after brave arrived at the shoreline—hundreds of them, all threatening. Abby felt lightheaded and started to breathe faster. She forced herself to take a few deep breaths to calm down. This wasn't real. She could leave at any time. But she had to keep going to find her parents and Grandpa.

Several Native Americans made large, arching gestures with their hands, urging Abby and the man to come ashore. Abby didn't know what else to do, so she paddled toward the army of Blackfeet.

The first brave to meet Abby pointed his arrow in her face and gestured for her to step out of the boat. She obeyed, her legs trembling, and stumbled onto the grass.

The braves also motioned for the man behind Abby in the canoe to come ashore. He didn't budge. They motioned several more times, but the man held his gun and pushed the canoe back into the water. Abby heard the whiz of an arrow; it lodged in the man's shoulder.

"Colter, I'm wounded," he cried.

"Come back in," Abby said, gesturing for her friend to row back to shore. He refused and instead aimed his rifle and fired back. A brave fell to the ground.

Abby turned to look at the dead brave as she heard countless swooshes cut through the air. She didn't turn back to the water to look, but heard a thunk. She knew the man on the boat had been riddled with arrows and had fallen hard against the wood canoe. Her heart felt heavy and seemed to pull at her throat. Her stomach churned inside her. The man had to be dead. She looked back. Colter's friend lay lifeless in the canoe.

Abby always knew things like this had happened, but she'd never realized how hard it would be. It was dangerous and heart-wrenching. She wondered why the man wouldn't come ashore. He said that he had fought the Blackfeet before. Had he known that something worse than arrows was waiting?

Abby felt arms grab her thick coat. They pulled her farther inland and threw her to the ground. The hands pulled her pouch and canteen from her shoulder and waist. They yanked the coat off her shoulders. She felt her hardened leather boots pulled from her feet. She rolled over only to see more arrows loaded in taut bows.

Abby sat on the ground feeling terrified and exposed. She watched as several braves counseled together. They had to be discussing what to do with her. Though she couldn't understand their words, she was able to piece together that some of them wanted to set her up as a target and let the braves see who was the most accurate. She imagined what it might be like for hundreds of arrows to hit her all at once. But the man who looked to be the chief walked over and lifted Abby up off the ground.

He spoke loudly and with authority. He seemed to be speaking something close to English, asking her a question, but Abby struggled to comprehend it. The only words she understood were *run* and *fast*. She shook her head no. She'd run track for several years, but she wouldn't consider herself that fast, especially running from a group of warriors.

The chief cocked his head to one side, and Abby thought she saw the hint of a smile. The chief turned to the party and made some kind of announcement. Abby heard the word *run* again. The braves took off their pouches and canteens. They set their bows and arrows on the ground and picked up spears. The chief held up his hand for them to stay where they were.

He led Abby forward. The men who had been guarding her joined the others. The chief walked with Abby over the hard soil for another three or four hundred yards. She was glad her feet felt calloused, at least somewhat prepared for the terrain.

Finally, the chief stopped. He looked Abby in the eyes and spoke slowly. Somehow, Abby could understand nearly every word.

"Run. Save yourself if you can."

The chief pounded his staff on the ground and gave out a shrill holler, and Abby heard a cacophonous roar— the screams of hundreds of braves. The war whoop echoed through the area, but Abby didn't dare turn around. She took off. She had no idea where she was going, other than *away* from the hundreds of braves chasing her. She could hear the muffled thunder of their feet.

Abby pushed over the hard ground, trying to find her stride. She hit something prickly with one foot. It felt like several wasps had stung her foot at once, but she didn't stop. She couldn't stop; she ran for her life.

When Abby raced during school, she used to imagine that she was running in the Olympics, or that some little girl was secretly watching and wanted to be like her. If her imagination was vivid enough, she could find energy she didn't know she had. She had no need to imagine anything now.

If she got out of this, from here on, she would just have to picture this moment to spark that extra length and speed out of her legs.

She knew the braves were coming up on her, and she knew what they would do if they caught her. But if she died in the simulator, would it mean she'd forfeited her opportunity to finish her grandfather's challenge? It had to. She'd let down her parents and her grandfather. She couldn't do that. Abby pushed forward, wanting to scream, but not daring to spend the energy. She willed her legs to push harder off the ground, to propel her forward a little more, a little faster.

Abby watched the brush go by, surprised at how fast she was able to go. She dared hope that her effort would be enough. Whoever the Colter guy was, he'd survived this. It was possible; she just had to figure out how to repeat it.

After nearly half a mile across a plain, she hazarded a glance over her shoulder. She felt both relief and panic at the same time. The hundreds of braves running behind her had scattered, many falling behind. She'd outrun the majority. Maybe she could survive.

But one brave, moving fast and clutching a spear, was

no more than a hundred yards behind her. He was gaining on her.

Abby concentrated, pushing herself harder. Her legs screamed as she went forward. All at once, she tasted something salty, something wet. There it was again. She lifted her hand to her mouth and pulled it away—blood. She'd pushed herself too hard, and her body was letting her know it. Abby didn't want to look back—the brave would be closer. She was already at her peak and didn't know how long she could keep it up. She spat blood to the side as she strode on.

Colter *had* survived. Whatever he did had worked. What did he do? If only she knew his history. But maybe she could guess. He must have run, and he must have pushed himself so hard that he would have started bleeding too. It was his pain she was feeling, right? He was a big mountain-man type. He was strong and bold. Maybe he could last longer than she could. Abby pushed forward. Blood dripped onto her shirt.

She ran and ran. She must have been nearly a mile away from the river, and had she been a little more relaxed, she would have realized that it was her best sprinting time ever. Of course, had she been a little more relaxed, it wouldn't have been her best time.

Then Abby heard the last sound she wanted to hear: footsteps. The brave was near. She expected to feel his spear drive into her back at any moment. She glanced over her shoulder. The brave was less than twenty yards away, spear raised.

THE FINISH LINE

Rafa and Derick pushed a large box on a dolly toward the elevator chute. Derick could already feel the strain on his muscles, though they had only pushed the box down one hall and into the next.

"What are you moving, boys?" a voice called out.

Derick turned around to see a group of girls following them down the hall.

"Nothing really," Derick said.

"Really?" another girl asked. "Why are you struggling so hard to push 'nothing'?"

"Yeah," another agreed. "You'd think 'nothing' would be really light. Plus, why don't you use a robotic dolly? Then you wouldn't have to work at all."

"We wanted the exercise." Derick was secretly glad for the work. He had a good excuse for his heart to be racing.

Otherwise, his hammering heartbeat might have given him away. If anyone discovered what he was smuggling in the box, it was all over.

"Can we see this 'nothing'?" a brunette asked.

"No," Derick said.

"Sorry, *meninas*," Rafa said. "We're kind of in a hurry."

"You might be able to refuse them, but not me," a deeper voice said. It was a woman Derick hadn't seen before, but by her professional pantsuit and hairstyle from 2052, he knew she was either a teacher or an administrator. "It is rather odd that two boys are pushing a box this size through Cragbridge Hall at this time of night."

Derick and Rafa both stopped cold. Derick spoke up. "We're just moving some things for Ms. Entrese. You know, trying to give back for our great educational opportunities here."

The teacher opened the top of the box and looked inside. She then looked back at the boys, and into the box again. "Why are you moving a huge box of hardbound books?"

"Ms. Entrese wants to take them home," Rafa explained. "She's checking out a van now, and we're supposed to meet her behind the building."

"I think she wants to see if she can auction them off online—get some extra cash or something," Derick said. He felt grateful that Ms. Entrese shared his grandpa's love for actual books and had them around for an occasion like this.

The administrator looked at the boys one more time. "Are you two serving detention?"

Rafa and Derick looked at one another. Derick tried to look guilty, which wasn't hard—he *felt* guilty.

The girls laughed.

"Hurry along, then," the teacher said. "I'll open the back door for you."

He was sure she wanted to check out their story with Ms. Entrese. Derick and Rafa pushed the box farther down the hall. The girls followed, probably waiting to see the boys get busted.

As they approached the back door, the administrator raised her hand to the scanner, and it opened.

"Oh, Vice Principal Fowers," Ms. Entrese said, looking the administrator in the face. "I see you've found my two detention slaves." Derick was impressed; she didn't look suspicious at all.

"I see you're maintaining discipline as well as always," Fowers said. "But you may want to reconsider selling these books. Perhaps one of those museum/libraries would want them."

Ms. Entrese flicked her finger, and the back door of the van opened. "I haven't decided what to do with them yet," she said. "But I've got to get them out of my office. It's getting too cluttered in there."

Derick and Rafa pushed the dolly down a ramp. Both grunted as they lifted the box into the van.

"Now go get the second box," Ms. Entrese said. "And I purposely made it several times heavier than the first."

Fowers smiled. "Carry on, Minerva."

Derick walked by Rafa as he pulled the dolly back up

the hall. The girls giggled as they passed. One of them said, "Enjoy detention, boys."

Neither Derick nor Rafa minded at all.

• • •

The brave would launch his spear soon—and guessing how much practice Native Americans had hunting, he probably wouldn't miss unless Abby did something drastic.

Another stream of blood hit her chin and dripped down her neck. She must look terrible. But it gave her an idea.

It was insane, but it was all she could come up with. Abby stopped running and turned around. She wanted to be able to see the spear coming, or at the very least, fight the brave one on one. Maybe she'd have Colter's strength.

The brave's eyes went big. He must not have expected his prey to stop so abruptly—and he probably didn't expect her to be splattered with blood, either. She might even be intimidating. Abby threw her arm forward as if she, too, had a spear to throw. He veered to one side to dodge what he thought was an attack. But as he shifted his weight to one side, the mix of momentum, exhaustion, and surprise threw him off balance. His spear drove into the ground as the brave fell, and it snapped in two against his body.

Abby couldn't believe it, but didn't dare sit around thinking about it. She quickly ran up to the brave, picked up the pointed half of the spear, and kicked the warrior. For a moment she thought about killing him, but she couldn't do it, even in a simulation. The brave began to rise onto his hands and knees. She kicked him again—hard—and he fell back to the ground. To be sure he wouldn't catch her again, she jabbed one of his feet with the spear. That would slow him if he tried to rise again.

Abby had no time to feel relieved. The next brave was only a hundred yards behind her. She took off running again even though her legs felt like lead. When she forced herself forward, it felt like she was running in thick boots. She didn't know how much longer she could keep her pace up. She had lucked out against one brave, but several hundred others were bound to catch up to her. She had to keep trying.

She heard another whooping sound and glanced back. The next warrior had come across his injured tribesman and was attending to him. That would buy her time. Maybe there was hope over the next hill.

Abby ran through cottonwood trees and over a landing. She saw a river below. As she moved closer, she spotted a beaver dam built against the riverbed and ran over to it. She wouldn't be visible to the braves behind her for at least a minute.

Abby dove into the river. The water felt like ice as it slapped her skin. It was a chilly relief from the blood and sweat. She swam as quickly as she could beneath the dam.

Abby remembered from a documentary that beavers always made their dams so they could enter them from underneath the water. That kept out most predators. Abby held her breath and went under the frigid water. She opened her eyes, searching for an opening. At first, she figured that the beavers that made this dam must have been a great exception to the documentary—all she could see was a wall of sticks and mud. Finally, she found a hole, and though she had to push and shimmy, she eventually made it up through the opening.

Her chest heaved up and down as she huddled inside the wood home. She moved her arms around as best she could to help her heart gradually slow down, but there wasn't much room. Had any of the braves seen her enter? If so, she was a sitting duck—or beaver, or girl in a simulator—whatever.

Splash. Someone was there.

Abby cupped her hand over her mouth, trying to muffle the little sound she made. She heard the footsteps pass through the river, onto the other side.

More splashes—this time one right after the other. They also continued to the other side. It appeared as though her ruse was working. Less than a minute later, she heard the screeching and yelling of more and more braves. There was a good size crowd. One brave yelled something from a ways across the river. Another responded. They had probably figured out that she wasn't still running ahead.

With her arms and legs freezing from the cold water, she tried not to move, not even to shiver. The Indians would be on the lookout. She knew the water would probably muffle the sound, but she wasn't about to take any chances.

She heard a brave moving through the river. Through a tiny hole in the dam, she could see his eyes.

He saw her. He moved in her direction. What could she

do? She looked around for a loose stick to defend herself with but couldn't find a thing.

Abby was so wrapped up in her terror that she hadn't realized that the warrior had stopped moving. She held her breath. He turned and looked in several directions. After a few more seconds, he moved to the other side of the river. He hadn't seen her at all.

Abby shuddered with relief and waited, shivering in the beaver dam, hoping her test was over.

ICE

Jefferson Cragbridge looked at his stolen watch. It was nearly 11:30.

"Perhaps this is a blessing," his wife said, hugging him in the cold air. "Maybe we should change what happens."

"No," Jefferson responded, pulling away. "You know the cost. Any attempt to intervene with events could be extremely dangerous. It will alter the course of people's lives. Then they in turn alter others. Key events in history may change or never happen. We've both heard my father warn us about that over and over again."

"But what if the cost isn't as high as we imagine?" she said. "At this point, it's all theoretical."

"And what if it is as terrible as we fear? Who are we to decide?" Jefferson asked.

She looked past him to the ocean waves. "I know,

I know. But I look into these people's faces, and I know what's about to . . ." She shook her head. "I don't know if I can just—"

"You can," Jefferson said. "And if we have to be part of this lesson in history, we will be." He looked at his watch again. "All we can do is hope that those with lockets will discover us. We still have a few hours."

• • •

11:40 P.M.

There was no moon out, the sea a mass of darkness. A man—the lookout in the crow's nest—pulled the collar of his coat up again, hoping to protect himself just a little more from the near-freezing temperature. He spotted something ahead, then peered for several seconds through the dark trying to identify it, squinting. His eyes widened. In a panicked flurry, he rang the bell three times and grabbed the phone. He called into the receiver, "Iceberg, right ahead!"

Officer Murdoch called out, "Reverse engines," and ordered the helmsman hard to starboard. The helmsman move the tiller to the right, hoping to make the large ship veer left, but the massive ship had too much weight and too much momentum to change direction quickly. It continued straight toward the iceberg.

The lookout watched in horror. The iceberg was at least six stories high and a few hundred feet wide, and that was only the tip. It looked as though they were going to hit it straight on. "Come on. Come on," he mumbled to himself.

He imagined the ship's metal crumpling against the icy blockade.

Finally, the massive ship swayed to the left.

"Farther left," the lookout whispered. "Farther. Farther."

He wanted to exhale with relief as the point of the ship missed the floating island, but he knew better. The danger wasn't over. A loud grinding rang out over the dark ocean. The right side of the ship scraped hard against the ice. The lookout didn't know it yet, but below the surface of the water, the ship's metal exterior buckled against the pressure.

From his perch, the lookout felt a small tremor—that was all. The monstrous ship collided with tons of solid ice, yet all he felt was a tremor. He knew most of the passengers were sleeping.

They probably wouldn't even stir. They would have no idea of the damage—a series of holes the length of a football field scratched into the ship's plates.

The *Titanic* had received its deathblow. It would not finish its historic maiden voyage. There were 2,223 people on the boat, but lifeboats for only 1,178.

SECRET

She had traveled for a little less than two hours from Cragbridge Hall. Ms. Entrese drove a van into the parking lot next to a lecture hall. Fences lined the building marked with "Under Construction" signs. She stepped out, and walked around to the back doors of the van. Before she could unlatch them, she heard a voice.

"Excuse me, ma'am. Please stop right where you are."

She froze.

"May I ask what you're doing here, and so late?" The man had an athletic build and spoke with a thick Southern accent.

"Just making a delivery," Ms. Entrese said, hoping to sound convincing. "The company lets me make them at night when there's less traffic."

"You're not a very good liar," the man said, and with a

flick of his finger, he triggered a gun barrel to slide out from under his sleeve and align with his index finger. "You're driving a Cragbridge Hall van. How stupid do you think I am?"

"Well, you do work for Muns," she said.

He pointed the gun barrel in her face. "I'd suggest you talk a little nicer if you want to live." His Southern accent had no hint of hospitality anymore. "Now keep your hands up, and let's step inside." Ms. Entrese turned and started toward the door of the auditorium.

• • •

Abby stood on the other side of the simulator. The river, the braves, the dam—all of it had vanished. She had passed the test. She had no idea how long it had taken, but it seemed like forever. Her legs still felt a little numb from the chill of the river.

An image of Grandpa appeared again, shining in the dim room. "Congratulations on passing such an arduous test," he said. "Because you must have had great cause to endure the simulator, I don't envy you for the fight that surely awaits you. You have earned the right to know, and perhaps even use, my secret." He paused for a moment before declaring, "The secret is this: I invented a machine that can travel through time."

Though Derick had already guessed that this whole thing had to do with time travel, hearing it from her grandfather felt strange.

"I heard of others who were pursuing time travel and

became curious. I began to study and tinker. Soon, time travel became another of my obsessions. It took me years and years to hit a breakthrough. I finally discovered the key to time travel in my university lab. At first, I was thrilled with the wonderful opportunities, but then I remembered someone I had met before—Charles Muns."

There was that name again. Abby paid special attention as Grandpa continued.

"For years, Muns had had a team researching the possibilities of time travel. Years before, he'd offered me a position."

Virtual Grandpa began to pace. "In our initial talks, I became very excited about the possibilities. I imagined being able to show people what had really happened in the past. I thought of all the mysteries of history we could solve, how we could teach people today to appreciate all that others had worked for and sacrificed to prepare the way for us.

"But as our talks became more serious, Muns's ambitions also became clearer. He wanted to travel through time to change the past. He wanted to right every wrong and reverse every tragedy.

"I admit that on its face, Muns's argument appears to be the very noblest of causes, but believe me when I insist that it is not. Though you have probably not had enough time to think about your own opinion on the issue yet, please consider mine. You are most likely one of my trusted friends, after all. Contemplate a world where we have known no tragedy."

Grandpa disappeared, and in his place stood two large

skyscrapers. They loomed large and majestic over a sea of buildings. Then a commercial airplane collided into one tower. Abby started. The image flickered, and another plane collided into the other tower. Abby remembered studying about this event in history. Terrorists had taken over planes and deliberately crashed them into the buildings.

Grandpa's voice came through the image. "Though we would not know such terror and fear by changing history, we would also miss the lessons such tragedies teach us."

The image switched to firemen rushing up stairs, helping people out of the buildings. Again and again, they rushed inside to get out as many as they could.

"Tragedies are where heroes are made," Grandpa's voice said.

One security guard moved up floor by floor with a bullhorn, making sure everyone else got out. As he moved to another flight of stairs looking for stragglers, he had his phone to his ear. "If anything happens to me, I just want you to know that you made my life," he said. Then the building crumpled to the ground on top of him.

"Tragedies help us forget lesser problems and come together," Grandpa said. Abby viewed image after image of volunteers combing through the rubble, bringing in aid, and taking people in.

Grandpa's voice continued, "Though we never wish for them, tragedies teach us. Not to learn from them is our shame. It is our loss. Others died to teach us, and we have a responsibility to learn."

Grandpa reappeared, walking in front of Abby. She

followed him with her eyes. "The second reason to not change the past is perhaps even more important than the first: doing so would most likely have horrendous ramifications. It would disrupt the balance between the past and present. If we prevented tragedies in the past, those who would have died would, of course, survive, changing human history. Our time would have people appear who hadn't existed before—the descendants of those who had previously died in the tragedy. We would also have other people *disappear*, because those who were saved could cause other circumstances that prevented people who live now from ever existing."

Abby listened closely, imagining the consequences her grandfather suggested.

"The very fabric of society could change," he continued. "Our whole government could be swayed by those who have not been humbled, who have not learned lessons from the past. This could lead to entirely new world wars, greater than those from the past. We may or may not be able to prevent wars from happening, for who knows how often or for how long we could change time? One wrong move, and perhaps I would no longer exist, and therefore, I never would have existed, and time travel would not be possible. Then we are stuck with how society turned out, or perhaps the consequences would be even more drastic than that. Messing with time could endanger civilization as we know it—our entire world."

Grandpa stopped his pacing. "After I discovered time travel, I felt that Muns would stop at nothing to have the ability. Once the experiments were published, it would just be a matter of time before he learned to replicate them. So I told no one. I worked for another three years before developing a shield between us and the past. That shield is what is in place today as you use the Bridge. You see only faint images of the past, because you are separated from it. You are not allowed to interfere with what you see. Nor are those from the past allowed to interact with you," Grandpa said. "That shield was supposed to solve the problem. It was supposed to allow students to study the past, not lead people like Muns to wreak havoc on our past and our future. Because you are listening to this, that shield has probably not been sufficient."

Grandpa cleared his throat. "You have now earned your final key." A rock slid out from the wall. It was hollow inside, and contained a single key, bigger than the others.

"This key, when placed in the console of the original Bridge, which all the other booths and copies are connected to, will allow you to enter the past—actually enter it. Please heed my caution, however. Do not interfere with the past unless it is worth risking the entire world."

Abby's mind swarmed with thoughts and questions. Was her situation that important? Her parents were about to die, but was that worth risking so much? It was up to her. She could choose.

Muns was likely the person holding Grandpa captive. Muns sought the same power, and if he got it, nothing would ever be the same. She had to have the key. She could save her parents from the past, where Muns had put them, then never change anything again. Muns had already messed it up; she would just fix it.

"The original Bridge lies on the other side of this door and farther below the school." Grandpa pointed behind him. "I have taken one more precaution. You will need three of these final keys to enter time itself, which means you will need two others who have keys. It is my hope that if your cause is dear then two of my other trusted associates will be sympathetic to your cause, and that together, you may make wise decisions for both the future and our past." Grandpa paused solemnly for a moment. "Do your best. I apologize if my ambition costs us our world. I was trying to help others learn and grow. I didn't realize the threats that my achievements brought. Best of luck."

And he was gone.

Abby was about to unlock the large door in front of her when she remembered Carol. She had left her behind on the other side of the simulator. She walked around the machine and found the door beside it. She used her new key and it unlocked. That was the purpose of the second door— to be able to come to the Bridge without having to return through the simulator.

"You did it! You did it! You did it!" Carol jumped up and down. "I can't believe it. I mean, I always knew you *could*, but it's great to see that you *did* it—not that I doubted you. Well, maybe a little, but I would have done that with anyone."

Abby told Carol what she had learned from her grandfather. Soon they faced another massive door. Abby stepped forward and used her new key to unlock it.

KEYS

Ms. Entrese stood, looking down the gun barrel.

In a flash, the back door of the van flung open, and a blur of black charged out. The man turned his gun on what he realized in horror was an attacking gorilla, but not in time. The gorilla knocked the gun barrel off of the track that held it in place, swung his long arms, and sent the man sprawling.

The man rolled to the side and struggled to push the gun barrel back into place. He nearly had it when his eyes grew even wider. A rhino ran out of the back of the van, lumbering at full speed. The man got only halfway to his feet before the rhino rammed him in the chest. He flew over ten feet and rolled onto the ground. Ms. Entrese quickly ran to his side and checked him.

"He's unconscious," she said.

Inside the lab at Cragbridge, both Rafa and Derick smiled as they moved their avatars into the lecture hall behind Ms. Entrese. The books they had packed around the avatars were scattered throughout the parking lot.

• • •

"Grandpa said that the original Bridge was below us," Abby said, beginning to climb down another ladder.

She noticed that other ladders on other sides of the cavernous basement also went down.

"Do you think those ladders are other ways of getting here?" Carol asked. "Like for other people with keys?"

"Could be." Abby admitted she didn't know for sure, but it made sense that each person would get a different set of clues specific to them. And each person could even have a different path to the original Bridge. Once at the bottom, the girls started down another dark hallway. They heard someone clear their throat.

"I thought I heard someone behind me." It was a man. Abby could only make out his silhouette. "But I didn't plan on seeing any students down here."

"Who are you?" Carol asked.

Mr. Hendricks stepped into the light. He looked ragged and tired. "I assumed only teachers would have lockets, but I guess it would make sense that Oscar would give one to his granddaughter."

"You have a key too?" Abby asked.

"I spent a full night in the simulator with Shackleton's

crew stranded in Antarctica for it," Mr. Hendricks said. "But I got it."

Carol shivered.

Relief swept over Abby. Someone else had a key, and it was Mr. Hendricks.

"Where do we go from here?" she asked.

"We continue down farther. There you'll see the real Bridge. I've come here several times hoping to find someone else, and fortunately, tonight I've found you."

"Has anyone else been here?" Abby asked, remembering her grandfather's instructions that they would need three keys to go back in time. They needed one more person, or they wouldn't be able to save her parents.

"There may be one other," Mr. Hendricks said. "I came late one night, and thought I saw someone leaving. Unless of course, that was you."

Hope swelled inside of Abby. It hadn't been her. There was one more person out there with a key. "It wasn't me. This is the first time we've made it this far, but we need to get to the Bridge as soon as we can. My parents are trapped in time."

"What?" Mr. Hendricks said.

"Somehow they were put on the *Titanic*," Abby explained. "And we only have"—she checked the clock on her rings—"less than an hour to save them before it goes down. It's already hit the iceberg."

"Then let's hurry," Mr. Hendricks said. He led Carol and Abby down the dark corridor. They walked fast but didn't dare run, through the twisting, dark corridor. The cave finally opened into a large room.

In the middle of it was one of the most unusual sights Abby had ever seen—what looked like a massive metal tree. A machine jutted up from the ground, with several thick supports anchoring it to the granite floor. It had a thick metal core, which, as it rose toward the ceiling, branched off into what looked like thousands of silver limbs that spread through the top of the room and disappeared into the ceiling. In the "trunk" was a console, complete with a screen and a shelf with three keyholes.

The real Bridge.

Abby stared at it. This was the invention that had now caused them so much trouble. It was one of her grandfather's great accomplishments—one of the greatest accomplishments in history. Abby imagined that the branches of the Bridge connected it to all of the booths in the school.

"Kids?" a deep voice asked aloud.

Abby looked across the room and saw two figures in the dark. As they walked closer, she recognized them: Coach Adonavich and Coach Horne.

"Not just any kids," Mr. Hendricks said. "One of them is Abby Cragbridge. And they have one key between them."

"Hello, Abby and Carol," Coach Adonavich said. Coach Horne repeated the greeting.

The girls said hello back.

"And do you have a key as well?" Coach Horne asked Mr. Hendricks.

"I do," he answered. "You?"

"No," Coach Horne said. "My locket was stolen over a month ago. I told Oscar about it, and he saw the theft as a warning that something might be about to happen. Ever since, I've been extra vigilant in trying to detect any signs of strange happenings around here. When I noticed a strange wound on Coach Adonavich, I followed her. She led me to the basement."

"I let him in past the simulator," Coach Adonavich said. "I'll vouch for his trustworthiness, as Oscar Cragbridge did when he gave him the locket."

"Or so he says," Mr. Hendricks said, stepping toward Coach Horne. "Does anyone else know that Oscar gave you a locket?"

"No," Coach Horne said. "But he did."

"Even if someone stole it, how do we know it wasn't because you traded sides in this whole adventure?" Mr. Hendricks asked.

"You don't," Coach Horne said. "But frankly, you don't have to believe me. I submit we destroy the keys. We have to assume that someone with bad intentions has my key, and we cannot risk someone gaining access to three of them."

"Or you and those you work for already have three, and you want to destroy the others," Mr. Hendricks suggested.

"*Listen!*" Abby burst out. "I don't have time to talk about this. We have to save my parents."

"Your parents?" Coach Adonavich asked.

"They're trapped on the *Titanic*," Abby explained. "And it sinks in a few minutes."

"I don't believe it," Coach Horne said. "I know they are just kids, but this could be a trick to keep us from destroying this danger."

"She's Oscar's granddaughter," Mr. Hendricks said.

"Yes, but another girl is with her," Coach Adonavich said. "I would never suspect betrayal from Carol, but you never know if Oscar's granddaughter was being coerced to come here. For that matter, they arrived with you, Mr. Hendricks, and no offense, but I don't believe any of us can afford to completely trust anyone."

"Point taken, and none of the offense," Mr. Hendricks said. "Abby, can you show us your parents using this Bridge? I've tried it, and I know it works like any other Bridge booth. There is nothing special about it—until the keys are in place. You work the console here." He pointed to the center of the Bridge, the trunk of the metal tree. "The image, however, only appears behind it—not all around us like in class. I believe that is because if we are to enter the past, we want a place to both enter into and exit from."

Abby moved to the Bridge and turned on her rings.

Mr. Hendricks stopped her. "You cannot sync to this Bridge," he explained. "Perhaps it was invented before the rings. You have to use the console."

Abby placed her fingers on the screen, and it flickered on. She quickly began punching in numbers—the date of the *Titanic* image Derick had shown her.

In moments, the space behind the Bridge filled with the ghost of a scene of chaos. The massive ship groaned, its front end dipping into the water. Passengers piled into lifeboats over the side. Other lifeboats floated in the ocean around the scene, some only half filled.

The ship groaned again. The front end sank deeper, and the back of the ship rose farther out of the water. Those who could not fit in the lifeboats were trying not to fall into the icy ocean as the vessel tipped. Passengers clambered over the deck gates that separated the first- and second-class areas from the crew portion, trying to get away from the water.

"Where are your parents?" Coach Adonavich asked.

Everyone in the damp basement gathered closer to the Bridge to see the scene.

"I'll check where we found them before—at the back end of the ship," Abby said. She used the controls to push the point of view to the stern. She searched the faces—a woman clinging to the railing, tears streaming down her face, a man screaming that he deserved to have space on the lifeboat—he had investments, family, and employees he was responsible for. Another man held tight to the rod and moved as best he could along it, shouting, "Loretta!"

They searched face after face, terrified expression after terrified expression. Finally, they found Abby's parents clinging to the same rail.

"I don't believe it," Coach Horne said. "That's them. Who would ever—"

"We don't have time to worry about that now," Mr. Hendricks said. "We have to get them out."

"Wait a minute," Coach Adonavich said. "We need to

consider whether this will send repercussions throughout time. We all heard what Dr. Cragbridge said."

"It won't," Mr. Hendricks said. "The deed has already been done. They are back in time but belong in the now. We're merely trying to put things right, make restitution. But we must be very careful to not interact with anyone other than Abby's parents if we can help it."

The ship slanted even more, creaking as it took on more water.

"Please," Abby pleaded. "Let us use your keys."

Mr. Hendricks walked to the console and pushed his key into one of the three holes. "Abby?" he said, motioning for her to join him.

She did, and she put her key into the second hole.

"Only one more," Mr. Hendricks said.

Coach Adonavich stepped forward and filled the third hole.

The *Titanic* disappeared, and Grandpa appeared, surrounded by blackness. "Hello," he said. "Apparently you have felt it necessary to use the full capacity of the Bridge to go back in time. I need to explain a few things and warn you. First, you must all turn your keys simultaneously. Because one person could turn two keys but not three, this ensures that at least two different people, and hopefully three, agree to the need for traveling back in time. The more heads in these decisions, the better."

He coughed and went on. "After you have turned the keys, you will notice a difference in the Bridge. The way into time is as big as this room. You can simply step in.

However, be sure to move the perspective to a stable location, one you'll be able to remember and find on the other side. You will, I assume, want to come back. You cannot see the Bridge portal from the past, so again, it is important to remember where it is. As long as you leave all three keys turned, you can travel in and out of the Bridge. Please be careful. Those from the past can mistakenly travel to our time if you leave the way open. Depending on the situation, it could be valuable to let someone into time, then turn the keys back to their original position to keep anyone else in the past from crossing over. To allow the time traveler back, turn the keys once again.

"Also, might I stress, you shouldn't change *anything* unless it is completely necessary. Our past has made us who we have become. We should not change that. If you are here trying to correct a large wrong that I started, I thank you, and I apologize." He disappeared, and the panicked crowd on the *Titanic* instantly reappeared.

Coach Horne spoke up. "Before you turn the keys," he said, "you're sure we should do this?"

"Yes," Mr. Hendricks answered. Abby was glad he was there; she didn't have to do the persuading. She nodded in agreement.

"Oh, I'm so nervous," Carol said. "This is historical and terrifying all at once. Kind of like the first time I had my ears pierced, except on a much, *much* bigger scale."

Mr. Hendricks gave a nod, and the three of them turned the keys.

The image from the Bridge warped as though a

transparent wave had washed over it. A gush of frigid, moist air rushed into the room. The *Titanic* sank more, its stern lifting higher in the air, but this time it was perfectly clear, no longer a ghost of the past. The image was vivid, real. It was as though the terror of the sinking ship was happening in the same room.

In fact, it was.

The group looked on in awe as the scene stood out in full color, and in reality, before them. Abby moved the perspective as close to her parents as she could. Moving another reality felt strange. It was no longer like watching a movie, but like shifting the entire angle of the room only feet away. And that room was huge. Everyone on the ship seemed completely unaware that they were being watched, or that an escape was right before them. Abby walked toward her parents.

"Wait," Coach Horne said. "Maybe I should go."

"No," Abby said. "I'm going."

"Perhaps you should go with her!" Mr. Hendricks nearly yelled, competing with the wind and confusion of the ship. "You can make sure that she comes back okay."

"Why not you?" Coach Horne asked, pointing her finger at Mr. Hendricks.

"Because I've taken it upon myself to make sure that the keys are turned off, and then turned back on, at the precise moment. I want Abby to return alive."

"Why not leave that job to Coach Adonavich and me?" Coach Horne asked.

"Because I'm not sure I can trust anyone else to do it!" Mr. Hendricks shouted.

"Perhaps it would be better if I went," Coach Adonavich said. "Abby can stay here, and then—"

But Abby didn't wait for the adults to figure out who should go in and who should watch the keys. The *Titanic* was nearly at a seventy-degree angle. It wouldn't be easy to leave the basement of Cragbridge Hall and board a boat on such a tilt. She focused on a railing. She should be able to grab on and be close to her parents.

Abby held her breath and jumped from the sturdy Cragbridge basement toward the railing. That one movement sent her back over a century in time.

RESCUE

M s. Entrese peeked around the corner into the lecture
hall, then turned back to the gorilla and rhino. "He's
in there," she said. "He's tied to a chair and surrounded by
at least six guards. He's . . ." She paused and swallowed hard.
"He's watching the *Titanic* sink."

Derick had suspected that was the case earlier, but hearing it confirmed made him feel sick. Perhaps it would have
slowed him down, if he were not so connected to his avatar rhino anatomy. Derick suspected that rhinoceroses had
much stronger constitutions than humans.

Derick watched Rafa's avatar gesture for Ms. Entrese to
stop. He pointed at the ground.

"You want me to wait here?" she asked.

The gorilla nodded. Back in the lab, Rafa said, "Give

me two minutes. Then Derick, you come in with everything you've got."

Derick nodded with his rhino and watched as the gorilla gave him a thumbs up.

"Two minutes exactly," Rafa said.

"How am I supposed to know how long it's been?" Derick asked. "I'm a rhino. I can't sync in and check the time."

"Count the seconds," Rafa said. "It'll have to do, but I think I'm going to need all the help I can get. Start . . . now." He crawled into the room.

Derick began counting in his mind—*one thousand one, one thousand two*. He tried not to go too fast. He didn't want to rush because of his nerves. *One thousand three*.

Derick brought his head low and peeked into the room. It was a decent-sized lecture hall with several hundred seats and a platform up front. There on the platform stood a bed, a series of simple chairs and several guards. And his grandfather, flanked by several men. Derick was sure they had guns.

How could they stop this?

He realized he'd stopped counting. Where was he? At almost thirty seconds. He skipped a few numbers, hoping he was close to where he should have been in the count.

One thousand thirty-four. One thousand thirty-five.

The gorilla crept across the floor, using the seats as cover. Rafa made it to the far wall, out of sight of those on the stage. With amazing dexterity, the gorilla climbed up a beam beside the stage and up to the lighting above. He was easily thirty or forty feet in the air.

One thousand fifty. One thousand fifty-one.

. . .

Crossing to the past felt strange, like taking a scalding shower for a fraction of a second, followed by the chills, and the same nausea Abby often felt after a long car ride.

She caught the railing with her hands, but her feet slid across the metal until her body was fully extended. After such a strange sensation crossing over, she was glad she'd caught on at all. Abby tried to stay calm and hang on, but her feet kept slipping.

"Dad! Mom!" she yelled.

Her father's eyes bulged for a moment before he hustled across the railing toward his daughter.

"Abby!" her mom cried out, racing behind her husband.

Abby clung on with everything she had. Finally, her father came close enough to extend his hand. Abby's mother held him securely. Abby took her father's hand, and he lifted her up to where another railing extended out toward the middle of the ship, giving her a secure place for her feet.

The lights of the huge ship flickered out. Abby couldn't see a thing.

"Brace yourself against the railing and the floor of the ship. We only have a few seconds," her father cried out.

Abby threaded her arms through the railing and pushed

one foot against the wooden deck. Abby felt her father and mother do the same, but surrounding her.

What sounded like an explosion, followed by the rattle of a massive chain, echoed through the night. The whole boat shuddered.

"Hold on!" Abby's mother screamed.

More explosions. Abby heard shattering glass and tearing metal. And then she knew she was falling. It felt like one of those rides at an amusement park where you free-fall for several stories, except this time, there were no safety restraints—nothing to keep her safe. The stern of the ship fell backward, over a hundred feet toward the ocean.

● ● ●

The gorilla managed to swing himself from one set of lights to another. In the background, the *Titanic* rose higher out of the water. Derick was counting his second minute. *One thousand seven. One thousand eight.*

Grandfather cried out. Had he seen something? Derick looked again to see his grandfather standing, watching the *Titanic* intently. The guards were too. Were his parents okay? What was happening?

The lights on the massive ship went out.

The gorilla swung to the next set of lights, catching it by only a few fingers. He dangled directly above the guards and Oscar Cragbridge. With the stage below him, the gorilla was less than thirty feet above the ground.

The *Titanic* fell, crashing into the water.

One thousand thirteen. One thousand fourteen.

One of the lights near Rafa shifted out of place and fell to the ground.

One thousand nineteen.

The team of guards, their attention ripped away from watching the *Titanic*, looked at the fallen light. In a second, they'd see Rafa. They'd shoot him before he could do any good.

One thousand—who cares? Derick couldn't wait. He barreled into the room, running his rhino in as fast as he could. He tried to roar, but it came out more of a groan. His entrance felt anticlimactic, but it would have to do.

The guards whirled, triggering their guns to come out of their sleeves and aiming at the charging rhino.

• • •

"Let's move the keys now," Coach Horne began, "back to the—" He didn't finish his sentence. He stared down the barrel of a gun, attached to Mr. Hendricks's hand.

"Everyone in!" Mr. Hendricks yelled, and motioned with his barrel for the group to enter the past, to go onto the *Titanic*.

"You're insane!" Coach Adonavich said.

"No, I'm not," Mr. Hendricks said. "This is a chance of a lifetime. We can change everything."

"Oh, this is bad. So bad. So terribly bad," Carol mumbled to herself.

"How do you know that we do not share your opinion on time travel?" Coach Horne asked.

"Because I know very well who is working for Muns and who is not," Mr. Hendricks said. "And none of you are. In fact, I appreciated receiving the locket you used to wear, Horne."

"It was you who took it?" he asked.

"No. We have a professional for those things, but I was happy to take it and work through its challenges from here in the school. Now go in."

Coach Horne looked at those on the *Titanic*, which was standing nearly vertical, and then back at Hendricks. "No," he said. "I think I'd rather make you shoot me, make you a murderer, than let you shift the responsibility to a tragedy in time. I'll die either way. If you believe in your cause so much, kill me. Eventually someone will come to this basement, and they'll discover—"

"Get in," Mr. Hendricks said. "I'll reverse the tragedy when the time is right, and you'll be back. But for right now, I need you out of the way."

"You don't know that," Coach Adonavich said. "You don't know for sure if you'll be able to reverse this whole thing or that we'll come back."

"It *will* work," Mr. Hendricks said.

"I know how he got to you, Hendricks," Horne said. "It was when your wife died. He's probably made you promises about bringing her back. You don't know that he'll be able to keep those promises, and even if he could, bringing her back might kill countless other people."

"It will work!" Mr. Hendricks shouted.

"I'm not stepping in there!" Coach Horne yelled back. "You'll have to kill me. You'll have to create your own tragedy that someone else will pine over, that someone else will wish hadn't happened. You'll have to take the responsibility."

Mr. Hendricks flicked his finger. A bullet rocketed out of the barrel.

DEATH TRAP

The *Titanic* broke in half. The weight of the front part of the ship under water put too much pressure on the rest of the ship, making steel plates, wooden decks, and cables to the smokestacks all splinter and snap. The back part of the ship that was still above the water slapped down against the ocean.

Abby couldn't believe how much the impact hurt. The ship beneath her took the brunt of the impact, but she still felt bruises on her shoulder and back. A trickle of blood dripped from her forehead to her cheek.

Abby's father groaned. She found him quickly and made her way to his side. He looked up at her. "We have to get out of here," she said. "It's going to sink."

"How do we get out?" Mom yelled, scooting next to her.

"They should be able to move the perspective on the

Bridge so we can walk out," Abby said. "Just reach out, search around, and look for anyone stepping in to get us."

They all moved around, waiting for some sensation, some portal back to their time. Nothing happened.

"Maybe they can't move it once someone comes in," Abby guessed. "Maybe we have to go back the same way."

"You came in way up there," her mom said, pointing up in the air.

"Wait for a minute," her father said. "The ship will rise again right before it goes down. We should be able to reach the portal then."

Abby clutched the rail and waited.

• • •

Derick loved the look of surprise in their eyes. Who could blame them? There was no way they would expect to see a charging rhino in a university's lecture hall.

A gorilla fell down on top of two of them and bashed the gun barrel of a third.

The three remaining guards shot at Derick. He thrust his rhino head to one side, and with a swing of his horn and the momentum of his body, he uprooted a string of metal stadium chairs from the floor and flung them in the air. Bullets ricocheted off the metal, but two pierced the rhino avatar's tough skin. He'd been shot. He felt like pieces of hot iron had poked through him.

In the lab, the real Derick screamed in pain.

Rafa leapt on top of another guard, and with a blow to

the head, knocked him unconscious. Another guard turned on him, but Rafa managed to propel himself with his long arms and kick the man right off the stage.

Feeling lightheaded and weak, Derick lost control of his body. He stumbled forward, trying desperately to somehow guide his huge mass toward the guards. He plowed through row after row of chairs. He lost control of his feet and awkwardly rolled over and over, seats flying in every direction.

Rafa ran toward the one remaining guard. The man raised his gun. Derick, his vision hazy, saw the guard aim at Rafa. Everything seemed to happen in slow motion. Just before the guard got off a shot, Derick hooked a nearby chair with his horn and hurled it in the man's direction. The chair only grazed the man's back, but it distracted him enough to make the gun's aim go wild, giving Rafa the chance to knock him over and dislodge the barrel from the man's wrist. The guard tried to rise again, but with a sweep of Rafa's long, hairy gorilla arm, he sent the last of the guards into unconsciousness.

From his seat, Grandpa spoke. "I really hope you are avatars, or I'm in some serious trouble."

"They are," Ms. Entrese said, running down the aisle. "Oscar, the rhino is your grandson."

"Derick?" he said, standing up and shuffling toward the edge of the stage. "Are you okay?"

Derick managed to get to his feet and shake his rhino head. Sparks erupted from the bullet wounds.

"You're amazing," Grandpa clapped his hands. "How did you ever learn to control something as large as a rhinoceros?"

Derick groaned in pain and fell down to his belly.

"Derick!" Grandpa moved toward his grandson. "Are you okay?"

Derrick managed a nod. "Abby's trying to get her key to bring Jefferson and his wife back," Ms. Entrese said, pointing to the screen.

"I saw her enter," Grandpa said, and turned to watch the deck of the *Titanic*. After locating Abby and her parents to confirm that they were still alive, Grandpa turned to the rhino. "Derick, are you and your friend in the lab at Cragbridge?"

Derick nodded, his vision tunneling.

"You must help your sister," Grandpa said. "I've heard enough while being tied up here to know that Muns has been monitoring the school. He must have a mole on the inside. He'll get the others' keys, and then he'll trap them all back in time."

• • •

Coach Horne grabbed his shoulder, where the bullet had entered.

"No!" Carol cried.

Coach Adonavich gasped and took a step back.

"Get in the Bridge!" Mr. Hendricks yelled.

"Never!" Coach Horne said. "You do it. You take responsibility. Put my blood on your hands!"

"Stop this!" Coach Adonavich screamed.

Carol started to cry.

Coach Horne took two steps forward, but Mr. Hendricks pulled the trigger again. The huge coach stumbled back, shot in the leg above the knee.

"Enough!" Coach Adonavich yelled. "Stop this."

"Fine," Mr. Hendricks said. He quickly pulled out all three of the keys and put them in the pocket of his blazer. The scene of the *Titanic* faded, and the sound from it died down. Mr. Hendricks spoke quieter now. "It will be just as easy to come back and change all this." He set his gun sight on Coach Horne's heart.

• • •

The stern of the *Titanic* groaned and rose out of the water again. The sinking half was pulling the stern up as it fell farther into the ocean deep.

Abby and her parents clung to the railing as they moved higher and higher into the air.

"The way back in should be here," Abby said, reaching for the air before her, hoping to feel the same sensation as when she'd come through. "They'll have it open for us."

"Is it working?" her mom asked.

"I don't know," Abby said. "I can't feel it. Maybe it's farther out. We might just have to jump for it." She reached again, but nothing happened.

"But what if it's not there?" her mom asked.

"Then we fall into the water with everyone else," Dad said. "We'll have to risk it."

SKID

O pen it," Carol demanded. "Let them back in!" She looked at Abby on the ship, feeling for the way back, but the Bridge was closed. "Please!"

"No." Hendricks wiped sweat from his temples. "She has to stay out of the way. And so do all of you."

"What are you going to do?" Coach Adonavich asked.

"It wasn't supposed to be this complicated," Mr. Hendricks said. "We were supposed to know the secrets by now. Oscar wasn't supposed to let anyone get hurt. He was supposed to tell us. But now I've got to . . ." He looked at the two coaches and Carol, and raised his barrel at them.

"I don't want to die," Carol sobbed.

"None of us do," Coach Adonavich said.

Coach Horne moaned, still nursing his wound.

Mr. Hendricks pointed the gun at Coach Adonavich,

then at Horne, then back at Carol. "I don't want to kill you . . . It's just that—"

"I have too many things to do," Carol cried. "I've never been married. I've never even gone out with Derick. I have a great idea for a new reality TV show, and I'll never get to pitch it, so they can tell me it's terrible—"

Mr. Hendricks walked toward her with the gun. "Look. There is a lot on the line, and I don't have many options at this point."

"I'll never get to go to that new water park. I don't remember its name, but it has the tallest waterslide—the one that drops you like fifty feet, but slows you down with air pressure. I don't want to die. I don't want to die." Her voice grew louder, but she didn't even look at Hendricks. "I don't want to die!"

"Calm down," Mr. Hendricks said, his finger poised on the trigger. "Don't worry. It'll be quick, and then before you know it, you'll be back."

"You can't promise that," Coach Adonavich said. "Don't lie to the girl."

"You'll hardly even feel it," Hendricks promised.

Carol erupted in wails and groans. She clutched at her hair. She fell to the ground, tears spilling over her cheeks. She opened her mouth and wailed. Her eyes, shifting back and forth, filled with tears over and over again. Her fear burst out anywhere it could. Her arms trembled. She clutched her hair. She swayed back and forth. She'd lost all control—completely crumbled under the pressure. She looked hysterical.

Only a foot away, Mr. Hendricks said, "It's time to calm down."

In one swift motion, Carol grabbed the gun barrel from Mr. Hendricks's hand and swept his feet out from under him. The gun fired across the room, and the bullet ricocheted off the hard walls.

Carol wasn't crying anymore.

Coach Horne lumbered forward and pounced on Mr. Hendricks, punching him unconscious with one blow.

"Get the keys!" Carol yelled.

• • •

Derick and Rafa tore the avatar suits off and raced down the hall. They whipped around one corner and then another, rushing out of the building and into Cragbridge Hall.

While running, Derick logged onto his rings. He tried to sync up to warn his sister. He had to warn her that men were coming. His computer screen simply read "Out of range."

She must still be back in time.

As he rounded another corner, Derick caught a glimpse of a shadow just passing the other end of the hall. Not many students roamed the halls at night. Derick slowed and shushed Rafa. They clung to the sides of a wall and quickly moved to the end. Derick peeked around the corner. Several men—perhaps ten or so—dressed in blazers, button-up shirts and khaki pants, approached a closet door. They looked like teachers. One glanced over his shoulder; Derick pulled back. In that split second, Derick recognized the man—he had a flat nose and thick eyebrows. He was the man who'd been disguised as a policeman—he took Abby's key.

After a few moments, Derick peeked around the corner again. The men entered the closet and closed it behind them.

"Must be another way to get back to the basement," Derick said.

"But they'll have to go through a simulator, won't they?" Rafa asked.

"I guess so, unless their mole already has and can let them in on the other side," Derick said.

"We could go the way you already know," Rafa said. "We might be able to beat them there."

"No," Derick said, thinking quickly. "Abby has our key, so unless she's waiting for us, we can't get in. These guys either have a key, or their mole has left the way open. We have to follow them if we want to help Abby."

They ran down the hall to the closet. They tried the handle—locked.

"To get in at the dead end," Derick thought aloud, "you have to push a part of the *Endurance* on the molding. It's different from the other things around it, but similar enough to blend in. Look around for any sign."

They both searched the area.

"The molding is all the same," Rafa said.

"Okay, so it's something else." Derick looked at the doorframe, hoping to find anything irregular. It all seemed uniform. Wait—the hinges. The bottom one was different. The phrase "small hinges" was written on it. Derick seemed to remember Grandpa saying that big doors always swing on small hinges. It was some metaphor about little things making a big difference. Derick pushed the letters and heard a click.

• • •

Coach Horne reached inside Mr. Hendricks's pocket and pulled out two keys. "The other one fell to the ground," he said.

Coach Adonavich dropped to the floor and joined Coach Horne in sweeping the ground with their hands. Carol looked at the Bridge. "Abby's feeling the air to get back."

"We need one more key," Coach Horne said, wincing as he moved his arm across the floor. The bullet wound sent a sting of pain through his arm. "It has to be here."

"I think they're going to jump!" Carol yelled.

• • •

"Are you sure the way back was right there?" Abby's dad asked.

"No," Abby said. "But I don't have any other ideas."

"Then let's risk it," he said. He looked at his wife, who nodded back.

"On the count of three," he said. "One—I love you

both. Two—Abby . . . thanks for coming back for us. Three."

Abby, her dad, and her mom all pushed off the railing, trying to jump toward the room in the modern-day basement of Cragbridge Hall.

Abby felt no scalding feeling followed by cold. There was no change of scene. Only terror. Freezing air whipped across Abby's body as she and her parents plummeted toward the icy waters below.

• • •

Derick tried to step gingerly as he and Rafa hurried down the hall toward the Bridge. He could hear the men a good distance in front of them, but he didn't want them to have a clue that someone was following them.

As Derick and Rafa moved forward, the voices grew louder; the men had stopped moving. Derick slowed his pace and Rafa followed suit. He could barely make out their mumbling words as two of them spoke.

"Is it unlocked like he promised?"

"Yes."

"We need to retrieve *all* the keys."

"Correct. Muns wants to add them to the one he has."

"Don't shut the door behind you. We may need to leave in a hurry."

They proceeded down the long tunnel to the Bridge.

• • •

Abby fell through the air in 1912. She only had seconds before she collided with the water. Why wasn't the portal open? What had happened? Had she risked so much, only to die with her parents?

Then again, would she have had it any other way? She'd done her best. She'd made it to the Bridge and crossed through time and found her parents. Now something was keeping them all from traveling back. Would they survive the impact of the ocean? If so, could they wait in the cold water for the others to find and save them? No. She couldn't take the space of someone who was on a lifeboat; those people needed to live. She couldn't change history. It was over. Staying in the water meant death.

• • •

"Found the last key," Coach Adonavich said. She stood and raced to the console, grabbing the two keys from Coach Horne as she went. Carol ran to the console to meet her. Once all the keys were in place, Coach Adonavich commanded, "Turn the keys." Carol and the coach simultaneously turned the keys.

Carol moved her hands across the screen, changing the Bridge's perspective.

"Bring them in on an angle," Coach Adonavich said.

• • •

Abby held her breath and braced for impact. A split second before crashing into the Atlantic ocean, she hit a slide—the hardest, most uncomfortable slide she had ever experienced. But it wasn't frigid, salty ocean. She skidded across the hard floor beneath Cragbridge Hall, careening out of control. She felt the heat of the friction against her jeans, tearing her flesh. Then she hit the back wall with a thud.

Someone was touching her. Someone was talking. Abby had to shake her head and blink several times before she could see straight.

"Are you okay?" Carol asked.

Abby managed to nod, and her vision became clearer. Behind Carol, a funnel from the top of the *Titanic* broke loose and careened toward the open Bridge. "Close the Bridge!"

Coach Adonavich turned to the open scene and quickly twisted the keys just before the huge metal cylinder could flatten them all. The image changed to a ghost of itself and crashed past them.

Abby felt her parents' arms around her. The three of them held each other for a few moments. They were back—and what was more, they were safe. She hugged them tightly. It didn't feel like it took any energy at all.

"Sorry we took so long," Coach Adonavich said. "Hendricks was working for Muns. He shot Coach Horne and took all the keys. If it hadn't been for Carol, you would be freezing in the ocean right now—if you were still alive at all."

With tear-stained cheeks, Abby turned to see Carol. Carol gave an enthusiastic wave. "I basically did a scene from *The Kidnapping of Jen Tusil*, a web movie I did a year ago. I faked being hysterical—which wasn't that hard to do under the circumstances. I mean, I was really *almost* hysterical, and then I attacked him when he got close enough. I can't believe it worked. I'll have to send a message to whoever wrote the screenplay and thank them for their accuracy."

"I'm glad it worked," Abby said. She exhaled slowly and rose to her feet. She'd done it—she had discovered all the clues, passed all the tests, and brought her parents home safe. A huge weight lifted from her shoulders.

Then her hand vibrated. Someone was trying to sync to her rings. She checked her ring and saw that it was Derick.

"Abby," he whispered. "You finally answered."

"Did you get Grandpa?"

"Yes, but there's more." His words were quick and urgent. "A group of about ten men are on their way down to the Bridge. We followed them in. I'm pretty sure they're armed, and they're coming after the keys. You only have a few minutes."

Abby turned to the group. "Some of Muns's men are coming."

"They'll do anything for the keys," Coach Horne said, wincing as he shifted his weight. "I'm afraid I'm not much good. Normally, I might have been able to take a few down for you."

Coach Adonavich looked at Mr. Hendricks. "His gun is no good to us either, unless we can hack into his rings and sync up to it. Chances are the code would be too hard to crack quickly." She began to pace.

Carol looked around, perhaps searching for anything that could help. Mom and Dad looked at each other. Abby eyed Mr. Hendricks. He caused this. He was a double-crosser all along. Even though he pretended to befriend her, pretended to teach her the value of history.

And then an idea hit Abby. "I know what to do."

"What?" Coach Adonavich said. "We are about to face who knows how many armed men who want to kill us for the keys."

Abby was surprised at how calm she sounded as she answered, "We make them think they've won. And then we ambush them. Just like Maynard and Blackbeard."

Coach Adonavich shook her head. "Like who?"

"Listen up," Abby said. "I'll need someone to help me turn these keys."

AMBUSH

The men bounded into the room, guns poised. "Everyone's hands in the air!" one yelled, from his position at the front of the group. He saw the figure of a girl at the console of the Bridge and approached her cautiously.

The other soldiers seemed dazed as they stared in wonder. Not only could they see the metallic, tree-looking Bridge, but the keys were all turned, and waves with lifeboats that were half-filled with passengers and debris filled the other side of the room. They hadn't expected to see an ocean in the school's basement.

One soldier looked up at the branches of the Bridge and yelled, "They're above us." He pointed two barrels, one attached to each of his hands, at the metal limbs, where Carol, Coach Adonavich, and Abby's parents clung to the branches. Both of Abby's parents kept their faces covered so they wouldn't be recognized.

"They were planning an ambush," the soldier said.

Two more raised their guns at the tree.

"Here's another," a different soldier called out, pointing his gun at Coach Horne, who stood in the corner, clutching the handle to a metal door.

The head soldier walked down the middle of the room toward Abby. "Step *away* from the console."

Abby turned to see the man with thick eyebrows and a flat nose. "I've listened to you before. Don't think I'll make that mistake again."

It took the man only a moment to recognize her. "I must admit, I didn't expect to find you here. You must be a very resourceful girl. But now you have lost your keys to me again. Now step away."

"Now!" Abby yelled. With one quick motion, she moved the Bridge's perspective to beneath the level of the ocean. A huge wave of freezing Atlantic water barreled in through the Bridge and into the room.

The soldiers only had time to widen their eyes before the water slammed into them. Coach Horne had already braced himself. Abby desperately held onto the console, the water mostly missing her as it flowed around the metal trunk of the tree.

The water stole the soldiers' footing and sent them crashing into the back wall.

Abby quickly moved the perspective above the ocean's surface again, and the water drained out nearly as fast as it had come in. She glanced over her shoulder to see one or two soldiers still conscious. "Again!" And she slammed them again.

As the water receded the second time, Abby yelled for everyone to take the men's guns. Within a few moments, they had removed the mechanisms from the invaders' wrists and were ready to hold them captive if they woke up.

"Abby," Coach Adonavich said. "It must run in the family, because that was pure genius."

Abby and Coach Adonavich retrieved their keys.

"You should probably take the third key," Carol said to Coach Horne, removing it from the console and handing it to him. "It was meant for you."

Coach Horne nodded and took the key.

Abby's mother found cuffs on a few of the men and now used them to restrain their owners. The others dragged the men, including Mr. Hendricks, out of the room so they could lock it up tight.

As they made their way out of the tunnel, Coach Adonavich and Carol helping Coach Horne, Abby saw two silhouettes coming toward her.

A voice broke the silence. "You're okay!" Derick ran through the hall and hugged his parents. "Abby, you did it!"

"Yes, she did," Mom said.

"We should have been here sooner," Rafa said. "We heard them enter, and we were trying to take them by surprise from behind, but then the door flew open, and we got hit by a wave of water. Knocked us both over and carried us down the passageway."

"And just when we were almost to the door again, another wave nearly knocked me out cold," Derick said. "Rafa, too."

Abby started to laugh. Carol joined her. Soon everyone but Derick and Rafa were laughing.

"I suppose someone will explain to me why that's funny," Derick said.

ASSEMBLY

Abby walked with Carol in Cragbridge Hall. She took her time, enjoying the fact that she didn't have to worry about keys or missing parents or falling off a sinking ship to her death. She didn't even have to worry about class, at least for the next hour or so. She was walking to some sort of surprise assembly.

"Hey, Abby," Jacqueline said, who approached from the other side of the hall. Her hair was pulled back into two braids, and her clothes matched flawlessly. "I saw on our grade updates that you're behind on a lot of your homework. If you need to, you can sign up for a tutor. Oh, wait, there *are* no tutors here. If you need a tutor, you should—"

"Oh be quiet," Carol said, walking beside Abby. "You'd think that with your intelligence, you'd be able to come up with something new to say."

Abby smiled at that.

"I'm glad Abby has at least one friend," Jacqueline said.

Abby faced Jacqueline. "Jacqueline." Her tone was commanding. She felt different—stronger, somehow. "You are beautiful and smart and talented and charismatic. And I'm not as pretty as you. I don't have my own business or great fashion sense. I don't have as many friends as you." Abby stood a little taller and stepped closer to Jacqueline. "But that doesn't change the fact that I'm not ordinary. I have something to offer, and if you were as much of a genius as you say you are, you'd see that I *deserve* to be here." Abby said the words slowly for emphasis. They felt good, and what's more, she believed them.

Jacqueline stood silently for a moment before breaking from her surprise. She let out a loud laugh. "Tell yourself whatever you need to, to help you sleep at night." Jacqueline turned down the hall and went into the assembly.

Abby shrugged at Carol.

"She gets under my skin," Carol said. "Little missy prissy sissy. I don't know where she gets off."

"Eh," Abby said, shrugging. "She doesn't bug me so much anymore."

"Really?" Carol asked as they left the hall and stepped into the large auditorium. Two floors overlooked one stage, which was set with lighting from the ceiling.

"Yeah," Abby said. "I guess I used to think her opinion was from one of the world's brightest, so she had to be right." They walked down the middle aisle, slowly making their way toward the front. "But now I think she's like a dog—a little one that always has to be barking about something."

Carol laughed. "You're right. Though she's probably the best-dressed little dog I've ever seen. Have you seen her new line of ruffle skirts? So cute! I wanted to ask if it would be a threat to our friendship if I bought one."

Abby laughed. She found a row, slipped in a few spots, and sat down. "Buy as many as you want."

A voice boomed over the loudspeaker as the lights dimmed. "Welcome, Cragbridge Hall student body. To begin this surprise assembly, we would like to introduce . . ."

Image after image flashed across the auditorium in the largest three-dimensional projection Abby had ever seen: earthquakes, armies, queens being crowned, Abraham Lincoln delivering a speech, people waiting in soup lines, a peace treaty being signed, a concentration camp, a tsunami. Each image was vivid and powerful—larger than life.

"The man who founded this school. He is responsible for many of the inventions . . ."

Images of the Bridge, the Chair, and the avatar lab flashed across the hall. Was Grandpa here, at the assembly? Why? Images of several other inventions appeared. Abby didn't recognize all of them. How many things had Grandpa invented?

" . . . that make this academy the premiere academy in the world: . . ."

The crowd cheered, a boy or two taking it upon themselves to yell louder than others at random times.

"Oscar . . . Cragbridge!"

The crowd erupted as Abby watched her grandpa walk across the stage. One after another, the students stood on their feet. Soon the entire auditorium had joined in the ovation. It was strange to be there with everyone cheering on her grandpa. Abby had seen moment after moment like this on the web, but this was the first time she had attended anything like it.

Yet her grandpa seemed somewhat at ease. He wore a simple button-up shirt, his Cragbridge Hall blazer, loose slacks, and his old unpolished, imitation-leather shoes. He was dressed up as he would be to go to the all-you-can-eat buffet with his family.

"Thank you, thank you," he said, motioning for the crowd to quiet down. They didn't respond right away, but eventually they calmed and sat. "Are you enjoying yourselves?"

Again the crowd erupted in applause and cheers.

"Good, good," he said, a huge smile on his face. "I invented these machines because I believe that young people's minds are our best investment. I think you're worth all the trouble, thought, and effort that went into them. Please do your best to live up to the great expectations we have of you. Don't worry too much. Don't stress too much. Just do your best, and everything will be just fine. You won't let me down."

The crowd clapped, less boisterously and more thoughtful.

"I give you my highest compliments. I know that some of you out there may well outdo my accomplishments, and do so soon. I wouldn't have it any other way. I hope I am of help."

Abby thought that if he wasn't her grandpa, he would have won her over.

"I'm here," he said, raising his cane in the air, "to honor someone. Actually, several people. As some of you may have heard, I have been missing for the past several days. It was because . . . I was kidnapped."

The crowd grew solemn.

A view of a press conference streamed in across the projector. A woman in a police uniform stood in front of several small microphones and made a formal announcement. "We are happy to report that Oscar Cragbridge, his son Jefferson, and Jefferson's wife, Hailey, have all been returned home safely. We will not release any details about their time in captivity." She flicked her finger, probably to bring up the next page of notes. "We have the perpetrators in custody. They will be prosecuted according to the severity of their crimes. There have been some allegations that implicate Charles Muns, but we cannot find any record or evidence as of yet that the perpetrators worked with him."

Another flick of the finger, and the woman continued. "Several people were instrumental in rescuing Oscar Cragbridge and his family members. He asked for the chance to honor them himself at an assembly at the school he founded, Cragbridge Hall. We'll go there live."

The auditorium appeared on-screen. The students went wild—standing, flailing their arms, whooping. Apparently even geniuses enjoyed a little attention. They were live on the air.

Oscar Cragbridge motioned for silence. "It is true. I was kidnapped and held against my will, as were my son and his wife."

Abby tried not to think about the nightmarish last few days.

"Although I will not share the details of that time, the end results could have been disastrous for me, my family, and the entire world—a calamity unlike any humanity has ever known—if it had not been for several people. Please honor them with me. First, Coaches Horne and Adonavich."

The two coaches stepped forward, and the students again erupted in applause. Coach Horne was on crutches, his shoulder and leg heavily bandaged. The students clapped harder, realizing he had been injured in whatever escapades he had been in.

"Minerva Entrese," Grandpa continued. The English teacher stepped forward, wearing a black dress. Her hair was pulled back with a black ribbon. Though she smiled, Abby thought she still looked nervous. Her actions over the last twenty-four hours had made it clear that she was against Muns, and this honor would remove any lingering doubts.

"But the greatest heroes," Grandpa said, "were four students." The crowd hushed. Abby gasped in shock. No. Would he really bring her up there? "First, Rafael Pereira Silva dos Santos. Rafa, would you please join me onstage?"

Rafa stood in an aisle to the far left, and the spotlight found him as he made his way to the stage. Grandpa put both hands on Rafa's shoulders, then hugged him. After he pulled back, he told the crowd, "Rafa is a man of exceptional talent—talent that proved vital to my escape."

"Second, Carol Reese."

Carol rose from her seat as the crowd clapped. She blew kisses in every direction and practically danced her way onto the stage. Grandpa gave her a hug too.

"Carol showed extreme bravery, even facing a gunman." The crowd hushed. "I owe her a great debt of gratitude."

"Finally, the two . . ." Grandpa's smooth voice broke. He took a moment to swallow and collect his emotions. Abby wiped her eyes. "Sorry," he apologized. "The two I owe the greatest gratitude to are those I love the most: Derick and Abby Cragbridge."

Abby felt the spotlight shine on her. She moved to her feet and slowly made her way to the stage, knowing that the whole school was watching. Part of her hated the attention, but she liked the applause coming from her classmates. Maybe she had a chance with them. Maybe she could fit in here. Maybe she could make it.

Abby caught a glimpse of Jacqueline, whose mouth hung wide open.

Derick joined Abby onstage. At the sight of Derick's T-shirt, she shot him a questioning look. It said "I'm in love" in bold red letters and had Carol's face underneath.

"Don't ask," Derick said. "I had to wear it today of all days." He shook his head.

Grandpa hugged them both together for several

moments. He let go, and then hugged them again. Finally, he addressed the crowd.

"If it were not for these two, this story would not have a happy ending. They have saved more than you will ever know. They faced fears and death, and just kept on going." Abby smiled wider to keep her bottom lip from quivering. She twisted her hair into a ponytail.

The projector flashed back to the news story. "Apparently Oscar Cragbridge's grandchildren and their schoolmates were instrumental in finding him trapped in an auditorium under reconstruction. The details of how they helped their grandfather escape and left his captors incapacitated are classified. All we can do is wonder, but in the end, we have to trust the word of one of the great geniuses of our time, that they are heroes."

The crowd again rose to their feet. Abby and Derick waved as hundreds of students applauded. Then the four students moved into a hug.

• • •

Abby stood once again on the porch of her grandfather's 1997 home. This time she was excited that he answered and let her in; seeing him at the door almost helped erase her terrible memories.

"So," Grandpa said with a smile. "Great to see you two again—especially when the world isn't watching." He motioned for Abby and Derick to follow as he hobbled back toward his study.

"Yeah," Derick said, following him, "you could have warned us about that."

"No, I couldn't have," Grandpa said. "Then you would have refused. I couldn't have that."

"Oh, I would have refused alright," Abby said.

"And I would have worn a different shirt," Derick mumbled.

"But the assembly was about more than giving you a little attention," Grandpa said, sitting in his old leather chair. "It was a strategic move. Now that everyone knows who the heroes are, they'll pay more attention to you, which will make it more difficult for Muns to do anything to you."

"Oh," Abby said, fingering some books on one of the many shelves. "I hadn't thought of that."

"How is school going?" Grandpa asked.

"The new history teacher isn't nearly as good of a presenter as Mr. Hendricks, but she's also probably not secretly trying to fight against my grandpa and kill my parents."

"That's good," Grandpa said with a laugh. "Mr. Hendricks won't be back."

"You never really trusted him, did you, Grandpa?" Abby asked.

"I didn't give him a locket. He had to steal that. But at one time, yes, I did trust him," Grandpa said. "At the time, he deserved my trust. But then Muns got to him. No doubt Muns made some promises to bring back Mr. Hendricks's wife. That would be very appealing to a grieving widower."

"Yeah, I can see that." Abby paused and then said, "Are we sure we shouldn't . . . I mean, save people like his wife?"

"Absolutely," Grandpa said. "I am sure. And I know that it's a difficult thing to accept, but we can't afford to play with time. Tragedies have their purpose; they teach us. True, many people have been broken because they've lost a loved one. But many people have grown. Many have gone on to change their lives, paying more attention to those they have while they still have time. These things bring people together. I know that ever since I lost your grandma, I . . ." Tears welled up in Grandpa's eyes. "I have loved you even more. She would want me to love you as I do, not bring her back."

"But don't they . . . I mean, doesn't Muns, have a key?" Derick asked.

"At least one, yes," Grandpa said. "We have to assume that after they stole it from Abby, they continued through the steps to gain the actual Bridge key. They also have my copy of the Bridge, which they stole from my basement. I believe it was what they used to show me the *Titanic* in the auditorium, but unfortunately, Ms. Entrese and I had no way of taking it back to the school before Muns's reinforcements showed up. We barely escaped ourselves. That Bridge, and the one in the basement of the academy, are the only two working time machines in the world."

Grandpa rubbed his temples. "So they have at least one key and a time machine. They could have persuaded others I've given lockets to. I'm in the process of communicating with everyone who has a locket to consult with them. The situation is more dangerous than ever."

"What about the energy burst, or whatever you said it

was, that they used to put Mom and Dad on the *Titanic?*" Derick asked. "Do you understand what it was? Couldn't they use that again?"

Grandpa leaned on his cane. "I think I understand a bit of the theory behind it, but not all of it. Unfortunately, they could use it again. We'll have to be on the lookout. Nothing is safe. No *time* is safe. But for now, we have avoided a disaster, and we have the upper hand." Grandpa looked at both of his grandchildren. "And we have you two to thank for it."

Abby smiled. She knew her grandpa had always believed in her and known she could do great things, but she finally felt like he might just be right.

"Now, let's go back in time and eat some original pizza," Grandpa said.

The twins looked at each other.

"I'm kidding," Grandpa said. "Though I have been tempted."

ACKNOWLEDGMENTS

So many people have helped and inspired me on the road to getting my first novel published—beginning with my parents. From letting me rig up makeshift string pulleys in my room so I could turn off my lights from my bed, to helping me buy my first drum set, to driving for hours to come to my comedy shows while I was in college, my parents have encouraged and supported my crazy dreams throughout my life. That pattern holds true with my writing. Thanks, Mom and Dad.

Thanks to Shane, Casey, Spenny, Michelle, and Brady. We had a great childhood that jumpstarted my imagination. Thanks for hiking mountains, cliff jumping, purposely crashing into each other on sleds, making homemade movies, and finding the secret talisman of Izynkz to become a clan of supernatural ninjas ready to save the world. (That

337

last one may or may not be true; the memory is a little fuzzy.)

My wife, Shelly, deserves special thanks. Not only did she encourage me when I thought this story was helpless, but she was my first reader, giving me feedback that set this book on its way to success. I based Carol on an exaggerated version of what I think my wife might have been like in junior high. Yeah, she's that fun.

I'd like to thank my kids too, for asking me to make up stories, for enduring all my crazy answers when they ask "Guess what?" and for being so creative and so alive. My ten-year-old son read the entire manuscript in a couple of days and gave me helpful feedback. My daughter tried very hard to do the same. I read a draft of this book to all my kids at night, and I thank them for often chanting "One more chapter! One more chapter!" when I said it was time to stop. And I forgive them for the times they fell asleep.

Thanks to David McCullough, who gave me (and the thousands of other people in the auditorium) a challenge that led to an idea—an idea important in the creation of this book.

I can't say enough good about Shadow Mountain, especially Chris Schoebinger and Heidi Taylor. They believed in Cragbridge Hall and took a chance on me. You are making a dream come true. Thanks to Lisa Mangum and Annette Lyon for using their editing skills to polish up my writing. Thanks to Brandon Dorman for having a great imagination and the ability to put it into an amazing cover and illustrations.

ACKNOWLEDGMENTS

Thanks to my agent, Rubin Pfeffer, for fantastic help and advice. And thanks to Deborah Warren for her support and enthusiasm.

Thanks to those who read this manuscript early on and gave me feedback: Dan and Sariah Reed, Matthew Crawford, Brittney Young, Parley Jenkins, Hailey Young, Lauren Sellnow, Randy Lindsay, and Will Mason.

Thanks to Brandon Mull for being an inspiration and a good friend. Thanks to Tyler Whitesides, who has given me advice and who let me follow him to school assemblies. Thanks to all the guys in Divine Comedy/DC Comedy who encouraged my creativity and writing. Huzzah!

Thanks to all the great people in history and literature that I cite in this book. Thanks for inspiring me. Though this book doesn't do them all the justice they deserve, I hope their stories inspire curiosity in a young mind. And few things are as powerful as a curious young mind.

And thank YOU. Yeah, *you*. To read this book, you trusted me with some of your time and imagination. If you enjoyed the ride, please tell your friends. Your recommendation makes a huge difference.

DISCUSSION QUESTIONS

1. Abby feels like she is ordinary. Have you ever felt that way? What talents did Abby discover she had? What talents do you have?

2. Abby finds it difficult to believe in herself, but Grandpa Cragbridge has confidence in her. Do you find it easy or hard to believe in yourself? Which people in your life believe in you? How do you know?

3. Abby and Derick studied various people in history, including Blackbeard, Frederick Douglass, and Ernest Shackleton. What impressed you about these figures in history? Why?

4. If you had the chance to sit in the Chair and read a book for everyone else to see what you imagine, what book would you choose? Why?

5. Derick loves controlling the avatars. Which avatar would you most like to control? Why?

6. When Jacqueline finds out that Abby got into the school because of her grandfather, she kicks her out of their room. She also picks on Abby several times throughout the book. How do you think Jacqueline should have handled her differences with Abby?

7. Carol stood up for Abby and became her friend when Jacqueline tried to bribe everyone to refuse to be her roommate. Have you ever stood up for a friend? Has a friend ever stood up for you? Have you ever become friends with someone who was struggling to make friends?

8. Derick's failure in the simulator had a strong effect on him. Have you ever failed at something? How did you feel? What gives you the strength to try again after you have failed?

9. Grandpa designed tests in the simulators that would require Abby and Derick to know their cause was truly worth it. What causes do you think are worth that kind of dedication today?

10. Charles Muns wants to change history. Grandpa teaches that we should learn from the past rather than trying to change it. What have you learned from history in general? What have you learned from your own past?

11. Grandpa also teaches that trials and difficulties give people the ability to become heroes. What heroes have you seen in your life? What hard times have you faced? How have they made you stronger?

RECOMMENDED READING

For more information on pirates and Blackbeard:

Matthews, John. *Pirates: Most Wanted*. New York: Antheneum Books, 2007.

Platt, Richard. *DK Eyewitness Books: Pirate*. New York: DK Publishing, 2007.

For more information about Annie Oakley:

Spinner, Stephanie. *Who Was Annie Oakley?* New York: Grosset and Dunlap, 2002.

Wills, Chuck. *DK Biography: Annie Oakley: A Photographic Story of a Life*. New York: DK Publishing, 2007.

For more information about Frederick Douglass:

Adler, David A. *Frederick Douglass: A Noble Life*. New York: Holiday House, 2010.

Sanders, Nancy I. *Frederick Douglass for Kids: His Life and Times, with 21 Activities (For Kids series)*. Chicago: Chicago Review, 2012.

For more information about James Naismith and origins of basketball:

Hareas, John. *DK Eyewitness Books: Basketball*. New York: DK Publishing, 2007.

Stewart, Mark. *Basketball: A History of Hoops*. New York: Franklin Watts, 1998.

For more information about Ernest Shackleton and his expedition:

Johnson, Rebecca L. *Ernest Shackleton: Gripped by the Antarctic*. Minneapolis: Carolrhoda Books, 2003.

Marcovitz, Hal. *Sir Ernest Shackleton and the Struggle Against Antarctica*. Philadelphia: Chelsea House, 2002.

For information on Mountain Men, including Hugh Glass and John Colter:

Collins, James L. *The Mountain Men*. New York: Franklin Watts, 1996.

Glass, Andrew. *Mountain Men: True Grit and Tall Tales*. New York: Doubleday, 2001.

For more information about the sinking of the *Titanic*:

DK Publishing. *Story of the Titanic*. Illustrated by Steve Noon. New York: DK Publishing, 2012.

Hopkinson, Deborah. *Titanic: Voices from the Disaster*. New York: Scholastic, 2012.